One Year in the Life of Benjamin Thomas

William C. Webster

PublishAmerica
Baltimore

ISBN: 1-4241-0195-6
PUBLISHED BY PUBLISHAMERICA, LLLP
www.publishamerica.com
Baltimore

Printed in the United States of America

To my wife, Kate

Acknowledgments

The author wishes to acknowledge and thank the following people for their help and support: my son Billy for his help in editing the manuscript and assisting in so many technical areas; my daughter Anne for helping with research, typing, editing, and more importantly, for encouraging me to continue with the project; my son-in-law Brandon for his skills with the computer and grammatical expertise; my son Tim for designing the cover; my wife Kate for her patience and advice; my parents and siblings for instilling in me a love for the land.

Author's note: Slim's ideas on Jeffersonian democracy come from an eighteenth-century intellectual named Jeremy Belknap.

November 4, 1995

I will be eighteen years old tomorrow. No one knows, or cares for that matter, that I am leaving this place forever. I hate the south. I hate the heat + the bugs + the lay of the land. Incredibly, I have been nowhere else. Only in pictures and film have I seen seasons change. I have never felt snow. I have never stood under a maple tree, or an oak. All is about to change. I am going to New England.

My mother died of cancer 3 years ago. It was a terrible death. For Me, it was also a great loss. She was literally the only person who ever loved me. I don't know my father. I have no idea who he is, or if he is dead or alive. It was the one secret she kept from me. All she said was that I was her great blessing from her great mistake. When she died, her parents took me in. They are her parents, but I cannot call them my grandparents. Nor, I am sure, do they consider me their grandson. They never forgave my mother for having me. When they took me in, it was from a sense of duty. I have not been abused or neglected by them... Nor have I been loved. The note of appreciation is written + ready to place on my bed. When they find it, they will be relieved. And so will I.
Tomorrow, November 5, 1995, is my birthday.
Chronologically I will be eighteen.
For me, it is the first day of my life.

Chapter 1

Dawn was approaching when he entered a small town in northern New Jersey. Daylight confirmed his fear that the ominous bluish gray smoke from his exhaust was getting worse. The empty bottles of 10 W-40 rattling in the trunk and the increasing number of remarks and gestures of passing motorists for the past two days had made him aware that the Dodge Reliant was on its last legs.

The city streets were quiet and empty when he entered the town. He eased to the curb in a residential area clearly not inhabited by the affluent. Garbage cans lined the curb as far as he could see. Leaning to the passenger side he removed the handful of envelopes from the glove compartment and shoved them into the worn backpack. He removed the keys from the ignition and slipped them under the floor mat. The backpack slung over his shoulder, he glanced into the back seat before walking away. He never saw the car again. Several days later it would be reported to the police. When they ran a check and discovered that the owner had no criminal record they had the car towed to the junk yard, filed their report and dropped the case. There was nothing to pursue. His was a faceless name recognized for what it was—a life of little significance.

* * *

He remembered the truck stop at the exit ramp of the interstate and he walked quickly in that direction. It was cloudy and very cold. He had never felt this cold before. He needed a coat and some gloves. He smiled at the fact that he had never owned either. The large Citgo sign came into view, serving as his beacon to the truck stop. It was still a good half mile away. He stopped outside a bank and checked his wallet. It contained one hundred sixty-eight

6

dollars and some change. Fear should have been his only companion. Instead he had a feeling of liberation and hope. The past was gone. Youth was his ally. The warmth of the diner and breakfast was his short-term goal. Beyond that—an empty page.

A blast of warm air hit him when he entered the diner. The closing of the door behind him muffled the sounds of diesel engines from the parking area. Those sounds were replaced by the clanging of cups and plates and the sounds of voices, mostly men's. He chose a stool at the counter. "You want coffee?" the girl said. "You look like you're freezing—look at you're hands; they're blue." He ordered the special. For three dollars there were two eggs, home fries and two sausage patties. Also toast and as much coffee as you wanted. He ate slowly listening to the conversations. At first there was nothing useful. When he had stayed longer than he should, a huge man rose from a nearby booth.

"I better get moving," he said to the man across from him. "It's a long way to Burlington and they're predicting snow."

* * *

"Excuse me sir," Ben shouted above the sounds of the engines. "I heard you say Burlington and I need a ride to Vermont. I don't have much money but…"

Interrupting him, the huge man shouted, "Get in the truck, boy; you look like you're freezing." Once in the truck the man said, "Let me see your bag, boy. You're a skinny runt but I need to make sure you ain't got no gun." Satisfied that Ben was harmless the man said, "I like to listen to country and I don't want much talking—understand?" Ben nodded. "Okay then let's get going—by the way, let me know when you want out and don't worry about money. You look like you need it more than me."

* * *

They stopped only once in the next six hours, and then only for a minute to relieve themselves beside the truck. The man ate sandwiches and drank coffee from a thermos. He offered nothing to the young man next to him. It wasn't a problem. Ben was more interested in the landscape than his stomach. Later he would learn that the autumn foliage was long past its prime but the pale orange leaves mixed with brown were new to him. Veiled against the stark gray bark on the trunks and limbs of trees whose leaves were completely off, it was a tapestry unlike anything he had seen in the South. It reminded him of a line he had once read in the large United States pictorial which he always looked at when his mother would take him to the library. There was a picture similar to what he was now seeing for real. The caption read, "The Earth Rests."

The two lane road winding through New York state into Vermont astounded the young man. Leaving the Hudson River Valley they climbed steadily into the Taconic Hills. The mountains were not huge, their beauty came from personality rather than size. There were no long continuous ranges but rather endless individual hills folding and overlapping each other. No two peaks were the same shape or size. All had a variety of hardwoods and evergreens—with a predominance of hemlock, oak, maple, and ash. He fell in love with the Northeast immediately. It was more than he had imagined. Someone had once told him that anticipation was always better than realization, but he knew that the visual unfolding before him was an exception to that rule. About an hour later they had made a delivery in Bennington, Vermont and were heading north toward Burlington. Other delivery points required the driver to take secondary roads. As they approached a small village the young man said, almost upon impulse, "I think I will get out here." Without a word the driver eased to a halt at the town's only traffic light. The young man said, "Thanks a lot," and as he stood on the street corner he watched the truck pull away. A clock on the bank said seven p.m. Cold and very hungry Ben started up the street.

* * *

It was a small town, much too small for homeless shelters or Salvation Armies or Red Cross centers. There didn't appear to be a hotel—not that he could have afforded one anyway. It was then that he approached the faded brick building with a flame and a cross emblem attached to its side. He started to pass by when he saw the dim light in a room off the main foyer. Without deliberation he entered. The hallway was cool but an improvement from the cold night outside. Tentatively he knocked on the office door. A voice from inside said, "Come in." He felt the warmth of the room on his face as he opened the door. He hadn't realized until then how cold he was. Book shelves covered three of the four walls from floor to ceiling. The fourth wall featured a large window looking out to a courtyard. Dimly he could see benches along a walkway. In front of the window sat a large, neat desk. A picture of a woman and a baby sat on one side. On the other side was a framed quotation from C.S. Lewis. It read "Good and evil both increase at compound interest." The man sitting at the desk took off his glasses as he turned in the swivel chair. "Hello, I'm Jim Braxton, the pastor. What can I do for you and boy, do you look cold."

The young man answered, "I just got into town and I need a place to spend the night. I don't have much money," he quickly added.

"How did you get here?" the minister asked looking perplexed.

"I hitched a ride with a truck driver after my car died somewhere in northern New Jersey," he answered. "I came from Florida and I want to try out New England."

The minister smiled. "We have some cots that the Youth Group uses for sleep overs. I'll set one up in the nursery and turn up the heat a bit. It's the last room down the hallway on your right. Go down there and I'll get the cot."

When he returned a few minutes later the minister's wife followed carrying a blanket and a pillow. She looked just like the picture on her husband's desk. Her smile was warm and friendly. "Have you eaten?" she asked.

"Not since this morning," the young man answered, "but I can go to a diner if you point the way."

"You better stay where it's warm. I'll fix you some soup."

A few minutes later the minister returned with a thermos of chicken soup, a tuna sandwich, and milk. Watching the young man eat he asked, "What's your name?"

The young man replied, "My name is Benjamin Thomas, and I appreciate what you have done for me."

"You're more than welcome, Benjamin Thomas. Well, you look like you need a good sleep. I'll see you in the morning. By the way, there is a bathroom through that door," he pointed.

* * *

Sleep came easy. Exhaustion coupled with youthful naivete allows for sleep when one's desperate situation should dictate otherwise. Years later Ben would recall that it was the only night of his life when he had no idea where he would spend tomorrow.

When he awoke there was beside his cot a box of cornflakes, some milk and a glass of orange juice. Sleep was so sound that he hadn't heard whoever left it. Beside the food he found the minister's note. It read, "Feel free to use the shower. I turned on the hot water. Please come next door to the parsonage this morning." The shower felt good. He also shaved using a bar of Ivory soap for lather. When he walked back into the youth room he was stopped in his tracks. Outside the ground was covered with several inches of snow. It was the most beautiful sight he could ever recall. He opened the window and reached out. At age eighteen he made and tossed his first snow ball.

* * *

"What are your plans?" the minister asked Ben.

"I need a job and a place to stay."

Realizing how ridiculous he must appear he stammered, "You must think I'm crazy but I'm not. I have wanted to be here a long time and I just came. I know it doesn't make sense to anyone else."

The minister smiled as he said, "Someday maybe you will tell me your story but now you need a job. Have you ever done farm work?"

"No, but I could probably learn."

"I know a farmer named Oscar Smith," the minister said. "He's looking for a hired hand. The pay is poor, twenty-five dollars a day, but he charges no rent for the trailer on his property. I took the liberty of calling him. If you want I will drive you out to his place. It's about five miles out of town."

"Thank you," said Ben. "I would like to talk to him."

On their way through town the minister stopped at a poorly painted building. "We have a collection center here," he explained. "People leave clothing they no longer use. Let's find you something warm to wear." Five foot nine, one hundred fifty-five pounds with size nine feet must have been a common size, for within minutes Ben came back to the car with his first winter coat, gloves and boots. They looked almost new. "Someone must have known you were coming," the minister remarked.

The minister stopped the car as they reached the top of the hill. Pointing his finger straight ahead he said, "That's the Smith farm." In total silence Ben took in the scene before him. The road ahead was straight for nearly a quarter mile. On both sides were large open fields—five all together separated by hedgerows. The fields on the right were bordered by a stream, about thirty feet wide. Directly to its right the woodlands began rising gradually to the height of several hundred feet. The forest was predominantly hardwoods— mostly maple, oak, and ash. There were also several stands of pine and hemlock. The fields to the left of the road were more contoured than those by the stream. They rose gently from the road. On a level area on top of a knoll sat the Smith home. It was a white two story house with a tin roof painted silver. Behind it was a large red barn with a tin roof also painted silver. It was surrounded by a very large area fenced in with page wire. A large herd of Holstein cattle stood in the fenced in area eating hay from two large metal feeders. To the right of the large barn stood a second barn, facing south. It had four huge sliding doors. There were two small sheds, also red, that sat nearer the house. Between them was a small trailer. It looked old despite a fresh coat of white paint. Ben hadn't asked the minister to stop the car, but he was glad for the chance to take it all in. It was one of the most beautiful scenes that he had ever looked upon. "It belongs on a calendar," the minister said.

"You're right," Ben agreed. "I don't know if I'll like Oscar Smith, but I already like his place."

Chapter 2

Oscar Smith was fifty-two years old. He stood six feet two inches tall and weighed one hundred eighty pounds. Since his high school years everyone called him "Slim." The name was still appropriate for his physical appearance had changed very little throughout the years. His medium brown hair was still thick with flecks of gray throughout. His face had a rugged look with soft wrinkles on his forehead. He had very blue eyes that mostly looked serious. But the feature that most people remembered when they met Slim Smith was the hands. They appeared slightly too large for his body. His fingers were very long, his palms hard and calloused. The back showed sinew and veins. His handshake was firm and sincere.

Slim Smith was a native of rural Vermont. He had never lived anywhere else nor had he ever considered it. His travels were limited to the northeast. The farthest he had been from his birthplace was his honeymoon trip to Canada. Slim's parents both had worked in a small factory that made men's shirts. Their work was steady but mundane. Even as a young child Slim knew it was a path he would not follow, for he loved to be outside. When he was very young Slim was cared for by his older sister while his parents worked. At age six he was allowed to walk by himself down the road from his house to a nearby farm. Every day during the summer he would climb the apple tree by the edge of the field and look at old Joe Thurston's herd of Holsteins as they grazed. He remembered counting them each day to see that nothing had changed. He remembered wondering why there were three Jersey cows in the herd of twenty-five Holsteins. Slim often smiled as he thought back through the years to those days of his childhood. For most people there is a dramatic event that forever changes their lives; perhaps a death, an award or even a war. For Slim it was different. The event that would change his life forever was the day, at age six, when Joe Thurston spotted him up in his apple tree at the edge of the field.

"What are you doing up my tree?" old Joe had said leaning out the window of the pick up truck.

"Sorry mister, I was just looking at them cows," a frightened Slim replied.

He remembered how Joe had laughed as he looked up at him. "You Fred Smith's boy?" he asked.

"Yes sir."

"You want to ride to my place and see the calves?" Joe asked.

"Yes sir, but I have to tell my sister where I am."

"Get in the back of the truck," Joe said. "I'll have my Mrs. call your sister and tell her you're with us." And so that day Slim's life changed forever. For the next ten years there was rarely a day, winter or summer, when he didn't spend every possible moment with Joe and Mabel Thurston. It was from them that he would learn to be a farmer. He would also learn a philosophy for life.

At first Slim's days with Joe Thurston were simply those of a small tag-along child. When Joe was cleaning stables Slim would play with the calves. At the chicken house Slim would look for eggs while Joe did his chores. He loved the March days when Joe was tapping trees for maple syrup. He loved riding with Joe on the John Deere crawler when they were pulling logs down from the wood lot for lumber or cord wood. He loved riding on the hay wagon while Joe loaded bales. He watched with wonder as the bales would ride up the elevator and drop into the loft. And to the amazement of Joe he loved to put on the netted hat and long gloves and without fear watch Joe work among his hives. At first he was no help except for amusement to Joe. But it was quickly obvious that the young lad had a love and talent for farming. "You're doing good, boy" Joe would say. It was years later that Slim would recognize why Joe was a successful farmer. "Keep it small and don't put all your eggs in one basket"; that was Joe's formula. It was the same formula that Slim was still using—a small herd of cattle, eggs, honey, syrup, and timber—all sold exclusively on the local level except for the milk that went to Boston.

Mabel Thurston adored Slim from the first day he rode home in the back of Joe's truck. On rainy days or when Joe was falling trees, a job the young boy was not allowed to be a part of, Slim would stay at the house with Mabel. It was from her that Slim learned the importance of "keeping things up" as she would say. "Tin roofs will last forever if you keep them painted," she said. She worked along side Joe when he painted the barns and sheds. The lawn and gardens were her domain, and they reflected her belief in order, simplicity and productivity. Young Slim was intrigued by the home's interior, especially the basement (cellar, as they called it) with the long shelves neatly arranged with fruits and vegetables preserved for winter.

Slim Smith loved his own parents but had no interest in a lifetime of making shirts and living in town. At age thirteen, with the approval of his parents and the Thurstons, Slim moved into the Thurstons' home and helped run the farm while finishing high school. Barely two months after his high school graduation while Joe and Slim were baling hay, Joe suffered a fatal heart attack and died in the field. The Thurstons' only daughter, married to a lawyer and living in Connecticut, insisted that Mrs. Thurston sell the farm and move in with them. Slim spent weeks traveling from bank to bank hoping for approval of a mortgage. No one would "take a chance" on an eighteen-year-old with no down payment, no credit and no collateral. When he had given up all hope of buying the Thurston farm, Slim was unexpectedly approached by a prominent businessman from town. The offer was simple. The businessman would loan Slim the money at eight percent interest over twenty years. There were to be no lawyers or legal documents. Everything was to be done "under the table."

"I hate the government and all their rules and regulations," the businessman had said. "I knew Joe Thurston and from what he told me about you, I'll take my chances." And so at eighteen years of age Slim Smith had legal claim to the farm he fell in love with as a child. For the next twenty years he never missed a payment—always in cash. When he made the final payment the businessman handed Slim the tattered notebook that was the only record of the transaction. Thus ended the successful business venture of two men who trusted each other.

Chapter 3

John Taylor was the town's only doctor. He would never be rich with money but he knew real wealth in his relationships. He was always on duty and made house calls to the elderly. People paid him what they could and when they could. He was probably taken advantage of sometimes, but he never paid attention to such things. His patients were his friends and neighbors. They viewed him with love and respect. Most of them also viewed him with pity for being married to Lucy Taylor. Lucy believed that John was wasting his talents and his life. She hated the small town atmosphere and longed for the "cultured life of the city" as she put it. She constantly reminded her husband of their modest home and modest income.

John and Lucy Taylor had one child, a daughter Mary. Much to her mother's dismay she was a shy and awkward child who preferred nature to culture. She inherited her father's excellent mind and his love for science. She also inherited his physical stature. By grade seven she stood five foot eight inches tall, nearly a foot taller than her classmates, especially the boys. She would grow no taller but for several years, until the others caught up to her, she was the skinny and ungraceful object of much teasing from her classmates. Mary had friends but preferred to be alone. She loved long walks through the woods and could identify birds, animals and trees in a way that amazed her father and irritated her mother. Her favorite possession was a camera which she used with a natural artistic skill. Her room was filled with photos that chronicled her love of the outdoors.

Mary attended the public schools where she excelled academically. Her mother constantly pushed her in the direction of a more urban private school and for one year during the eighth grade Mary and her father yielded to the pressure. It was the worst year of her life. Her classmates were from wealthy backgrounds and the tall and gangly Mary spent the year alone in her room homesick for the paths and brooks of her home and for her father. Realizing the futility of her efforts, Lucy consented to let Mary return home for her high school years. She did little prodding after that because she knew that Mary would end up "just like her father."

During the summer after her third year of high school Mary changed dramatically in many ways. She became a very attractive young woman. Gone were the freckles and the awkward body. Her shoulder length hair, dark brown or auburn depending on the light, was soft and silky. Her eyes were very brown and accented by long dark lashes. It was as if a transformation had occurred, as indeed it had. During her senior year heads turned when she walked by as they had never done before. Still, it was too late for close social relations to develop and on the night of her senior prom Mary sat at home alone. Mary Taylor graduated from high school never having gone on a date.

The September following her graduation from high school Mary Taylor went away to the state university where she majored in biology and prepared for a career in teaching. She loved the rigors of academic life and even took part in the school's social activities. Young men pursued her, but she found them for the most part immature and mainly interested in what she was not prepared to offer. Many weekends she went home and took long walks or bicycle rides, always with her camera. One such Saturday found her several miles outside of town sitting on a large rock by a small stream. When she finally climbed the bank back to the road where her bicycle was parked against a telephone pole, she discovered that the rear tire was flat. Mary pushed the disabled bike nearly a quarter of a mile to the well kept farm house sitting on a knoll. She hoped that the occupants would be home so that she could use the phone to call her father. As she pushed the bicycle up the driveway she saw a tall young man walking toward the house from the nearby barn. Almost immediately she recognized him as the boy everyone called Slim who had been a class ahead of her in high school. He also recognized her but could not recall her name. He was quite certain that she was Doc Taylor's daughter. "I have a flat tire," Mary said. "Do you think your parents would mind if I use the phone to call my Dad?"

"Actually," Slim returned, "I live here alone. I bought this place when I graduated from high school."

"Wow. It's such a beautiful place. I've always loved this spot."

"Thanks," Slim replied as he slowly spun the flat tire on her bicycle. "There's your problem," he said pointing to the small roofing nail lodged in the tire. "I can put a patch on that in ten minutes if you want." Mary watched how easily Slim removed the wheel, separated the tube from the tire, applied some sticky material to the tube and placed the patch over it. When he had filled the tube with air and reattached the tire Mary remarked how quickly he had made the repair.

"I've patched a lot of tires," Slim said.

As Mary was about to leave she offered to pay for the repairs. "Not necessary," Slim answered. "Glad to help." Noticing her camera he asked if she was working on a project.

"No," Mary replied, "just trying to add to my collection of birds and animals.

"I saw a real nice owl up on my mountain yesterday."

"Really? The only one I ever saw was on a day I didn't have my camera. Do you think I could walk up there sometime? I might get lucky and see it."

"I know the tree he was in," Slim replied. "I'll show you sometime if you like. It's quite a hike."

Surprising herself Mary said, "How about next Saturday?"

"Sounds good. I finish milking by eight. It's about an hour's walk each way."

"Would nine be all right?" Mary asked.

"That's good," said Slim. "See you next week." As Mary rode away Slim thought to himself, "I'll never see her again."

* * *

That evening Mary worked on a project for her Children's Literature course. Alone in her room, she took a break from her work and walked to the window that overlooked the quiet street lined with huge maple trees. She loved this time of year—November, a time most people hated. She loved the stark gray look of the lifeless trees, a look they seemed to have no other time of the year. By mid winter they would already have a reddish tint as new buds began to develop, but now they were completely dormant, resting, Mary would say, sending the message to busy humans of the necessity of rest. A message mostly ignored, she thought. As she left the view from her window, Mary stopped at the large book case along the wall across the room from her bed. She removed the high school yearbook from her junior year. Going to the section of senior portraits she found the picture of Oscar "Slim" Smith. Under his name it said: "basketball 1,2,3,4; Future Farmers of America 1,2,3,4." In addition to names and activities, each senior class member was given a remark that reflected their personality. These remarks, Mary recalled, were written by the yearbook staff along with their faculty advisors. Under Slim's picture were the words, "Solid as a rock—he knows where he stands." Admitting that she didn't know Slim Smith very well, Mary still suspected that the statement was accurate. She did recall one specific incident from Slim's high school days. It had occurred in the school's cafeteria where a group of rowdies were unmercifully teasing a boy with Down Syndrome. Mary remembered Slim getting up from his table, walking over to the boys and saying, "That's enough."

Her recollection was that one of the boys had made the mistake of saying to Slim, "Mind your own business, dirt farmer."

Slim had responded by picking the startled boy up by the shirt, pinning him against the wall and simply repeating the words, "I said that's enough." She also recalled that the boy with Down Syndrome had, from that time on, eaten lunch at the table with Slim and his friends.

* * *

Slim finished milking at eight o'clock. He went back to the house and had his usual large breakfast. After washing his face and hands he took a large comb and ran it through his wavy brown hair. It was then that he heard the sound of her car as it came up the driveway. She was wearing jeans with a red sweatshirt under a dark blue vest. Around her forehead she wore a head band with what looked like an Indian design. Strapped to her belt was the small canvas case that held her camera. Slim watched as she approached the door.

The first few minutes were awkward, filled with nervous small talk. They fell silent as they walked across the well worn path to the stream at the base of the mountain. When they approached the stream, about thirty feet across, Mary noticed that piles of rocks had been placed approximately three feet apart across the stream. "Poor man's bridge," Slim said. "It's a bit tricky but if you're careful you can get across with dry feet." When he had reached the fourth pile of rocks he looked back and saw that Mary was negotiating her way without difficulty. The final jump to the bank on the other side was tricky due to the upward incline. Slim, standing on the bank and looking back at Mary on the last pile of rocks, put out his hand for Mary to grab as she made the final jump. As they started up the mountain trail, Mary thought about the strong yet gentle grip of Slim's large hand.

To make conversation, Mary remarked that the "poor man's bridge" looked like a lot of work. "It took quite a while," Slim answered, "and I have to do some rebuilding each spring after the ice clears." They started up the trail that worked its way up the mountain. Faintly Mary could see tracks left by a small bull dozer.

"You bring a machine up here?" she inquired.

"Yes," Slim replied, "I harvest some trees each year. Some I sell for lumber but mostly I clear dead ones for firewood. We lost a lot of oaks two years back when the gypsy moths were so bad. Hopefully their cycle has run its course for a few years. The woods need time to recover."

"The new young saplings look healthy" Mary said pointing.

"Most of the new ones I planted. Joe Thurston, who owned this place before me, taught me how to harvest trees carefully and always plant a new one to replace the one cut. Joe had an expression—'Treat the land light.' I must have heard him say it a million times. 'Treat the land light, boy; treat it light.'"

They walked silently for a while. "There's a cold spring just off the trail here if you're thirsty," Slim said.

"That would be nice."

Mary watched as Slim cupped his hands and took a drink and then she did likewise. When they reached the spot near the mountain's top Slim looked at the tree and said, "I'm sorry but he's not there. Maybe it's too early in the day. I don't know much about owls."

"Don't worry about it," Mary replied. "It's been a great walk. Anyway now I have an excuse to come back." As soon as she said it Mary wanted to take back her last remark. "*Too pushy*," she thought to herself.

But before she had time to fret, Slim said, "We could try it later in the day next Saturday if you want."

"I would like that," Mary said as they started down the mountain.

* * *

Mary was angry. Bad enough that her Children's Literature professor thought hers was the only course the class was taking, but now she had announced that they must attend a special lecture on Saturday. And why did she wait until Friday to tell them? Mary stormed back to her room and called her father's office. Remarkably he was in and available to talk. "I can't come home this weekend," she said explaining the situation. "I was planning on a hike with Slim Smith on Saturday. Can you look his number up for me? I need to call him and cancel."

"Isn't he the kid who bought Joe Thurston's place?" her father asked as he looked up the number.

"Yes," Mary replied hesitantly.

"So you're hanging around with a farm boy," her father teased. "Better not let your mother find out."

"Oh Dad," said Mary. "He's taking me to a spot where he saw an owl."

"The old owl routine," her father said laughing. "Hey, I've got to get to the hospital. Call me this weekend, okay.

"Okay Dad. I love you," Mary said as she hung up the phone.

* * *

"Hello Slim, this is Mary Taylor calling. I can't come home this weekend. My Lit professor has scheduled a surprise Saturday lecture. Do you think we could go next weekend?"

"That will be okay if there's not too much snow. The report calls for some snow around Wednesday. I'm sorry about your class. I was looking forward to…"

Surprising herself, Mary interrupted him and said, "Why don't you come over here on Sunday? We could hike the trail they use for cross country skiing."

"I don't know about that," Slim replied. "I'm not used to that college crowd."

"Oh stop being silly," Mary answered. "Can't you come around eleven? I'll be in front of Aikens Dorm."

"Well okay," Slim said, "if you don't mind being seen in a pickup truck."

"I'll see you Sunday," Mary said. And as she hung up she thought to herself, "I can't believe I just did that."

* * *

It took Slim a few minutes to locate Aikens Dorm but soon he saw her standing by the curb. Talk came easier this time. They had lunch at a snack bar near campus and then started up the ski trail. The day was sunny but cold. The view from the mountain top was spectacular. Mary took some pictures including one of Slim. As they came to an overlook, they stopped to look at an especially beautiful scene. They stood silently for several minutes. Then surprising himself, Slim reached out and took Mary's hand. For a moment he was terrified until he felt her squeeze his hand gently. They said nothing as they began the descent from the mountain. But as they walked silently, hand in hand, they both wondered if their lives had changed forever. Later as Slim prepared to leave campus, Mary reached up and kissed his cheek. "I'll see you on Saturday," she said. Slim arrived back at the farm an hour and a half later. He didn't remember much about the ride home, but he knew that he was falling in love with Mary Taylor.

* * *

By Tuesday Slim had convinced himself to forget Mary Taylor. He decided that she was from a different world than his. Her father was a doctor, her mother a socialite, Mary herself a beautiful college girl surrounded by young men who would soon join the professions. It was foolish, he thought, to think that she would be interested in a twenty-year-old trying to make a go of an old farm. Besides, Slim thought, he had moved too fast grabbing her hand up on that mountain. True she hadn't resisted but what could she do? He did think about the kiss she had placed on his cheek when he left. "Probably a farewell kiss," he thought. He went ahead with his work resolved to put the past two weeks out of his mind.

It was different for Mary. During high school when she was transformed from the awkward girl with freckles to the beautiful young woman her attitude was also transformed. She became a very confident person who knew who she was and what she wanted in life. She wanted to teach science and help kids. She wanted to pursue her love of photographing nature. She wanted to spend much time out of doors experiencing the wonders of mountains and streams. It was so wonderful, she thought, that the tire on her bicycle had gone flat. Otherwise she wouldn't have met Slim. She thought that he was so genuine. She liked his gentle strength. She could see the love and respect he had for the outdoors, especially the farm that he could already call his own. Her reaction to holding hands on the mountain was the opposite of Slim's fear. To her it was a sign of the bond that had formed between them almost from the start. Rather than an aggressive act by a brash young man, it was the beginning of a connection between two people and Mary hoped to see that connection strengthen.

Mary Taylor did have one concern. It was her mother and how she would react to Slim Smith. Mary feared that she would resist the relationship and let

Slim know in no uncertain terms that he was not Mary's social equal. This problem resolved itself when Mary returned to her room after classes on Tuesday afternoon. There she found a note on her door telling her to call her father's office. Quickly she dialed the number and her father picked up on the first ring.

"Mary," he said, "I won't waste any time on this; your mother has left me. She has been seeing a doctor for several months now and wants a divorce so they can marry. She has already moved out of the house and wants the place sold so that she can have her half." Dr. Taylor stopped speaking and waited for Mary to react. He didn't have to wait long.

"Good," Mary said. "She's always treated you like a dog, pushed you down, kept you from being the doctor you want to be. I'm sorry Dad but I can't be upset because I'm glad. You deserve so much more. You have so much to offer. Now you can start the clinic you have always wanted. Sell the stupid house. That's all it ever was anyway. It was never a home. Our real home was those three rooms above your office where we played games and watched TV when mother was off at her club meetings. We'll move in there. There's more space than we'll need." Mary caught herself. "I'm sorry, Dad. I didn't mean to react that way. It's just that I'm so angry—and so relieved."

She heard her father reply, "That's okay, Mary. I'm relieved too. This whole thing has been a nightmare for years. Still I'm glad for it because without it I wouldn't have you."

Mary asked, "Do you want me to come home?"

"Absolutely not," Dr. Taylor answered. "The lawyer has already been contacted and I'll call Tom Reilly's real estate agency tomorrow."

"Let's move into your office this weekend," Mary said.

"I'm not sure I can arrange for a truck and movers by then," her father answered.

"Don't worry about that," Mary replied. "I know a real strong guy with his own truck."

As soon as Mary concluded the call to her father, she sat down on the edge of her bed and cried for an hour. Later she would wonder if they had been tears of sorrow or of hope. When she had calmed herself down she walked to the window and looked at the mountains. The sun had gone down and darkness had set in. She could see the silhouette of the mountain tops against the night sky. Looking at her watch, Mary saw that it was seven thirty. "He might be done milking," she thought and dialed Slim's number. When he answered she could sense the surprise in his voice. "Are you tired?" Mary asked.

"Not a bit," Slim answered.

"Will you come to see me?" Mary asked. "I need someone to talk to."

Slim could hear that she was crying. "I can be there by nine."

"Thank you," Mary replied. "I'll be waiting out front for you.

Slim showered and left without eating. The trip seemed to take forever. His mind played games with him. What was wrong? Was she sick? Did she want to end their relationship? She was waiting when he pulled up to her dorm. Before he could shut off the engine she was in the truck. With no self consciousness at all she leaned across the seat and kissed his cheek. "Thank you for coming," she said. "I found out today that my parents are getting divorced. I need someone to lean on for a while—actually I need you to lean on for a while. There's an all night diner about a mile from here. Will you take me there? Oh Slim, I'm all mixed up. I'm supposed to be upset but instead I'm all excited."

* * *

They picked a booth near the back of the diner. The seats had high backs and gave them privacy. They sat across from each other. "Order what you want," said Mary. "I'm buying." Slim hadn't eaten that night so he ordered two cheeseburgers and french fries. Mary asked only for a coke. For two hours she talked. Slim said barely a word. She poured out her life's story. She talked of her awkward childhood, her love for her father and her dislike for her mother. She defended her father and talked at length of his hopes and dreams to start a clinic that would be open to all people. She said that today's events would allow him to pursue his dream. She said that she sometimes felt guilty about the negative feelings for her mother but that she couldn't help herself. She said that today felt like a day of liberation for her and her father. And then she looked at Slim and said, "My mother wouldn't have approved of you. She wanted me to end up with a rich lawyer or something like that. I want you to know that it wouldn't have changed anything," she continued. "Still it will be a lot easier for us with her gone."

She told Slim of the plans to move out of the house this weekend. She asked if he would help and if they could use his truck. When she finished she was exhausted physically and emotionally. She had never talked this openly about her personal affairs. Still she had no regrets. It all had needed to be said and for her it needed to be said to Slim Smith. Reaching across the table they held hands. Slim told Mary that he would help her in any way she needed. He said that he would be there for her whenever she wanted. Leaning across the table their lips met for the first time. It was a moment they would always remember. Slim's head was spinning as he looked across the table at Mary. Her hair was so silky, her skin so smooth and soft. Her brown eyes sparkled between her long dark lashes. "You are so beautiful," he said quietly.

Looking back across the table Mary said simply, "I love you."

* * *

It was after three a.m. when Slim returned to his farm, but he was not in the least bit tired. Never again did he doubt. Never did he try to convince himself that he was mistaken. Yes it had happened quickly. True they had been in each other's company for an extended period on only three occasions. But so what! Some things were meant to be. This was one. He knew what he wanted—he wanted to be with Mary Taylor. Better still he knew that Mary Taylor wanted to be with him. Everything that he loved—his farm, nature, the outdoors had a new dimension. Now the farm had to be beautifully kept and successful for Mary. Now the paths and trails that he loved so much were for Mary. Now his hopes and dreams for the future included Mary. On that night, Slim Smith looked at himself in the mirror and said out loud, "You are the luckiest man on earth." He had no way of knowing how many times throughout his life he would look into the mirror and think those words again.

The next night Mary called at nine o'clock. They talked for an hour. She called again on Thursday night. "I'll be home by four tomorrow," she said. "Can I come right to your place? I'd like to see how you milk your cows. Maybe I can I help you. Do you have any baby calves? Do they like to be petted? Do they have names? Why not? Do you mind if we have dinner with my Dad? He has office hours until eight o'clock. He really wants to meet you. I'm rambling, aren't I?"

* * *

The next day Slim went to the store where he bought his work clothes and bought a pair of coveralls that would fit a person five feet eight inches tall. The clerk asked if he wanted a name stitched on the pocket. "Yes," he said. "Mary."

The next afternoon as she slipped them on over her jeans and shirt Slim thought, "She's even pretty in coveralls." She watched him work and asked lots of questions. She helped him feed the calves. They finished at seven. Mary went to her house in town while Slim showered and changed at his place.

They met at Jensen's Restaurant at eight and Mary's father joined them shortly after. By then most of the town knew that the Taylors had separated. The news had spread like wild fire. Nearly everyone was glad, although most did not say so openly. "It's the best thing that could happen to Doc," one man said. "She was wearing him down. He'll look ten years younger in a month." And after having dinner at Jensen's more news began to spread. "Mary Taylor's seeing the Smith boy, the one who bought Joe Thurston's place. They sure look good together."

* * *

John and Lucy Taylor's home could have sold easily. John's friend, Tom Reilly, found buyers less than two weeks after listing the property. The problem was Lucy. "We can get more than that," she exclaimed. "You insist on using the locals for everything, and they know nothing about the modern world. I won't sign anything for that puny little amount."

John called Tom Reilly and apologized for wasting his time. From that point, Lucy took charge of the process. The out-of-town realtor whom she employed suggested several improvements for the house that he felt would make it more marketable. The most expensive work was renovation of the upstairs bathroom. Lucy insisted on out of town carpenters. "We're not using any of those local handymen who call themselves contractors," she insisted. Six weeks later when the work had been completed the new realtor listed the property for sale. For several months the house stood vacant with no serious offers. "No one wants to live in this godforsaken place," Lucy said. "We'll have to cut the price and take the loss." The house sold nearly a year later. When the calculations for the improvements, plus another year's tax bill were figured into the sale price, the Taylor's actually sold the house for three thousand dollars less than they would have received from Tom Reilly. John was so relieved to have the deal completed that he said nothing.

Mary, who attended the closing with her father, was not so silent. "Gee Mother," she said looking at the final figures, "we only lost three thousand dollars doing it your way. Maybe you should go into the real estate business." Lucy glared at her daughter but said nothing. Later, on the way back to their apartment, Mary apologized to her father for the sarcastic remarks. "I'm sorry," she said, "but I just couldn't resist pointing out those numbers to Mother."

John looked over at his daughter and smiled as he said, "You're a feisty one, all right." And then he added, "I think that is the only time I ever saw your mother speechless."

The next day Dr. Taylor called his friend Tom Reilly. "What's the status of that double lot where Castle's Lumber Company was located?" he asked. Tom told him that it was just sitting there.

"It's a great piece of property but no one wants to pay for the clean up from the fire. That will be more expensive than the property itself. Why? What do you have in mind?"

John told him that he was going to build a health clinic. He wanted a place where people could come regardless of their financial or insurance status. He said that he wanted a large, single-story building with several well equipped rooms. He wanted one of the rooms designed to accommodate minor surgical procedures. And he wanted a large community room where groups ranging from the Boy Scouts to Alcoholics Anonymous could hold meetings.

The word spread quickly. Within a month the local clergy association met with John Taylor and formed a permanent board of directors. A women's auxiliary was created, made up primarily of members of the Methodist church in which John was an active member. A local demolition company agreed to clear the double lot at cost. Dr. Taylor began meeting with an old college friend who had majored in architectural engineering. There were meetings with officials from the local bank, building contractors, medical suppliers and the nearby university. Within two years from the day John Taylor called Tom Reilly, the ribbon was cut and the health clinic/community center was open for business.

Dr. Taylor hired as a full-time nurse, Joan Keller, a medical missionary who had recently returned from a twenty year tour of duty in the poorest areas of India where she had known and sometimes worked with Mother Teresa. Joan Keller was a humanitarian with boundless energy. She threw herself into the work of the new clinic. Within five years this gentle lady would not only win the love and admiration of the entire community, but also the heart of Dr. John Taylor. They would be married in the community room of the clinic. The Methodist minister presided.

* * *

It took a good part of Saturday and three hours on Sunday for John Taylor and his daughter Mary to move their things into the three room apartment above his office. The doctor liked Slim immediately and was impressed by his strength, efficiency and abilities. "That sink has leaked for years," he said as Slim replaced the washers and carefully tightened the connections. The doctor took them out for lunch to celebrate the move. Then he went to his office to meet a young couple whose baby had an ear ache.

Slim and Mary went back to his farm and hiked up the mountain trail. It was a clear day with a bright blue sky. As they neared the summit, Mary saw Slim motion for her to be quiet. There atop the dead oak tree sat the big owl staring at them. Quietly Mary removed her camera from around her waist and attached the zoom lens. She took nearly a dozen shots from different angles, adjusting the light meter skillfully to compensate for the bright blue sky in the background. Then she removed the film and inserted a new cartridge. "I want to get some in black and white," she whispered to Slim. When she was done they left the area quietly with the owl still watching them. Mary would have the best shot made into an eight-by-ten and framed in oak. She gave the photograph to Slim for his twenty-first birthday. That picture would forever occupy a prominent place on the wall of their living room.

For the next two years, while she finished college and secured a job teaching science in the local public school, Slim Smith and Mary Taylor spent most of their free time together. Mary came home from school every weekend, and Slim drove there to see her at least twice each week. Their favorite times were in the summer when Mary was home for an extended period of time. Each day she would leave her father's apartment by nine in the morning and spend the day on the farm with Slim. Whatever he did she joined in. She especially enjoyed harvesting the hay although Slim was always careful to see that she avoided the strenuous lifting jobs. He was also careful to protect her from injury from the machines. "You need those fingers for teaching and photography," he would say. Still she wanted to become a part of his career and soon was driving tractors and doing her favorite thing, feeding the calves. Their special times were Saturdays and Sundays. Slim had a philosophy, right from the beginning, that he would only do necessary chores on the weekends and use the rest of those two days to rest and relax. He followed that rule strictly except during May and June when hay harvesting was at its height. Together they hiked and explored every area of Slim's nearly two hundred acre farm. It was during these times that familiar meadows, trees, stone walls and views became like old friends to them. Slim especially liked the mountain behind his house and barns because it provided the best view of the distant mountain ranges. Often they would climb to what Slim called the upper pasture with a blanket and picnic lunch. Mary always took her camera and intrigued Slim with her vision of things. Once she spent several hours photographing the life that went on in a giant ant hill that she had discovered. Years later some of those pictures appeared in a high school entomology book.

Mary's favorite spot was across the road from the house. They would cross the open field until they reached the creek that ran along the base of the mountain. There beside the stream and under the shade of huge maple trees they would talk for hours. Often on hot summer days they would swim in an area where the pool of water was nearly five feet deep. It was here that Mary learned of Slim's deep convictions. He talked openly to her in ways that he would never reveal to anyone else. Mary learned that Slim, without the benefit of a college education, was a deep thinker and an avid reader. Mary discovered that early in his life Slim had been deeply influenced by old Joe Thurston. Joe had always been vocal in his distrust of anything organized, be it government, unions or religion. Joe's hatred and distrust of government, especially the government in Washington, bordered on radical. "Cheat 'em whenever you can," Joe would say whenever the subject of taxes came up. "They'll just steal the money or waste it anyway." And when it came to religion Joe would say, "They're all a bunch of hypocrites looking for a way to get your money. I've got no use for any of them." Slim told Mary that as a young teenager he accepted Joe Thurston's philosophy thoroughly. As he grew older, during his high school years, Slim's thoughtful mind began to question Joe's ideas although he never argued with them openly.

Slim's beliefs had especially been challenged by his American History teacher during his junior year. He remembered well listening to her lectures on the Great Depression of the nineteen thirties. For her master's degree, she had interviewed dozens of people whose lives had been dismantled by the economic disaster. "These people weren't lazy," she would say as she shared their stories. "They wanted desperately to work. They were victims of a system over which they had no control." Slim could still remember that in these interviews most of the victims had praised the efforts of government— local, state, and national—for creating programs to relieve the suffering.

"If it hadn't been for the CCC," one interviewee had said, "there would have been a violent uprising of young men, and I'm afraid that I would have been one of them."

Slim looked at Mary and could tell that her mind was intent on him. "What are you thinking?" he asked.

"That I want you to continue," she answered.

Slim told her that this same teacher had required that the class read Steinbeck's *Grapes of Wrath*. Most of his classmates had hated the book, but he couldn't put it down. He said that the book had so many dimensions for him that it often kept him awake at night. It made him hate banks. They were so impersonal and uncaring about the lives they were destroying. But he was also frustrated and irritated with the farmers who were forced off the land. Couldn't they see that renting land or worse yet having huge mortgages was a recipe for disaster? And why did they lean so heavily on one crop? Wasn't it obvious that if the prices on the one commodity fell or a drought came along they were doomed? It was so obvious. Joe Thurston was right. If they had kept it small and varied they could have survived. Slim said that he was moved by the loyalty the displaced farmers had for one another. He liked the way they looked out for each other the way a good community should, even though their community was moving rather than stationary. He said that it angered him when government officials treated the dispersed like common criminals. He wondered what kind of a government would act in a way that would make the lives of the displaced people worse rather than better. How could government expect to be part of the solution when it was part of the problem? Slim said that the book had made him think more deeply than ever before. It raised questions in his mind that were still for the most part unresolved. Still he said that the book had convinced him that he wanted to create a situation for himself where he was secure and separated from the dangers that had destroyed the people described by Steinbeck. He wanted to be free and independent. He didn't want to have to answer to any bank or government official. They would leave him alone and he would do the same to them. "So," Mary asked, "are you more like Joe Thurston or your history teacher?"

"I'm somewhere in between," Slim answered. "I still feel like Joe did, that the best life is where you are in control of your own situation and don't need to depend on other people for much of anything. Still I have come to realize that not everyone can do that. Some people just aren't smart enough. Others live in cities and towns where they can't be independent the way I am out here with all this land." He paused, and then continued, "Do you remember from your history classes studying about Thomas Jefferson and Jeffersonian democracy?"

Mary shrugged her shoulders and said, "If I studied it I don't remember. What does it mean?"

"Well," Slim began, "I guess it is basically what I believe. It's what I am. I am a supporter of Jeffersonian democracy."

And so there along the banks of the creek, beneath his grove of maples, and beside his freshly mowed field, Mary sat in quiet amazement while Slim explained Jefferson's philosophy for living. "Jefferson liked small towns nestled among hills and valleys and streams. He liked small farms with good fences and cleared fields. He wanted an honest local government that would keep the roads and bridges in good condition. He thought that every town should have a good inn where travelers could stay. Most people would be farmers but there would also be craftsmen and a few traders—shopkeepers, we would call them. Every town would have a doctor and a lawyer as well as a church with an upright minister. Of course there would be a school with a teacher who knew his stuff and kept good discipline. And maybe most of all there would be a library that was well-used and always growing." He stopped talking and immediately looked embarrassed. "I guess that I got carried away," he said. "But basically that's what I believe. I am a local person. I don't like big national or global things."

Mary had a very serious look on her face as she replied. "You have a greater depth and understanding of things than any of my college classmates. You have gone intellectually where most of them have never thought of going. I am so proud of the way you are thinking things through. It's all right that you haven't resolved everything yet. Neither have I. We're not supposed to yet. We're still in our early twenties." Mary continued. "We have so much to learn from each other. My experiences are so different from yours. My dad has always loved Franklin Roosevelt and what he did for the little people. He often says that madmen like Huey Long would have led us into fascism if Roosevelt hadn't saved capitalism by reforming it. Dad talks about social security and unemployment compensation with near reverence. He would have liked Joe Thurston's abilities as a farmer, but he wouldn't agree with his cynicism and skepticism about government. And would he ever disagree with his opinions on organized religion." Mary told Slim that her father was a lifelong active member of the Methodist church in town. She told how he admired its unselfish motives and its outreach programs. "Your friend Joe Thurston was just plain wrong," Mary said. "At least when it comes to the churches I'm familiar with. Those people aren't perfect but their hearts are in the right place."

* * *

Mary loved the times together when they talked for hours about important and serious issues. Slim was less comfortable verbalizing his deepest thoughts. He was by nature introspective. The people who knew him best gained their perspectives more by the way he lived than by what he said. Still, alone with Mary, he would talk openly in a way that would have amazed even his closest acquaintances. It was a part of Slim that Mary loved. Knowing that Slim would share with her what he would share with no one else, made him even more special to her. But more often those weekends on Slim's farm were times of fun and laughter when two young people, healthy, vibrant, full of hope and very much in love, would run and play like happy children. Those summer days of the two years before they were married would always be remembered as truly special times in their lives.

* * *

Slim Smith married Mary Taylor in the middle of August following her graduation from college. The ceremony took place in the Methodist church. Nearly one hundred people attended. The reception was held beneath a large white tent next to the stream in the lower field of Slim's farm. Mary's mother attended the ceremony but refused to come to the reception. "I am not going to sit in some hayfield," she had said.

For a wedding gift two of Slim's friends took care of the farm for a week while Slim and Mary traveled through New England and into Canada. It was the only official vacation they would have for nearly thirty years.

Thus began the very happy married life of Slim and Mary Smith. Mary began her career teaching science to middle school children in the local public school. Her career as a photographer also blossomed and throughout the years her nature photographs not only adorned the walls of people's homes but also were found in calendars and even in numerous magazines and science textbooks. She also became a farmer and played a major role in caring for the animals as well as harvesting crops of hay and corn. Slim followed the philosophy of his mentor Joe Thurston and ran a small diverse operation with money coming from many sources that included milk, lumber, firewood, maple syrup, honey and snow removal. He also sold the excess hay from his property and for a while kept chickens which he eventually gave up, saying that they were too much work with not much to show for it.

* * *

Slim and Mary Smith lived a life of very private passion. They found happiness on the land they had both come to love. The one great sadness of their lives was that there had never been children. After several years of trying they went through a series of tests; the results told them that a serious bout with the mumps at the age of fifteen had left Slim sterile. They often talked of adoption but eventually decided against it. "We have each other," Mary had said. "Let's just be happy together." And so they were. Now in their early fifties Mary had convinced Slim to look for a hired man so that there would be more time for relaxation and perhaps even an occasional weekend away. In response to Mary's urging, Slim purchased an old trailer which he completely refurbished by replacing the flammable insulation, rewiring all the electrical fixtures, and painting both the inside and outside. They had hoped to find an older man with farming experience. Instead a nervous young man climbed the steps of their porch accompanied by Pastor Jim Braxton.

Chapter 4

Ben stood nervously on the porch as the pastor rang the bell. Mary answered the door, and as they entered the house Ben saw Slim sitting at the kitchen table. The room was very large and equipped with all the modern conveniences. Still it had a rural, almost nineteenth century look to it. Especially noteworthy were the black cast iron skillets and pots hung neatly on the walls. The large kitchen table and chairs matched the solid oak cabinets. From the kitchen he could see into the spacious open living room with hard wood floors and colonial style furnishings. No walls separated the kitchen from the living room, but the division was made clear by the huge circular double flue chimney that rose through the center of the house. From the kitchen side, Ben could see the wood burning behind the glass doors. He would learn later that there was a similar fireplace on the living room side. A circular seat made of thick gray slate went around the entire stone chimney.

Pastor Braxton spoke first. "Slim, Mary, I want you to meet my friend Ben Thomas. He just arrived from Florida and he's looking for work." Mary smiled and extended her hand. Slim followed and Ben noticed the firm grip of his huge hands.

"It's nice to meet you," Ben said. "You have a beautiful place."

"Thanks," Slim responded. "We like it."

An awkward silence that lasted a few seconds was broken by the pastor. "I have a few errands to run. Why don't I give you some time to talk? I'll stop back in an hour or so."

Looking relieved, Mary responded, "That would be good. I'll see you out." She walked to the pastor's car and as he was about to leave she said, "Thank you Jim, I assume your errand is to go home and give us some time alone with this young man. If things work out, I'll call and save you a trip back out."

The pastor smiled and replied, "I'll wait for your call."

33

When Mary returned to the house Ben was sitting at the kitchen table with the cup of coffee that Slim had just poured. Their large golden retriever, Anabel, had wandered into the room and was sniffing Ben's shoes. As Mary joined them at the table, she glanced at Slim and then, looking at Ben, said, "Tell us about yourself."

Ben spoke hesitantly but honestly. He told them that he had never been anywhere but Florida and how he had always disliked the tropical climate. He said that he had always been fascinated with mountains and seasons and snow. Then he spoke of his mother's death and how he had stayed with his grandparents until completing high school. He told of the trip north and how his car had given out somewhere in New Jersey. He said that he had caught a ride in a trailer truck the rest of the way and that stopping at this particular place was more by impulse than design. He said that he had spent the night in the church and that he hoped the minister knew how much he appreciated all the help. Then, looking up from the table, Ben said, "I really need a job and a place to stay, but I have to admit that I don't know the first thing about farming."

Mary had listened intently as he spoke. When he finished, she looked at Slim and then said to the boy, "Why don't you try it for a couple of days on a trial basis and we'll see how it goes."

Ben nodded and said, "Thank you, I would like that."

"Good. Slim, you take Ben out to the trailer and I'll try to get hold of Jim Braxton and save him the trip back here."

* * *

Ben picked up the large backpack from where he had left it on the porch. He followed Slim to the trailer that was located behind the main house, between two red out buildings. Slim unlocked the door and they entered the main living area. Along the wall, opposite the door, was the kitchen. In the corner was a small refrigerator. Beside it on a counter sat a small two burner hot plate. The sink was located in front of a window that looked out at a large field. The counter to the right of the sink held a small toaster oven. The rest of the room was completely open. A platform rocker was the room's only piece of furniture. The back part of the trailer was separated by a wall with a door in the middle. Slim opened that door and entered. Ben followed. There was a small cot against the back wall. To the right was a toilet, sink and shower stall. Along the opposite wall was a metal clothes rack. Ben set his

34

back pack on the cot as Slim began to speak.

"You have electric heat with a thermostat in each room. Don't turn them below fifty-five degrees or the pipes may freeze. You are responsible for the electric bill. Otherwise there is no rent. That's part of your pay. These old trailers were fire traps. They were insulated mainly with cardboard. I removed all that material and replaced it with good insulation, including the floor and ceiling. You'll stay warm in here."

They returned to the kitchen-living area just as Mary entered. She was carrying a large grocery bag in one arm and two blankets and a pillow in another.

"Here are some things to keep you going till Friday when Slim pays you," Mary said. "You can return the blankets when you have your own. Let us know if you need anything else."

Slim looked at his watch. "It's one thirty. Why don't you get settled for a couple of hours. I'll knock on the door at four when I'm ready to start chores."

Slim and Mary left Ben alone in the trailer. He turned the thermostat to sixty-five degrees and felt the room begin to warm almost immediately. He sat down in the platform rocker and rested for a half hour.

By three thirty Ben had made up his cot and put away the items that Mary had brought. They included bread, a package of hot dogs, a dozen eggs, a tub of margarine, and several cans of soup and pasta meals. He emptied his back pack, hanging up the clean clothes and putting those that needed laundering back in the pack. He put on his oldest jeans and a sweatshirt and was waiting when Slim knocked on his door precisely at four.

* * *

Ben followed Slim to the barn. They entered a large room attached to the main barn. It was hygienically clean. The smooth gray concrete floor was spotless. A great stainless steel tank stood on one side of the room. A clear plastic pipe ran from the tank, through the wall into the main barn. Buckets, some stainless steel and some plastic, lined a rack on the opposite wall. There was a large double basin sink above which were shelves containing various types of cleaning fluids. Slim took off his coat and hat and hung them on a nail in the wall. After removing his work shoes, he pulled some dark blue coveralls over his pants and shirt. He slid his feet into a pair of rubber boots and headed to the door of the main barn. Ben followed Slim into the barn and was immediately aware of the warmth created by the bodies of the thirty-five cows standing in their stanchions. The cows were mostly black and white Holsteins, along with a few Guernseys. It was the first time Ben had ever seen cows up close, and he was impressed with their enormous size.

"Are you afraid to climb?" Slim asked.

"No," Ben answered.

Slim took him to the end of the barn and showed him the ladder that went to the top of the tall silo. He pointed out that small doors appeared beside the ladder every few feet. They were closed, he said, because the silo was full of ensilage. He pointed to the door at the very top, and Ben could see that it was open.

"Climb through that door and throw down a hundred forkfuls of ensilage."

Ben hung tight to the metal ladder as he climbed the chute to the top of the silo. When he reached the door he crawled into the silo and found the fork. By the time he had thrown a hundred forkfuls of the sweet smelling ensilage down the chute, his back ached. When he climbed down the ladder, Slim stood waiting.

"I guess my forkfuls are larger than yours," he said. "You'll have to go back up and throw some more down. Keep counting and I'll yell up to you when there's enough."

Embarrassed, Ben climbed back to the top and had thrown thirty-seven more forkfuls when he heard Slim's voice. "One hundred and thirty-seven", Ben thought to himself, hoping that he could remember that number for the next time.

Slim had Ben fill a large wheel barrow with ensilage and showed him how much to place in front of each cow. As Ben worked his way down the line, he could see Slim move from cow to cow with two milking machines. Before attaching the machine to each cow's udder, Slim would dip it into a solution in a stainless steel pail. He would also wipe each cow's udder with a clean paper towel dipped into the same solution. Ben could see the milk running from each machine through the clear plastic pipe into the room with the stainless steel tank. "So that's how it works," Ben thought to himself.

When he finished distributing the ensilage, the pile at the base of the silo was almost gone. He was feeling good about that when he saw Slim coming toward him.

"Good," said Slim. "I don't like any left over. It gets stale and they won't eat it."

Next, Slim had Ben feed the fifteen calves that were tethered in an area at the far end of the barn. "Put a cup of this powder into a pail of lukewarm water and give each calf about half a pail," he said. "When you're finished, open up some bales of hay and give each calf two pads. You'll use about three bales altogether."

By the time Ben finished the calves, Slim had completed milking and was cleaning and sanitizing the machines and the plastic pipe. He stopped long enough to show Ben how much hay to place in front of each cow. It was after seven o'clock when they finished the work. As they left the barn Slim said, "Good job. I'll see you here in the barn tomorrow morning at five thirty."

Ben returned to his trailer tired but encouraged. He felt certain that he could do this job. He had to. Otherwise he faced the cold winter with no money and no place to stay. Slowly he took off his clothes and hung them up. The hot shower revived him and made him aware of his hunger. He looked at the groceries Mary had left and chose a can of ravioli. That, along with a glass of milk and several slices of bread, was his evening meal. He washed the dishes and put them away. Ben had always had a need for things to be clean and orderly. He was also aware that Slim and Mary had very high standards. That was clear wherever he looked. Ben sat quietly for nearly an hour thinking of the events of the past few days. He was pleased he had mustered the courage to take this chance. He liked this place and these people. He was determined to succeed.

Ben turned the thermostat in the living quarters to fifty-five degrees and went into the bedroom. He set the alarm on his watch for five o'clock and climbed beneath the blankets. Sleep came quickly and Ben remembered nothing until he heard the beep of the alarm.

* * *

Ben was watching from the window, and he went out before Slim could knock. The sky was still dark as they approached the barn. While Slim changed into his coveralls, he told Ben that the cows received grain and hay for their morning feed. Inside the barn he showed Ben the large metal bin that contained the grain. Slim placed the wheelbarrow under the bin and opened a small sliding door. Ben watched as the grain flowed smoothly into the wheelbarrow. Taking a large coffee can, Slim showed Ben how much to place in front of each cow.

"When you're done with the grain, give them the hay just like last night and then feed the calves." With those instructions, he started milking and the two didn't speak until Ben had finished the calves.

When Slim finished milking he opened the large doors at the end of the barn that led to the barn yard. Pointing to the two large metal feeders he told Ben to place two bales of hay in each. When Ben had finished, Slim showed him how to open the stanchions to release the cows. Ben was intrigued that the cows knew exactly what he was doing and that they walked directly to the barn yard and began eating.

"They sure do have appetites," Ben remarked.

"That's what makes milk," Slim answered, smiling.

It was seven thirty and they were nearly finished with the chores when Mary came into the barn.

"I'm leaving now," she said to Slim. "I'll see you around five. We have a faculty meeting after school." Looking over at Ben she asked if the trailer was warm enough.

"It's fine," Ben answered, "and thanks again for the food."

Ben helped Slim finish washing the pails. As they left the barn Slim told him to take an hour for breakfast. "Meet me back at the barn around a quarter to nine," he said.

Ben fixed a large breakfast of eggs and toast. He drank some milk and thought how good it would be to have some orange juice and hot coffee. He checked his watch calendar and made sure it was Wednesday. He hoped that Slim would pay on Friday without his having to ask. Then he could go into town for supplies. He remembered that he still had over one hundred sixty dollars in his wallet, but he hoped to save that for emergencies.

Back in the barn, Slim gave Ben a shovel and showed him how to scrape the floor. Everything but the hay bedding was pushed into a concrete gutter that ran in a large oval around the barn directly behind the milking cows. Most of the cows' waste fell into the gutter but some missed. Ben cleaned the right side of the barn while Slim did the left. When they finished, Slim flipped a switch to start the track located at the bottom of the gutter. Blades, welded to the track, pushed the manure to the end of the barn and into a waiting spreader. Before Slim took the tractor and spreader to the field to empty, he told Ben to remove any soiled bedding to a compost pile behind the barn. He showed him how to apply fresh bedding. "Be sure to use the hay over there," Slim said, pointing to a section of the loft located on the second floor of the barn. "That's poor hay that I don't use for feed. It's from the swampy area down by the creek that doesn't get dry enough to work on till late August. By then the hay has lost its nutritional value, but it's perfect for bedding. Most farmers buy sawdust for bedding, but I figure why pay for sawdust when this is just going to waste? Anyway, the cows seem to like to lay on hay better than sawdust."

Together they threw the loose, unbaled hay down to the milking area. While Slim took the load of manure to the field Ben began to remove the soiled hay. He was nearly finished putting down the new bedding when Slim looked into the barn and said, "Good job."

* * *

Slim took Ben to the edge of a field near the barn where a large stack of logs stood higher than Ben's head. The logs ranged from ten to twenty feet in length. Nearby was a huge pile of firewood that had been cut into sixteen inch lengths and split by the hydraulic splitter that sat nearby. "We're in the firewood business for the next few days," Slim announced. Ben helped remove the plastic tarp from the wood pile. Slim filled the splitter with gas and checked the oil. The machine started on the second pull and Slim shouted to Ben, "It needs to warm up for a few minutes." Then Slim went to the five-yard dump truck parked nearby and took a chainsaw from the floor of the passenger side. He filled it with gas and bar oil. Without speaking he went to the stack of logs and began sawing the wood into sixteen-inch lengths. Ben could see that each piece was almost exactly the same length even though Slim never measured them. When a large pile of wood began to build up around him, Slim stopped the saw and said to Ben, "Get the wheel barrow from the barn and start moving this wood over to the splitter. Stack it in a neat pile."

Ben began to work and Slim returned to sawing. When Ben had wheeled and stacked several loads, Slim shut off his saw and came over to the splitter. "I want you to be real careful with this machine. Never put your fingers here," he said pointing. Slim took a piece of wood from the stack. "Split them about this size and throw them on the pile," Slim demonstrated as he ran it through the machine until it was quartered. "Any questions?" Ben said no and began to work. It was a cold day but soon he was warm with perspiration, except for his toes. The machine worked easily and Ben caught on quickly. For the next three days, Ben and Slim milked the cows and worked on firewood. At night Ben was exhausted. He would eat his dinner, shower and fall into bed. He had never worked so hard. Still he found himself challenged and eager to please Slim.

Friday night they finished milking at six thirty. "You're getting faster at this," Slim said with a smile. He took his wallet from his pocket and gave Ben eighty-five dollars. "That's twenty-five dollars a day plus ten for helping with chores the first night you arrived."

"You should keep the ten for the food you gave me," Ben said.

"Don't worry about that," Slim answered. "By the way, I don't work on Saturdays and Sundays except for milking. If you help, I'll pay you ten dollars a day or you can take the weekends off."

"I'll work," Ben quickly responded.

"Good. That way Mary won't need to be a weekend farmer. She's already too busy with school." Slim continued, "We'll be gone for a while tomorrow. We're leaving around nine."

"Could I get a ride into town with you?" Ben asked.

"Sure thing," said Slim. "See you in the morning."

Chapter 5

Ben ate and showered quickly. They had hurried with Saturday morning chores and he knew Slim and Mary were anxious to get started. He put on his last pair of clean jeans and shirt. His laundry was already stuffed into the worn back pack, and he quickly left the trailer when he saw Slim get the car from the garage. He sat quietly during the five mile ride to town and thanked them when they left him at the curb. As they rode away Slim said to Mary, "I wonder if we'll ever see him again."

"I'm guessing that we will," answered Mary.

* * *

Ben walked down the main street for the first time since arriving in town in a tractor trailer. So much had happened; he couldn't believe that it had only been five days. Without having to ask for directions, he came to a laundromat. An attendant exchanged his ten dollar bill for a roll of quarters. Within an hour his clothes were washed and in the dryer. A woman with two small children who called her Grandma was using the machine nearby and smiled when Ben looked up. Later, while folding his laundry and putting it back in the pack, Ben asked the woman if the town had a grocery store and a clothing store. She told him that the malls had pretty much ended the businesses that used to be in town. "We do have a good size IGA one block down and around the corner," she pointed. "As far as clothes, the only thing in town is the thrift shop one block up," she continued. "They have a big variety and great prices," she added.

Ben went first to the thrift shop. The clerk was friendly and very helpful. "I'm looking for warm work clothes, especially boots," Ben said. She quickly found two pairs of heavy wool socks that looked almost new. She also located a heavy denim jacket with a lining that zipped in for the cold weather. Next she found some lined leather work gloves and, best of all, a pair of rubber boots insulated with a soft lining. They were size ten and a half, slightly larger than Ben's shoe size but the clerk said they should be fine with the wool socks underneath. "How much does this come to?" he asked and was pleased that the total bill was only fifty-two dollars. The clerk put everything into a large plastic bag and Ben headed toward the IGA with his new clothes over one shoulder and the pack with his laundry on his back.

When he entered the IGA he asked the clerk at the register if the town had a taxi service. "Yes," she said. "It's three buildings down from the Methodist church."

"That will be easy to find," he thought, recalling his first night in town. Ben asked if he could leave his two bundles by the register while he shopped and the clerk pointed to a good place.

Ben knew that he had to be a careful shopper. He had to keep the grocery bill under thirty dollars. Figuring each item as he went along, he chose six cans of soup, a box of macaroni, a block of cheddar cheese, a can of instant coffee, sugar, a box of corn flakes, and a small canned ham that was on sale. He didn't need milk because Slim gave him as much as he needed. On his way to the register, Ben walked through the snack aisle and chose some oatmeal raisin cookies and a bag of chips. The bill for the groceries was twenty-two dollars. "Good," Ben thought, "there is still eleven dollars left from my week's pay." He still needed to go to the drug store and then pay for the taxi. Maybe he could do both without dipping into his emergency funds. At the drug store he bought a small tube of toothpaste, one bar of Ivory soap, a tablet and a box of envelopes. As he started toward the taxi building, he realized that he was overloaded for the walk of nearly five blocks. Part of the way had sidewalks but the final two blocks Ben walked along the edge of the street.

It was along this section that Ben set the two bags of groceries on the ground to rest his arms. One of the bags tipped over and several cans spilled out. It was when he reached for a can among the leaves under a privet hedge that he spotted the small worn leather pouch. Opening the clasp, Ben was startled to find a large roll of bills inside. As he counted in amazement, Ben discovered that the pouch contained seventeen hundred-dollar bills. Ben put the money back into the pouch and slowly turned it over. On the reverse side he could see very faintly the initials NLZ. Ben picked up his belongings, but instead of going to the taxi he went up the steps of the porch leading to the Methodist parsonage. Mrs. Braxton recognized Ben at once and called to her husband. Jim Braxton extended a friendly hand and looking at all the bundles said, "It looks like you could use a ride."

"I'm on my way to get a taxi," Ben said, "but I was wondering if you knew anyone in town with the initials NLZ."

The minister smiled. "That would have to be Nellie Zenger. She goes to our church. I've been real worried about her lately. She just hasn't been herself for a month or so."

"I think I know why," Ben said and he handed the worn pouch to the Pastor. He and Mrs. Braxton appeared stunned as they looked at the money.

"That explains it," Mrs. Braxton said. "She lost all that money and she's such a private person that she didn't tell anyone."

"Can you see that she gets it back?" Ben asked.

"Sure," the minister answered, "but don't you want to deliver it yourself?"

"No need, and please don't make a big deal out of it."

"Well, at least let me take you home," insisted the pastor.

As they left, Mrs. Braxton looked at Ben and said, "Thank you. You've really helped a nice lady today and you've restored my sense of optimism."

When they arrived back at the farm, the minister said to Ben, "I'm glad you chose this place, Ben. By the way, Mary says you're doing a great job."

* * *

It was nearly four o'clock when Slim and Mary approached their farm. Slim had been quiet on the trip back and Mary knew he was wondering if Ben had moved on. As they pulled into the driveway they noticed the light in the barn. Before going to the house they walked to the barn and Mary saw Slim smile as he heard the familiar sound of ensilage falling down the chute.

By nine thirty Sunday morning Ben was feeling good. Slim had noticed the new work clothes and remarked that he should be much more comfortable working outside. Now the morning chores were done and Ben looked forward to the relaxing day. At ten thirty, after a large breakfast that included hot coffee, Ben decided to walk up the road that wound around a sharp curve where the Smith property line ended. He started down the driveway just as Slim and Mary were leaving for church. He noticed what an attractive couple they were. Mary knew how to dress and she was also very pretty. Slim wore a tweed jacket and a good shirt open at the collar. "I bet she picked that out for him," thought Ben, smiling. It was strange. He had known this couple for less than one week and yet he had a feeling of pride as he watched them leave together.

* * *

On Tuesday evening, around seven fifteen, Ben had already showered and eaten his evening meal. Mary was driving to town for a church meeting, and she was dropping Ben off at the public library which stayed open until ten o'clock on Tuesdays. "I think you will like our library," she said as they drove towards town. "We take a great deal of pride in it." Then, changing the subject, she asked if Ben remembered that Thursday was Thanksgiving Day. Ben admitted that he hadn't. "We have a good time on Thanksgiving, and Slim and I are hoping that you will join us for dinner at noon."

"I would like that," Ben replied.

Mary's car eased to a stop in front of the library. "Meg is our librarian," she said to Ben. "Tell her that you are a friend of Slim and Mary Smith. She will process your card immediately and you can sign out books tonight if you like." Ben was excited as he walked up the steps to the library. He had always loved books. Even as a child he had enjoyed his mother's weekly trips to the library. In school, he loved his English classes, especially when they studied great literature. One of his fondest memories of high school was the day his American Lit. teacher had kept him after class and urged him to consider college. He had always remembered with appreciation, that recognition of his potential.

When Ben identified himself, the lady at the desk smiled and said, "Oh yes, Mary said you were coming." She added, "Mary has been on the board here for a long time. This library wouldn't have grown the way it has without her."

"First things first," thought Ben as he left the desk with his new card. He went to the computer and got online. With little difficulty he found the name and address of the mayor of the northern New Jersey town where his car had broken down. He wrote the information on a slip of paper and put it in his wallet. Next he logged on to the card catalog for the library and looked up the topic "Vermont History." He was pleased to find a large selection and immediately located the area where the books were shelved. He was so deeply involved in the books that he lost track of time until he heard Mary's voice as she talked to Meg at the desk. Quickly he chose a large pictorial of Vermont and a small book entitled *Vermont By Choice*.

As Meg checked out the books she remarked, "It looks like you want to know about your new state." Then, looking at the pictorial, she added, "Did you see any of Mary's pictures in here?" Seeing Ben's surprise Meg said, "I guess Mary hasn't filled you in on her photography career. You will find her work in many places if you look."

"Not that many," Mary said.

"There you go selling yourself short," Meg said, and looking at Ben she added, "Have her show you her gallery sometime."

On the way home Mary told Ben that she had loved photographing nature since she was a child. She said that Slim had built a dark room for her in the basement of their house and that she was fortunate enough to sell some photographs each year. "What about the gallery?" Ben asked.

"Oh that's a room upstairs where I store everything. You remind me and I'll show you on Thursday."

Chapter 6

Thanksgiving Day at noon Ben walked from his trailer to Slim and Mary's front door. Two unfamiliar cars were parked in the driveway. Ben was wearing his best jeans and shirt. On his feet were the newer sneakers he tried to keep clean. He wished that he owned some slacks and shoes. When Slim paid him again on Friday he would be able to do some shopping in a real store. For now this would have to do.

The house was filled with talk and the odors of cooking food. Mary began the introductions before Ben had time to feel nervous. First he met Mary's father and stepmother. Her father was a tall distinguished-looking man with pure white hair. He had a friendly smile and told Ben how glad he was that Slim had some help on the farm. Mary's stepmother was very soft-spoken and her manner immediately made Ben feel very much at ease. "Ben," she said extending her hand, "it's so good to meet you. We've heard such nice things."

Next Mary introduced Slim's older sister Carol and her husband. "So Slim's making a farmer out of you," she said and before Ben could respond she continued, "You couldn't have a better teacher."

Finally Mary introduced Ben to a young man named David Burnham. David, Ben learned, was a college student who worked part time at the medical clinic run by Mary's father. "David lives too far away to go home for Thanksgiving," Mary said. "I think you two are about the same age."

"I'm nineteen," David said as they shook hands.

Ben replied, "I turned eighteen earlier this month." Before any further conversation could take place Slim called everyone to the dinner table.

It had been a very long time since Ben had enjoyed a meal like this. The menu was traditional New England Thanksgiving from the fruit cup appetizer, through the turkey, dressing, potatoes (both mashed and sweet), cranberries, rolls, squash and finally apple, mince, and pumpkin pie served with squares of sharp cheddar cheese. Both the meal and the company relaxed Ben. The adults, particularly Dr. Taylor, were conscious to include him in the conversation. He especially liked David who, though quiet, seemed pleased to have another young person at the table.

After dinner Ben joined Slim and the other men in the living room for football and coffee. The fireplace was bright and cheerful. It was during this time that Ben noticed two of Mary's photographs framed and hanging on the wall. He especially liked the one of the large owl sitting atop a dead oak tree. Sitting in the overstuffed chair and surrounded by these kind people, Ben felt good. He looked up from the television in time to see Slim watching him with a look of satisfaction.

* * *

That night, long after all the guests were gone, Ben and Slim were finishing chores when Mary came into the barn. She looked at Slim and then said to Ben, "It was nice that you could join us today. Slim and I were so pleased to have you." Before Ben could respond she continued, "We know that you are a private person, Ben, and I hope that you won't be upset with Pastor Braxton, but he told us about you finding and returning Nellie Zenger's money. We want you to know how pleased we are that you chose to do that. Most people would have ignored those initials and kept the money, I'm afraid."

"I'm not upset," Ben replied. "I guess I'm glad he told you. Honestly, though, I never thought about keeping the money. My Mom was really strict about things like that."

"Nellie is a long-time friend of ours," Slim said. "I have to deliver a load of wood to her place on Monday. She's hoping that I'll bring you along. She would like to meet you."

That night Ben sat in his trailer thinking of the day's events. Could it be, he wondered, that he had been at this farm for only just over two weeks? How could he have such a feeling of attachment to this place and these people in such a short time? It was almost like a dream. He hoped that it wasn't. Later, before going to bed he took his writing tablet and wrote two short notes. First he told his grandparents that he was living in Vermont, working on a farm and liking it very much. The second note was to the mayor of that small New Jersey town. In it he explained that circumstances had forced him to abandon his car there in early November. "I know that I shouldn't have done that," he explained, "but I was in desperate straits at that point." Then including his address he told the mayor to notify him if there were any fines or expenses for which he was responsible.

* * *

It was the Friday morning after Thanksgiving. The day was clear and cold. When the morning chores were completed, Slim and Ben took their usual breakfast break. At nine thirty, Slim knocked on the door of Ben's trailer and said, "Dress warm, we're heading up the mountain to cut fence posts. Make yourself a sandwich for lunch. I'll bring a thermos of coffee." Slim was surprised to see the look of excitement in Ben's eyes. "Something wrong?" Slim asked.

"No," Ben replied. "It's just that I never climbed a mountain before. We didn't have any in Florida."

They started up the hill behind Ben's trailer. It was open pasture for nearly a quarter mile. The pasture, where Slim kept his milking cows during the warmer weather, was enclosed with cedar posts and three rows of barbed wire fencing. Slim told Ben that each spring, after the frost was out of the ground, they had to walk the entire fence line checking for rotted posts and broken wire. "If you do it every spring," Slim said, "it's never a real big job." He went on, "You need a real tight fence to keep cows in. They have a tendency to get out if they can."

When they reached the point where the pasture ended and the woodlands began, Slim lifted the wire for Ben to slip through and once through, Ben did the same for Slim. Slim carried a chainsaw, two splitting wedges, and a small can of gas. Ben had a jug of bar oil and an axe. Their lunch and the thermos were in a small pack which Slim carried on his back. Once within the woods the mountain became more steep. They followed a stone wall that was in remarkably good condition. In a small opening near the wall Ben spotted a small green building with a tin roof painted silver. A pipe ran out of the building from which flowed a stream of water. Slim told Ben that the building was the reservoir for the water that was piped to the house and barn below. Opening the door to the reservoir Slim showed Ben two pipes running into the building from behind. "Those are the two springs that feed into the reservoir," Slim said pointing. "One is right behind this building and the other is up the mountain another hundred yards or so. It's a good water system. We've never run dry and you know that cows use a lot of water."

They moved upward in silence for nearly a half hour. The forest was a combination of hemlock, pine, oak, maple, and ash. Quite suddenly they came to an opening and entered what Slim called the upper pasture. "I don't keep cows up here anymore," he said. "It's a perfect spot for cedar trees," he said pointing. "They reseed faster than I need them for posts. If we have time I'll cut more than we'll need and sell the extras."

Ben turned around and looked down the trail they had just climbed. He could see the silver of the tin roofs of the barns and the house. He could see the open fields across the road from the house and the creek that flowed at the base of the mountain on the other side of the valley. Then looking into the distance, Ben had his first good look at the Green Mountains of Vermont. The view went on for miles—range after range of snow-capped mountains. Standing there in silence Ben knew that he would return often to this spot. It would become his favorite place on earth. A strange and wondrous feeling came over him. He had been on this farm for less than a month and on this mountain only a few minutes. Still he felt somehow that he was home. It was a feeling he had never before felt, and he knew that he did not want it to end.

Slim sawed down a cedar tree that was about twenty feet high and a good ten inches thick at the base. He showed Ben how to trim off the branches with the axe and then proceeded to cut down nearly twenty-five more trees. Ben had finished removing the branches of only two trees when Slim stopped cutting. "I'll trim the rest with the chainsaw," Slim shouted. "You begin piling the branches in one spot." For nearly an hour they worked steadily. Slim stopped only to refuel. "Pile those branches as high as you can," he told Ben. "I want them consolidated as much as possible."

When all the trees were trimmed of their branches, Slim measured them to the appropriate lengths and sawed at each mark. By noon all the branches were piled and the posts lay in a large stack. The two men sat in the sun on the stone wall while they drank coffee and ate sandwiches. Slim seemed pleased that a section of the upper pasture was again clear of trees. "I like to keep it open even though I'll probably never put cows up here again. I hate to see the old mountain pastures grow over."

After lunch, Ben watched with keen interest as Slim began to split the posts. Placing a wedge against the end of a post, Slim would tap it with the back of his axe until it lodged in the wood. Then with one swing of the axe he would drive the wedge into the post and a crack would develop up the side. By placing the second wedge into the new crack, and hitting it with the axe, the post would split further releasing the first wedge. Repeating this process

49

one more time would split the post completely. When he had split several posts he told Ben to start carrying them, two at a time, down the trail to the fence at the top of the pasture. Two hours later when Slim said, "Let's stop for today; it's almost chore time," Ben was exhausted. Later that evening as they completed milking, Slim asked Ben how he was holding up.

"To be honest, I'm worn out."

"Get a good night's sleep," Slim said smiling. "I know tomorrow's Saturday but I would like to get those posts down here. I think we can finish by lunch time if we get started by nine."

* * *

The next morning while they were milking, Mary appeared at the barn with coffee and buttered rolls. "Breakfast on the run today," she said to Ben. "Slim is determined to get those posts down this morning. He thinks we will have our first big snow next week and he is usually right."

They finished chores at nine o'clock sharp and started up the mountain. Slim drove the John Deere crawler with a sturdy wooden sled attached behind. The sled's steel runners slid easily along the ground even though there was no snow. It had oak two-by-fours, three feet high bolted to the sides. There were three on each side so that the fence posts, when loaded on the sled, would not slide off. Ben followed behind the sled and was surprised to see Mary running to catch up with them. Her camera case was attached to a strap around her waist.

When they reached the upper fence, Slim left the crawler and the three of them walked to the upper pasture. Slim and Ben began carrying posts down the trail to the crawler and Mary continued up the mountain with her camera.

Up and down the trail they went for over two hours. By noon all the posts were down to the upper fence and loaded on the sled. Almost on cue Mary appeared from the woods. "Any luck?" Slim asked.

"No animals but some good shots of the ice on the brook," Mary answered. Then she added, "I did get a few shots of a couple of guys lugging fence posts."

"I hope you took my best side," Slim said and he started the crawler.

* * *

Slim backed the dump truck up to the huge pile of split firewood. Together Slim and Ben removed the huge tarp from the woodpile. The truck had two ten-inch planks attached to its sides to nearly double its capacity. "You climb into the back, and I'll throw it up to you," Slim said. "Stack it in rows from front to back." Ben quickly figured out why Slim had chosen to throw the wood into the truck. He watched as Slim selected smaller chunks while throwing the larger ones aside. "He knows which pieces he wants to take to a little old lady," thought Ben. "The bigger chunks will go to the stronger, younger customers."

Both men were warm with perspiration by the time the truck was filled. They drove into town, past the church two blocks, and turned left onto a quiet street. Nellie Zenger's house was a small white salt box. The front had a steep roof that attached to a single-story section with a nearly flat roof in the back. Next to the house was a single car garage. The garage was empty except for some tools hanging from nails. "We put a good size pile on the side porch near the door," Slim said. "The rest goes in the garage and every week or so we come back and replenish the porch. That way Nellie can reach what she needs without leaving the house."

They began to work and said little until the job was complete. Then taking a quart of honey from the truck Slim went to the door where Nellie was waiting. Ben saw Nellie take the honey and hand Slim some cash. Then after a few moments of conversation Slim called for Ben to come over and he introduced him. "I have to run over to the bank," Slim said to Ben. "I'll be back to get you in a half hour."

Ben was nervous, but not for long. Nellie took him into a very open kitchen. Through a curved archway Ben could see a bedroom filled with antique furniture. A small bathroom was visible just off the bedroom.

The kitchen, while large, was cozy and warm. There was a wood-burning cooking stove along one wall near the sink. On the other end of the room was a brown stove that Nellie used as her main source of heat. Ben would learn later that she used wood for fuel during the day but just before bed time she would fill the stove with coal for the night. The walls of the kitchen were papered with a design of small pink flowers and green leaves that resembled dogwood. Several pictures done in crewel hung on the walls—all rural scenes. Near the brown stove sat an oak rocking chair with brown cushions. Beside it was a basket filled with all kinds of cloth, thread and sewing utensils. A large yellow-orange cat slept by the stove. The middle of the room was dominated by a wooden table with four chairs.

Nellie Zenger was a plump woman of eighty years. She had a warm smile that seemed to remain on her face even if her talk was serious. She wore a house dress beneath a large blue apron with yellow flowers. The house was very warm.

"Take off your coat and sit at the table," Nellie told Ben. She brought two cups from the counter and poured hot tea. "Let me add some of Slim's good honey," she said without asking. "And have some cookies," she added, removing a towel from a plate of large oatmeal raisin cookies with walnuts. They were homemade and still warm from the oven. "So you're the nice young man who found my money," she said. Then she explained how she had walked to the bank on a warm October day. On her way back she had stopped to remove a handkerchief from her coat pocket. It was then, she speculated, that the small purse had fallen from the pocket. She said that she went back several times the next few days but that the fall leaves were coming down and she knew that she could never locate it. Besides, she had thought, it was probable that someone had found it anyway. She explained that she was too desperate and embarrassed to tell anyone. She just sat at home trying to figure out how to get through the winter without that money. She said that she had nearly decided to confide her situation to Slim and Mary when Pastor Braxton had returned the purse. Ben realized that he had yet to speak as, handing him another oatmeal cookie, Nellie continued to talk. Before she was done, Ben knew that she was a widow, that her husband had worked in the same shirt factory as Slim's parents, that they had one child, a son who was severely retarded and had died just before his fourteenth birthday. Finally she said, "Oh dear, I've done all the talking and I don't know a thing about you."

Ben smiled and said, "That's okay, I'm sure that I'll be back again."

"You will," Nellie quickly answered. "Slim says he will send you next time to replenish the wood supply on the porch."

It was then that they heard Slim pull up to the house and beep the horn.

"I have something for you," Nellie said, and she handed him a large bundle wrapped in brown paper and tied with a white cord. "Open it at home and put it right to use. Hurry along now; I don't want to keep Slim waiting."

On the way home Slim asked Ben if he had been able to get a word in edgewise.

"Not really," Ben said smiling.

"She loves to talk," Slim said adding, "She's a real nice lady who's very close to Mary. They talk on the phone several times a week." Then looking at the bundle Slim said, "I'll bet Nellie made you one of her famous quilts. I'll guarantee you'll never get cold under it and you'll still have it when you're my age."

That night Ben slept soundly under the dark blue quilt. Beside his bed lay the white envelope that he had found inside the bundle. It contained a crisp fifty dollar bill.

Chapter 7

The first big snowstorm of the season came on the Wednesday following Thanksgiving. It was nearly a foot deep but the extreme cold had produced a light, fluffy snow that blew and drifted as much as two feet deep in some places. The day before, Slim had attached the plow to the dump truck and checked all the hydraulic hoses. On the back of the truck Slim had rigged up a small portable steel platform just large enough to hold the Toro snow blower that was used for narrow paths and sidewalks. He showed Ben how to use the snow blower, especially the various ways that the chute could be adjusted and directed. In the back of the truck were two snow shovels and a barrel filled with calcium chloride. "We do ourselves first," Slim told Ben, "then I have twenty places to clear all around the area. You'll sleep well tomorrow night."

The snow began after dark on Tuesday night and continued until late Wednesday morning. Ben had trouble sleeping. He kept getting up to look out the window. When he heard Slim start the truck around four a.m. he dressed quickly and went out. While Slim used the plow, Ben used the snow blower. He found that using it was more complicated then he expected. Slim was particular about protecting plants and shrubs. Also it was important to avoid blowing the snow in the direction of windows, people, cars and anything else that could be hurt or damaged. Ben learned quickly how to point the chute in the proper direction and angle the moveable tip of the chute to determine how far to throw the snow.

They rushed with morning chores, skipped breakfast and were on the road by nine o'clock. As they traveled to the first place, Ben told Slim that he was nervous about using the machine in unfamiliar places. "I'll show you how I want things done," Slim said, "and don't be afraid to stop me when you have questions."

For the most part the day went smoothly. Some places were quite large while others, like Nellie Zenger's, took only a few minutes. Once Ben caught a stone in the auger and Slim showed him how to remove it with a hammer and a pinch bar. "Never put your hands in there," Slim said, "even when you have removed the spark plug wire. You're too young to be missing fingers."

They finished just before five in the afternoon. During the day Mary had caught up with them long enough to bring sandwiches and sodas. At home, Ben was surprised to see that Mary had started chores. The ensilage was down from the silo and in front of the cows. About a third of the cows were already milked. Mary noticed the surprised look on Ben's face and said, "I did this a lot before you came along. See how much easier you have made things for us."

Ben went back to his trailer exhausted but feeling good. As he stood in the hot shower he thought about the day. At each stop, the people had seemed appreciative. They were mostly older people whom Ben could see really depended on Slim. They all handed Slim cash, which he shoved into his pocket without counting.

Ben was about to make dinner when he heard the knock on the door. Slim said, "Get your coat, Ben; Mary's taking us out for pizza."

* * *

The second week of December was cold but there was no new snow. Temperatures were below zero each morning. Ben was glad that he had increased his winter wardrobe to include long, thermal underwear and a warm hat that covered his ears. On Thursday night they were done with chores by six thirty. It had pleased Ben that Slim had noticed and mentioned his increased efficiency at completing his job of feeding the cows and calves. Because Ben was now finished nearly an hour before the milking was complete, Slim had brought out a third milking machine and taught Ben how it worked. This night Ben had milked five cows completely without assistance.

They left the barn and stepped into the light of a nearly full moon. Its reflection on the snow made it seem almost daylight. "I think I'll take a walk up the road," Ben told Slim as they reached his trailer.

"It's a good night to walk," Slim replied. "Watch for icy spots on the road."

Ben turned left at the bottom of the driveway, which took him up the county road in the opposite direction from town. The road turned sharply right after Slim and Mary's house, and Ben had never been there before. He could see clearly the barbed wire fence built along the stone wall that marked the end of Slim and Mary's property. Immediately he came upon a new farm, much smaller than Slim's, but neat and well kept. There were two large open meadows on the left hand side of the road. Between them sat a white farm house smaller than Slim and Mary's. Behind the house Ben could see the shape of a foundation for what had clearly been a large barn. The house was dark and there was no sign of activity. The snow in the driveway had not been plowed and was untouched except for the tracks of birds and rabbits. There was less open land on the right side of the road. Ben walked across the field to the ice-covered creek and followed the shoreline for nearly half a mile. Before turning back, he stopped and listened to the sound of the creek as it flowed. And as he stood there in the darkness his thoughts fell on Slim Smith.

He had known this man for only a month. It seemed unreal that he could have developed such an interest and admiration for someone he hardly knew. Slim fascinated him. He was always busy but seldom hurried. He did everything well. In one month Ben had watched him milk cows, split wood, sharpen posts, plow snow, weld a broken axle, and deliver a calf. He was enterprising: besides his dairy business, people were always calling him for a load of fire wood, a jar of honey, or a load of hay. Twice Ben had seen men come to the barn and give Slim cash. Both times Slim had taken a small notebook from his pocket and made an entry. Wherever Slim Smith went people looked at him with a respect that was obvious. And yet Slim never appeared anything but modest and equal. All these things Ben saw and admired. He wanted to stay in this place and learn from this man. But the thing Ben most admired about Slim was the relationship that he had with his wife Mary. She was clearly his equal and his confidant. He was obviously proud of her abilities as teacher, photographer and community leader. And it was very apparent that he worshiped the ground she walked on.

* * *

The next morning Ben asked Slim about the farm up the road. Slim told him that it had belonged to an elderly couple until about five years ago. The husband had died, and shortly after his death lightning had hit the barn, burning it to the ground. Fortunately all the cattle had been sold so only the building and some farm equipment were lost. Slim continued by saying that the wife had moved to live with her daughter. Before she left she made arrangements with Slim. He could have the hay each season and could also cut timber from the woodlands in exchange for keeping an eye on the place and paying the taxes. "We'll be going over there to cut wood in a few weeks," Slim said. "I may even tap some of the maples come late March."

"I'll look forward to that," Ben replied. "It's a nice-looking farm."

* * *

Friday night Slim gave Ben his pay for the week. It was the usual one hundred forty-five dollars, twenty-five dollars per day Monday through Friday and twenty dollars more for helping with chores on the weekend. Taking the glass jar from beneath his bed and counting the money it contained, Ben found that his savings had grown to over four hundred dollars. Soon he would have enough to open an account at the local bank. Ben put one hundred dollars in his wallet and replaced the rest in the jar. He was about to settle down with his book on Vermont history when Mary knocked on his door. "David Burnham just called," she said. "He is going to the mall and will stop by in a few minutes to see if you want to go along."

* * *

The two young men talked easily during the forty-minute ride to the mall. Ben learned that David was a pre-med student who wanted to be a general practitioner. David told him about college, and how much better he liked it now that he rented a room off campus. He asked Ben how he liked farming and told him that the college had an agricultural division. "I'll keep my eyes open," David said. "I know that they often have guest speakers and the public is invited. There may be some things that would interest you."

At the mall they split up, agreeing to meet at the food court at nine. Ben looked at shoes, tried to find a Christmas gift for Slim and Mary but ended up buying nothing. He enjoyed the holiday decorations and thought that they looked more authentic in Vermont than in Florida. He was drinking a soda when David met him at the food court. They returned to the farm by ten o'clock and Ben thanked David for inviting him along. It had been an exciting night for a young man who had grown up very much alone except for his mother. He had never had a really good friend and he hoped that David Burnham would become one.

Chapter 8

One morning in mid December Slim asked Ben if he would ride into town with Mary to help her do some shopping. After they had left Slim entered his barn and hooked the latch from the inside. He took out his wallet and sat down on a bale of hay. It had been a good month. He had sold several loads of hay, delivered wood to a dozen customers, plowed snow and sold honey. Unlike the check he received from the milk company, which he always deposited in his checking account, all of these transactions were done in cash. From this cash, Slim paid Ben and took care of his day to day expenses. Counting through the bills Slim saw that he had at least five hundred dollars beyond what he would need for the next two weeks. He walked through the main part of the barn, past the area where the calves were tethered, to an unused section in the back corner. This end of the barn was unchanged in appearance from when it was originally built over a century and a half ago. All additions and modernizations had been made at the other end. Like many New England barns it was built against a bank so that the back of the first floor was under ground. To enter the second level of the barn, where the hay was stored, you could climb the wooden ladder through a hole in the ceiling or enter through huge sliding doors behind the barn that were at ground level with the second story. Slim stood looking at the huge flat stones that formed the foundation wall for the back of the barn. They were arranged one on another to a height of nearly ten feet. On top of them sat the huge hand hewn oak sills where the second level began. Slim often marveled at how those rocks had been lifted and arranged without the assistance of modern equipment. "This was built when men were men," Slim often said to himself.

The frame of an old, steel wheeled wagon sat in this unused corner of the barn. The wagon had been used by Joe Thurston to load loose hay before he bought his first baler. The flat bed that fit on top of the frame had been removed and rested against the large rocks of the barn's foundation. Using the leverage of his six foot two body and the enormous strength of his hands and arms, Slim pushed the flat bed away from the wall until it came to rest against the frame of the wagon. He then eased his way along the foundation wall for approximately six feet where he found the spot where two rocks could be worked loose. Carefully he sat the rocks on the ground beside him. The opening behind the two rocks revealed that a small area of earth had been removed from the bank. The area had been lined with half inch steel carefully welded by Slim. A padlock secured the front of the encasement. When the lock was removed, the front panel, hinged from the inside, opened to reveal a small water proof, fire proof safe. No one except Mary knew of the safe's existence. Slim had built this encasement shortly after their marriage over thirty years ago. Through the years it had been his private bank where all his financial transactions, except for the milk check, were conducted. To the world, including the Internal Revenue Service, Slim Smith was a dairy farmer. His other activities were conducted in cash with friends and neighbors.

Slim added the five hundred dollars to the money already in the safe. He had not counted the money in the safe for over two years, but he knew that the total was in excess of eighty thousand dollars. Carefully he replaced the lock and slid the two rocks back into the foundation. After easing his way along the wall to the end of the wagon frame, he pushed the flat bed from the frame until it rested once again against the barn's foundation.

* * *

Saturday morning chores were nearly done when Slim asked Ben if his driver's license was still valid. Ben said that it was and that he hoped to have it transferred from Florida to Vermont after the New Year. "I was wondering if you could do me a favor," Slim said. "Mary and I are going Christmas shopping today and Nellie Zenger called to have some wood transferred from the garage to her porch. Could you take the pickup into town and do the job for me?"

"Sure," Ben answered. "I need to do some laundry and pick up some things at the IGA anyway."

"Feel free to take it for a spin," Slim said, handing him the keys. "It could use good a run."

Ben was happy to be driving again. He went carefully with the Ford 150.

He felt good that Slim had trusted him with it. It was another sign for Ben that he was becoming a part of Slim and Mary's life. He wanted to say "family" but forced the thought out of his mind.

Ben worked quickly re-supplying Nellie's porch with wood. In less than twenty minutes the job was complete. When he was stacking the last armful, Nellie opened the door and said, "Thank you, Ben. Have time for some tea and cookies?" Ben sat down at the kitchen table as Nellie fixed the tea. As she poured she acknowledged the thank-you note that he had sent regarding the quilt and money. "Most young people don't remember thank-you's," she said.

"Well, that's something that was important to my mother." Ben answered.

"Your mom isn't living?" Nellie inquired.

"She died several years ago," Ben said. "Cancer."

"Were you alone?" Nellie asked.

"I stayed with my grandparents until I finished high school," Ben said. "We weren't very close, and I left on my eighteenth birthday. I always hated the South; too hot, too many bugs, no distinct seasons. I always looked at pictures of Vermont in a book at the library. I must have signed that book out a hundred times. I knew since I was ten that I would come here someday."

Nellie looked at Ben and said, "I asked Mary and Pastor Braxton about you but they both said you were a very private young man. I want you to know that they were careful to respect your privacy, even to a nosy old lady like me." She continued, "Slim and Mary are very fond of you. They haven't said so but I can tell. You feel free to talk to them when you need to. They're wonderful people. You couldn't have found a better place."

"I know that," Ben said. "I hope they like my work. I'd like to stay here."

"Oh they do like your work," Nellie said. "Slim says you're a quick learner. And we know you're honest," she continued and she tapped her hand on the faded leather pouch that sat on the table.

As Ben was leaving, Nellie said, "Thank you for listening to an old lady. I hope that I didn't speak out of turn but some things just need to be said." She put her hand on his arm and said, "Ben, it wasn't an accident that you ended up here. I'm sure of that."

Ben smiled and said, "I hope you're right." He could see her watching from the window as he drove away.

* * *

Ben bought some groceries for the coming week and returned to the farm by lunch time. He gave the trailer a thorough cleaning and curled up in his chair with the book *Vermont By Choice*. The book fascinated him; books always had. He read about the extreme primitive conditions endured by the early settlers of the eighteenth century. Many had first seen the land when they had traveled across it during the French and Indian War of 1754-63. Later other soldiers from the Revolutionary War had marched through the area. After these wars, when cheap land was becoming scarce in places like Rhode Island, they moved north into this wilderness claimed by both New York and New Hampshire. This disputed area would, in time, become the state of Vermont which was fractured French for "green mountains." Ben also learned that Scottish soldiers who had fought in the French and Indian War were among Vermont's earliest settlers. They had been charmed by the land and also saw it as an escape from the grinding poverty of Scotland where they were trapped in a class system in which wealth was in the hands of an elite nobility. Ben read how these first settlers, with no conveniences, had survived the cold and the Indians to become the first Vermonters. They were fiercely independent, ambitious and resourceful. Further, they were civic-minded with deep loyalty to their communities as well as their families. As Ben read about these early settlers, he found himself thinking more than once, "They sound like Slim Smith."

* * *

The second big storm of December hit on Sunday night. It was a wet snow and difficult to handle. The snow blower clogged often and shoveling by hand was exhausting. The snow was even difficult to push with Slim's big plow. "We have to get them done today," Slim said. "It's going to turn bitter cold tonight and this stuff will be like solid ice."

* * *

It was nearly six o'clock when they returned to the farm exhausted. The chores had not been started. Mary met them in the driveway, looking tired. "Anabel is much worse," she said to Slim. "I think she's in a lot of pain."

"Have you talked to the vet?" Slim asked.

"Yes," Mary answered. "He's home if we need him."

Slim looked at Ben and said, "Can you start the chores alone? I'll be gone

61

for a while. Get the milking done first. The calves will be hungry, but they can wait."

Ben was nervous. He had never done the milking process by himself. Some things were straightforward and easy to remember, but he was concerned about turning on the pumps and mixing the solutions. He started by throwing the ensilage down from the silo and feeding the milking cows. That would keep them satisfied when he started milking. Nervously he flipped the switch that would draw the milk through the pipe from the barn into the tank. He mixed the solution that sterilized the udders and began to milk. Everything worked and he began to feel relaxed. He forgot the fatigue of the day and the fact that he had barely eaten since early morning. This was his opportunity to prove to himself and to Slim that he had come a long way since his first day here over six weeks ago. Once the milking machines were working he literally ran to the calf pen with two pails of water at a time. He found that he could mix the powder with the water and feed two calves before running back to the main barn to move the milking machines to the next cows. By the time he heard Slim enter the barn, he had finished feeding the calves, gave them their hay and was over three quarters done with the milking.

"We had to put Anabel down," Slim said. "She was seventeen and too old for an operation."

"I'm sorry," Ben said. "How is Mary?"

"She's pretty sad right now," Slim replied, "but she'll be all right. She knew it was coming." Slim continued, "It looks like you've got things under control here. You start giving them their hay and I'll finish milking."

Within the hour they had washed everything clean and were ready to leave the barn. "You earned your pay today," Slim said. "Thanks for taking over. I'd have been in trouble without you. Now get a good sleep. We'll just do chores tomorrow and take it easy the rest of the day."

* * *

Slim was more quiet than usual the next morning, and Ben knew that Anabel was on his mind. As they were washing the pails and sterilizing the equipment, Slim began to talk. "She was just the second dog we've had since we were married. The first one looked just like her and was also named Anabel. Amazing how attached you can get to a dog. I'd like to get another golden retriever and name her Anabel the Third. It would be good for Mary. Better wait till school's out so Mary can train her. They're a lot of work when they're puppies. It's a long time till June, though."

Ben listened as Slim continued talking. It wasn't really a conversation, more like Slim was thinking out loud. After a few minutes Ben said, "You could get one now and keep her in my place during the day. I don't have any carpets and it would be easy to clean up if she makes a mess."

"You mean when she makes a mess," Slim said smiling. "I'll think about that," Slim added. "It would be good to have her for Christmas." They left the barn and headed for breakfast. "Get some sleep this morning," Slim said. "Maybe we'll work this afternoon. Right now we need some rest."

Ben slept soundly for over three hours. He woke at twelve thirty feeling rested but famished. Realizing that he hadn't had much food in well over a day he made himself a meal of ground beef, boiled potatoes and peas. Ben knew that his appetite had grown in the last six weeks. He also knew that his young body was developing a new strength and stamina that he had never felt before, a development that greatly pleased him. He was cleaning the dishes from his big meal when Slim knocked on his door. "How are you feeling?" Slim asked.

"Stuffed and rested," Ben replied.

Slim said that he was going to start the tractor and move snow away from the sliding doors of the various barns and sheds. He told Ben that once that was done he would clear snow from the barn yard so that the cows could more easily reach the feeders. "I've also got to clean a spot to pile manure," he added. "It'll be a while until we can get it out on the fields." He asked Ben to do the hand shoveling in spots where the tractor couldn't reach. "Dress warm," he said. "It's already turning cold and windy. Tonight will be the coldest of the winter." As he was leaving, he told Ben that he had called the pet store and could have a female golden retriever before Christmas. "Don't tell Mary," Slim said. "We'll surprise her in a few days. By the way, I'm taking her to Jensen's for supper. I want to get her mind off Anabel. Why don't you plan to come with us."

* * *

Jensen's was a family restaurant located in the middle of town. Slim and Mary ate there often. Its menu had a good variety but was most well known for its hot turkey sandwiches served with mashed potatoes, cranberries and vegetables, which Slim, Mary, and Ben all ordered. The evening was good for Mary and kept her mind from dwelling on the loss of Anabel. Several times during their meal people would stop by their booth to chat. Some expressed their sympathies about Anabel, each saying that Nellie had called to tell them. Mary made certain to introduce Ben whenever people stopped by. "I would like you to meet Ben Thomas. He's doing a great job working for us on the farm," she would say.

Slim and Ben had pie and coffee for dessert. Mary had only coffee. As she talked, Mary told Ben that her father was having his annual Christmas party at the clinic on Sunday afternoon. "He told me to be sure to ask you to come," she said. "It's very informal and David Burnham will be there," she added.

Ben hesitated for a moment and then said, "I really don't have any good clothes. Would it be possible to use the truck on Friday night to drive to the mall?"

"We're going there ourselves on Friday," Mary said. "Why don't you come with us? It will be fun."

"Thank you," Ben replied. "I would like that."

* * *

Tuesday morning the thermometer read minus thirty-four degrees and there was a driving wind. Even the bodies of thirty-five milking cows couldn't keep the barn warm. When the morning milking was done they put the cows outside just long enough to run the cleaner through the gutters and then brought them back inside for the day. "It's not fit for man or beast outside today," Slim said. After breakfast, Slim and Ben carried cedar posts from the big shed where they were stacked to a smaller shed equipped with a small wood stove. Once they were inside and away from the wind, the stove made the shed comfortable. Slim sharpened his axe until it was razor sharp. Then he had Ben hold the post on a large block of oak. Ben would turn the post slowly while Slim would skillfully sharpen the end. Ben was fascinated at the precision of Slim's work. When he had completed a post it looked as though it had been put in a huge pencil sharpener. "I'll let you practice on some posts another day," Slim said. "I'm selling these twenty-five to a man who owns horses. He'll be over for them in a day or two."

After lunch Slim told Ben that someone had called for a load of wood. "Not one of my regulars," Slim said, "but we've got plenty of wood and they sounded desperate." It turned out to be a big job in the bitter cold. First they had to shovel snow from the huge tarp that covered the wood pile. Twice, while loading, they went inside to get the feeling back in their fingers. When they arrived at the house where the wood was to be delivered, the woman told Slim that her husband had run off leaving her with three children and little money. Also she said that the stove wasn't working quite right. Slim checked the stove, discovered that the pipe leading to the chimney was nearly clogged, and while Ben stacked the wood by the back door Slim cleaned the chimney.

Ben heard the woman ask Slim if she could pay for part of the wood now and the rest later. "My husband will be back sometime," she said. "He's off drinking somewhere." Slim asked the woman if she had enough food for the children. When she said she had enough for a few days, Slim told her to use the money for them and pay him when she could.

On the way back to the farm Slim said, "I doubt we'll ever see that money. The old man was probably hiding in the bedroom. I guess we did our good deed for today."

That night while they were milking, Mary came into the barn. Ben heard Slim tell her about the woman who needed wood. "Maybe you can call Jim Braxton about her," Ben heard Slim say. "I'd hate to see those kids go hungry."

* * *

"Are you sure that you want to help with this puppy?" Slim asked Ben on Monday morning.

"I can't wait," Ben answered. Slim said that he would pick up the new little Anabel at the pet store after lunch. He asked if Ben would keep her in his trailer the rest of the afternoon and bring her over to the house after evening chores. When Slim returned to the farm around two o'clock he was carrying the little golden puppy under his arm. She already loved humans and wiggled with delight as Ben kneeled on the floor of his trailer to pet her. At chore time, Ben took her outside where, remarkably, she squatted and relieved herself. "See, she's trained already," Ben said to Slim.

"You'll eat those words before long," Slim answered.

Ben took the puppy back to his trailer and placed her in a cardboard box with high sides. Exhausted from an afternoon of play, the puppy curled up on the towel that Ben had put in the box and fell asleep. When evening chores were completed Ben hurried back to his trailer to find the puppy still asleep. Quietly he went to the bathroom and showered quickly. Before he could finish dressing he heard the puppy begin to cry. Quickly he removed the excited little dog from the box and sat her on the floor where she promptly made a mess. Within a few minutes Ben had the floor clean, and taking some bailer twine that he had brought from the barn, Ben attached a homemade leash to the little dog's collar.

Quietly Ben climbed the steps leading to Slim and Mary's front door. Carefully he attached the leash to the door knob, rang the bell and moved away from the door into the shadows. He heard Mary's shriek of delight when she opened the door and saw the puppy. Slowly Ben came out of the darkness and stood in the open doorway. Mary was on the floor holding Anabel and Slim stood over them smiling. "Come in, Ben," Slim said. "We're having homemade chicken noodle soup for supper and you're invited."

Chapter 9

Mary and Slim missed the Sunday worship service. Instead, as soon as Slim finished the morning chores, they drove to the clinic to help prepare for the Christmas party. Mary knew how much this event meant to her father. It was one way that he could show his staff and supporters how much he appreciated their efforts. When she entered the community room, Mary stopped to enjoy the scene before her. A large Concolor fir, grown, pruned, cut and delivered by Slim stood in the far corner. It was slightly larger than the one Slim had given to the church and much larger than the one that stood in their living room. It was covered with colored lights, red and silver balls and wrapped with gold garland. Beneath the tree were gifts for the children of the clinic's staff. Throughout the room tables for eight were decorated with red table cloths and green napkins. At the center of each table there were sprigs of fresh Yew that Slim had brought from the farm. The candles on each table were new this year. Slim had found white birch approximately six inches in diameter which he cut into one-foot lengths. Next he had carefully planed the bottom of each piece so that it would sit firmly on the table. Finally, in the top of each piece he drilled three holes. The center hole was large enough to accommodate a large red candle while the two holes on either side were drilled with a smaller bit and contained slimmer candles. Across the front of the room sat a long row of tables covered with white table cloths. Just before the guests arrived at twelve thirty, the buffet would be placed on these tables. At the end would be the punch bowl. The food would include vegetables with dip, fruit, cheese and cold cuts, rolls, pickles and olives, potato and macaroni salads, Swedish meatballs served in gravy, ziti and lasagna. Later in the afternoon cookies, coffee and hot chocolate would be served for dessert.

Dr. Taylor and Jean were already working when Slim and Mary arrived. Mary joined them as they cut up fruit and Slim began to unfold the chairs and arrange eight at each table. By twelve o'clock everything was ready and shortly thereafter they heard the caterer's truck pull into the parking lot. Dr. Taylor breathed a sigh of relief when he heard the truck. "I'm always afraid they'll be late," he said. Around twelve thirty the guests began to arrive.

It was twelve fifty when Ben eased the Ford pickup into the parking lot of the clinic. He was nervous. This was another first. It seemed beyond belief but Benjamin Thomas had never been to a Christmas party or any kind of party for that matter. His mother had avoided social activities completely and always had a reason for Ben to do so as well. Then for two years, when she was so sick, Ben remained by her side almost constantly except when he was in school. After his mother's death when he moved in with his grandparents, Ben had withdrawn even further, rarely leaving his room. He had not even attended his high school graduation, choosing instead to pick up his diploma at the school office the next day. And so, an event that for most would be a time of relaxation and enjoyment was, for Ben, something to be feared. He did look good, and he knew it. Born with good looks and pleasant features, his six weeks of vigorous farm work had strengthened and toned his young body. Two nights ago he had walked into an Eddie Bauer store at the mall and purchased a completely new outfit. On his feet were casual brown leather shoes that looked good with his khaki slacks and brown woven belt. Beneath a new dark blue jacket with brown leather collar he wore a light blue shirt under a bright yellow V-neck sweater. The clothes had been expensive, but Ben was beginning to feel confident of his future on Slim and Mary's farm. It was this confidence that allowed him to spend considerably more than a week's wages on the new outfit.

* * *

Ben was standing in the doorway that led from the foyer to the community room when he heard his name. Judy Braxton, holding her year-old son Jamie, said, "I'm so glad you could come, Ben. It's good to see you again. You're seated at our table. Come, I'll introduce you." Ben followed her to a table located near the tree. Jim Braxton welcomed him warmly and let Judy do the introductions. First he met Charles Weston, a shy man with a friendly but cautious smile. Charles had Down Syndrome. Judy told Ben that Charles was the faithful sexton of both the clinic and the Methodist church. "He has been a friend of Slim's since high school," she added. Next Ben met Mr. and Mrs. Johnson, a couple similar in age to Dr. Taylor. Mr. Johnson was the long-time president of the local bank and a life long friend of Dr. Taylor. The Johnson's welcomed Ben warmly. It seemed clear that they were aware of Ben's identity and his uneasiness in this large gathering. The chair next to Ben was empty. Soon he heard a familiar voice and looked up to see David Burnham.

"Hey Ben, Merry Christmas. I'm glad to see you. I'll be leaving for the holidays on Wednesday and I'll be gone for a month. How have you been?" Before Ben could answer Dr. Taylor went to the microphone and welcomed everyone to the party. His voice was serious and sincere as he thanked everyone for making the past year such a good one. He reminded the group of a January planning meeting for the annual April fund-raiser. He told everyone to eat heartily. He told the children that after dinner they would find gifts under the tree. Then he asked Pastor Braxton to give the blessing and the dinner began.

Ben was surprised that he was feeling quite relaxed. It seemed that everyone was friendly but not aggressively so. Several times he noticed that Mary had glanced his way. He was certain that she was checking that he was not alone, and he felt good that she was concerned. Twice during the afternoon Slim had come to the table for a brief time. "Getting enough to eat Ben?" he said as he moved on. Nellie Zenger spent most of the day in the kitchen but she had called to Ben as he moved through the food line. Ben had quite a discussion with the Johnsons. He learned that Mr. Johnson had been a vital part of the clinic since its beginning. At one point Dr. Taylor came by and in the course of their conversation told Ben that without the backing of Mr. Johnson's bank, the clinic would never have become a reality.

When they left, Mr. Johnson told Ben to stop by the bank if he needed to open an account. "Be sure to ask for me," he added. And as he was leaving he said to Ben, "Slim tells me that you're doing a great job on the farm. I'm so glad he found you."

As the afternoon went by, Ben met many people. Most of the names he would have to learn again. Still he sensed a oneness with the group. It was a spirit of unity that he liked and one that he had never felt before. Clearly, he sensed these people believed in what they were doing. They cared about each other. He wondered if he could ever have that feeling himself.

At three forty-five, Slim came to Ben and asked if he was ready to do evening chores. They left Mary to help clean up from the party. On the way back to the farm, Slim asked Ben if his head was spinning from meeting so many people. "Yes it is," Ben answered truthfully, "but I enjoyed myself. Everyone was nice."

"They're good people," Slim said. "I'm not much for big events but I don't mind them." And he repeated thoughtfully, "Yes, they're good people." The rest of the drive back to the farm they were both silent, deep in their own thoughts.

Chapter 10

Monday morning the thermometer read minus thirty-five degrees. A driving wind from the north created a chill of minus seventy. Schools were closed; people were advised to stay inside. Faucets were left open to keep pipes from freezing. Ben left his trailer at five thirty and entered a world he had never before experienced. A bone chilling cold overtook his body before he could reach the barn. His face burned in the wind. He went inside the barn and was about to climb the metal ladder up the side of the silo when Slim entered. "It will be brutal up there this morning," Slim told him. "Take the pickaxe with you to break through the frozen ensilage. Don't stay more than five minutes before coming down to warm up. You'll probably need to make around five trips to keep from freezing. Be real careful. This is as bad as it gets around here." Slim brought a large electric heater into the barn and plugged it in. "This will help," he said. "Get yourself good and warm before you go up."

Slim was right. Ben made five trips up and down the ladder. Each time his fingers and toes ached by the time he returned to the heater. Chores took much longer than usual and Slim decided to leave the cows inside all day. They would come back to the barn throughout the day to check the water pipes and throw more hay in the cows' feeders. Even in the barn the cows were restless and uncomfortable.

When they went to breakfast, Slim took another electric heater and placed it in the garage next to the dump truck. "Maybe if I warm it up a bit it will start," he said. "Three people called last night who need wood. We're going to try and make the deliveries today. Have a hot breakfast. I'll stop by your trailer in an hour or so."

Ben's trailer was warm. Slim had insulated it so well that the cold wind could not penetrate the walls. Ben made coffee and it warmed his body while he cooked eggs and toast. Within minutes he was warm and energized. He found the extreme cold exciting and challenging. He was anxious to go outside and face the elements. He hoped that the truck would start. Delivering wood to people who were desperate to get it gave him a sense of worth. He was ready to go when he heard Slim's knock on his door. Slim was wearing a hooded mask that covered his face except for the area around his eyes. In his hand he carried a second hood that Mary had sent for Ben to wear. He also had special gloves that provided extra protection. "Wear these," he said handing them to Ben. "They'll help a lot when you are throwing that cold wood into the truck."

The dump truck started. Slim left the engine running while they loaded. Twice they went to the house to warm themselves. Mary had coffee for them while they stood next to the fireplace. "I took Anabel to the dirt floor section of the cellar," she told them. "It's too cold for her to go outside." She smiled as she added, "She didn't want to do her business down there. She trained so easily that she already knows she isn't supposed to go inside. I think we got another smart one."

Throughout the day they worked and warmed themselves. Slim checked the water pipes between each delivery. On their way home from the third load Slim stopped to look in on Nellie Zenger. After checking her water pipes in the basement he told her to increase the trickle in her kitchen sink. "Better safe than sorry," he told her.

Late that afternoon while they were milking Slim said to Ben, "Listen! I think the wind is beginning to die down. Maybe the worst is over. It's supposed to cloud up tomorrow and snow on Wednesday. We'll hook up the plow in the morning. By the way, Mary's serving leftovers from the party. Come over around six thirty and eat with us."

* * *

When they finished eating, Ben played on the floor with Anabel while Slim helped Mary put away the food and load the dishwasher. The house was warm from the two fireplaces, and Christmas, exactly one week away, was everywhere evident. Ben had previously noticed, Mary's gift for decorating, but it was even more apparent now. Christmas decor was everywhere and yet nothing looked cluttered. Slim told Ben that they usually had his old electric train around the tree but Anabel couldn't resist knocking it from the tracks so he took it down. "She'll be old enough to leave it alone next year," he said.

Ben, nervous about staying too long, was about to thank them for the meal and return to the trailer when Mary asked if he would like to see the gallery. They went upstairs where she first showed him the dark room that Slim had built for her to develop her photographs. A door led from the dark room to a smaller room which served as Mary's office. It contained a large desk and long wooden shelves that held between thirty and forty gray letter-sized file boxes. Each box was labeled by year and Mary told him how she catalogued all photos worthy of keeping. Each envelope in the file drawer contained three items; a three-by-five print, a slide, and a negative. "How many are there all together?" Ben asked.

"Thousands," Mary answered. "Someday I hope to get everything recorded on the computer but for now I'm doing it the old-fashioned way."

They left the office and walked down the hallway to a large room approximately twenty by thirty feet. On the walls dozens of pictures were mounted, ranging in size from small five-by-sevens to large twenty-by-thirties. Some were in color but most were in Mary's favorite medium, black and white. It was difficult to categorize the photographs with a particular label. Generally one could say they were outdoor scenes that emphasized the wonders of nature; yet that description would not be totally accurate, for many of the pictures included people and the creations of people; buildings, tools, boats and machines. As Ben worked his way around the room, he could sense a feeling of unity and connectedness in Mary's work. The pictures made him feel that all living things and their creations could complement each other in some harmonious way. The pictures showed a harmony so contradictory to the way Ben had viewed the world. His world had always been filled with conflict and disagreement. He had learned to believe that the world was an uneasy place where people were essentially at odds with one another and with their environment. Mary's gallery, and indeed this place where he had lived for over six weeks, seemed the opposite of that and he wondered if the dream would end, and he would reawaken to the world he had fled.

Ben was lost in time. He stopped for long periods in front of pictures that especially intrigued him. A series of colored photos showing the interior of a honey bee hive captured his attention. Another colored print of baby foxes peering from their den amongst some rocky ledges impressed him. There were spectacular wide angled photographs of mountain ranges and lakes along with scenes of stony brooks, maple trees being tapped and new born calves. But there were also the people: painting barns, under the hoods of cars, welding broken tools, planting trees and sitting on park benches. These also fascinated Ben. Mary's pictures made people appear to be a part of things rather than a master of things.

Mary's work was much more than pictures from a camera. The angles, lighting and use of shadows showed a talent that could never be taught. It was a visual gift given only to a few.

Suddenly Ben realized where he was. Embarrassed, he asked Mary what time it was. She smiled, "You have been here for over an hour."

"I'm sorry," Ben stammered. "They are so special. I lost track of time."

Mary laid her hand on his arm and said, "That you forgot to think about time is the nicest compliment you could have given. I hope that you will come back often and look some more. There are thousands of pictures in the files."

They walked along the hallway until they came to another room. "Slim's den," Mary said pointing. "Want to see it?" Inside there was a large sofa chair with a huge round hassock in front. There was also a large oak desk behind which sat a high back leather swivel chair. "Slim made the desk," Mary said. "It's from our own lumber." Across the room from the desk, the wall was lined with book shelves from floor to ceiling. "Slim's the reader in the family," Mary said.

"What does he like?" Ben inquired.

Mary said that he had a wide range of interests. She thought that American history was his favorite and she pointed to a book on the Lewis and Clark expedition that sat on the hassock. "He loves Wallace Stegner books," she said, "and Wendell Berry and David Grayson." Ben had to admit that he had never heard of them. "He likes biographies too," Mary added pointing to a series of books on one of the shelves. Ben couldn't see all of the titles but he did notice one on Thomas Jefferson and another on Charles Lindbergh. As they left, Mary said almost to herself, "How Slim loves this room."

Before they returned to the downstairs Mary showed Ben the very large guest room with a full bath. It was beautifully furnished with antiques and beige wallpaper with pale green leaves.

"You must have received the long tour," Slim said when they came downstairs.

"I lost track of time looking at the pictures," Ben said. "They are incredible."

With a look of pride on his face, Slim responded. "And there aren't many places around this area where you won't see some of Mary's photos. They're in books, on calendars, postcards as well as galleries and museums."

"Stop it," Mary protested. "You'll give me a big head."

Chapter 11

Wednesday's storm didn't arrive until evening. It was nearly six inches of white, fluffy snow. Removal was easy and by mid afternoon on Thursday they were on their way back to the farm. The temperature was cold but not extreme. It was expected to remain like that through Christmas. "What are you doing for Christmas?" Slim asked as they drove home.

"Nothing, I guess," Ben answered, feeling a twinge of embarrassment.

"Mary and I would like you to spend the day with us," Slim said. "Come over around noon. We'll have the same people as Thanksgiving except for David Burnham. He's back home with his family for the holidays."

Ben felt good. He hadn't looked forward to spending Christmas day alone. Still he feared that the invitation was from a sense of obligation rather than desire. Ben's feelings of doubt and insecurity played games with his mind for the remainder of the day, but he knew that in the end, his desire to be with Slim and Mary would win out over his fears.

* * *

Ben entered the trailer and placed the small manila envelope on the kitchen counter. He removed his hat, coat and gloves and hung them on the rack in his bedroom. Sitting on the edge of his bed he removed his heavy boots. As he undressed he put his clothes in the large laundry bag. Tomorrow would be a busy day; besides laundry he had several issues to take care of. Christmas was only three days away, and Ben knew that he had already waited too long.

He dressed slowly, went to the kitchen, put a large pot of water on the stove, and when it came to a boil he poured in an ample amount of macaroni. Mixed with cheese sauce it was his favorite meal. In another dish he heated a can of green beans. That along with a huge glass of milk and several slices of buttered bread would be his supper.

Ben ate slowly and made a mental list of what he needed to accomplish tomorrow. When he finished eating he washed and dried all of his dishes and put them away. He kept the trailer spotless at all times mostly because that was his nature but also because he wanted the approval of Slim and Mary. Now that Anabel spent so much time with him, Slim and Mary were in his trailer often. They had never mentioned his habit for cleanliness, but he was certain that they noticed.

Ben took the manila envelope from the counter and sat down in his easy chair. It was then that he noticed the extra thickness. Inside he found a note, hand written by Slim that said simply, "You are doing a real good job. Enclosed is your Christmas bonus." Instead of his usual one hundred forty-five dollars he found five crisp one hundred dollar bills. Ben knew that combined with the money in the glass jar under his bed he now had over a thousand dollars. Never in his life had he saved that much money, and he felt like a millionaire. Next week he would go to Mr. Johnson's bank and open two accounts, savings and checking.

* * *

His laundry was done in a little more than an hour. He folded it carefully and returned it to the laundry bag. He placed a few items on hangers to prevent wrinkling. Back in the truck, he drove to the IGA and bought his groceries for the week. Jobs like these were easier now. He had developed a system and knew where things were located. Stability, even in small things like these, was satisfying to Ben. Someone had said that familiarity breeds contempt, but Ben did not agree. At least not in this place. He drove to the local florist shop and entered. He was pleased to find that deliveries were being made that afternoon. He ordered two small arrangements. Taking two of the cards from the rack on the counter, he began to write. Nellie Zenger's card read, "Thank you for the encouragement you have been to me. Merry Christmas. Benjamin Thomas." On the other card he wrote, "Pastor and Mrs. Braxton, Thank you for the help you gave me when I arrived here. I would have been in real trouble without you. Merry Christmas. Ben Thomas."

They seemed like such simple sentiments. To most they would have been easy to express, but to Ben they bordered on terrifying. His life was filled with doubts and insecurities. How would these people react to what he said?

Would they think him silly and sentimental? Would they be right?

Ben left town and drove to the shopping mall. Last Sunday at the clinic party he had over heard Mary mention a favorite restaurant for her and Slim. Ben remembered seeing it in an area near the mall and he found it easily. Before going to the cashier he stopped to read the menu posted in the lobby and looking at the prices determined that he should get a gift certificate for fifty dollars. The girl at the register called the manager who filled out the gift certificate and signed it. Ben was pleased when she placed the certificate in an elegant handkerchief-sized box with a silver bow. Finally Ben drove to the mall and went directly to the Hallmark store. It was very crowded and the selection of cards was limited but after a considerable effort he found one that seemed simple but appropriate. He stood in line for a half hour and reminded himself not to put things off till the last minute. The trip back to the farm gave him time to think about what to say on Slim and Mary's card.

Back in his trailer Ben found that he was more confused than ever. His mind played games with him again. The past few weeks must be a dream. How could he feel so close to this place and these people in such a short time? It didn't make sense. His doubts and insecurities grew and sleep was restless both Saturday and Sunday night. By Christmas morning he had made up his mind, and taking the card from the envelope he wrote, "The last seven weeks have been the best of my life. I want you to know how grateful I am for all you have done. I hope you know how much I want to stay here. Merry Christmas. Ben."

It was exactly twelve o'clock on Christmas day when Ben walked across the yard from his trailer to Slim and Mary's front door. In his hand he carried the gift and the card.

* * *

Mary met him at the door and wished him a Merry Christmas. She thanked him for the gift and said, "I'll put it under the tree and we will open it later."

Everyone was friendly. Dr. and Mrs. Taylor told Ben how pleased they were that he was able to attend the party at the clinic and they hoped that he would come to the meeting in January to plan the spring fund-raiser. "It's a big event," Mrs. Taylor said, "and we need all the help we can get." Ben also shook hands with Slim's sister and her husband and felt good when she expressed her gratitude that Slim had such good help with the farm work. "Slim still thinks he's sixteen," she added.

The dinner was extraordinary. Along with the traditional turkey, Mary had also prepared a roast of beef and breaded fillets of flounder. There were also several vegetable dishes, cranberry sauce, rolls, pickles and olives. For dessert Mary served a Christmas pudding with whipped cream on the top. "We only have this once a year," she told Ben. "It's so rich that we would all weigh five hundred pounds and suffer from high cholesterol if we had it more often," she added.

The company left at three thirty explaining that they had other Christmas stops to make. Ben and Slim went to the barn to do the evening milking. Mary drove to Nellie Zenger's for a Christmas visit but told Ben to come back with Slim when the chores were finished. Ben felt restless inside as he did his work. He wished that somehow he could retrieve the card that sat with his gift beneath the Christmas tree. He convinced himself that it was too personal, maybe even too aggressive for someone who had been here less than two months. He knew that Slim and Mary were private people. They would probably react negatively to the hired man telling them that it was the best seven weeks of his life. He found himself embarrassed just thinking of the uncomfortable scene that would occur in just a few minutes.

When Ben and Slim entered the house, Mary had coffee and turkey sandwiches waiting for them. The house was warm and cheery with both fireplaces burning brightly. When they finished eating, Mary brought a gift from the tree and handed it to Ben. It was a large flat present elegantly wrapped with a card attached. She also brought to the table the card and gift from Ben. Silently the two cards were opened and read. The three looked nervously at each other and then suddenly began to laugh. The card from Slim and Mary was written by Mary and read, "It has been so wonderful having you here these past few weeks. You are doing such a good job. We hope that you will stay and be a part of our lives."

"I guess we were thinking the same thing," Slim said and extended his huge hand to Ben.

Ben returned the hand shake and said smiling, "I was worried that maybe I would say the wrong thing. I really feel relieved."

Mary rose from her chair and came around to Ben. She bent down and gently kissed his forehead. "You are a very special boy," she said quietly. And as Ben looked up at her she could not help seeing the tear in the corner of his eye.

* * *

"Oh look, Slim," Mary exclaimed. "It's for our favorite restaurant, and so generous. How did you know?" she asked. Ben told her that he had overheard her at the clinic party and hoped that it was the right place. "It's perfect," Mary said. "We will use it soon, you can be sure."

Ben opened his gift and found a large picture frame designed to hold an arrangement of eight different photos. In each opening was a picture from Mary's collection. Ben took time to look at each picture. He especially liked the one of himself and Slim walking down the mountain trail with cedar posts over their shoulders. "Thank you," he said with sincerity. "Is it all right to put a hook into the wall of my living room?"

"I'm a step ahead of you," Slim said and he took a picture hook from his pocket and handed it to Ben.

Mary reached into her purse, and took out a small rectangular box and handed it to Ben. "A gift from Nellie Zenger," she said. "I think you will like it." Inside Ben found an intricately designed gold pocket watch. The numbers were Roman numerals. On the face was the word Elgin. "She had it cleaned and polished," Mary said. "It was a gift to her husband on their first wedding anniversary. She really wants you to have it." Ben said that it was beautiful and asked if they thought it was all right to accept it.

"She lost her only son years ago," Slim said. "She thinks you're pretty special. Of course you should keep it."

"Then I will," Ben responded.

* * *

Sleep did not come quickly for Slim and Mary. Well past midnight they lay in bed talking. "In his own quiet way," Mary said, "he is screaming for help. Do you realize, Slim, that in nearly two months he has never received a single letter or phone call from Florida? It's almost like he didn't exist before he came here."

Slim lay silently for a few moments and then he spoke slowly. "I suppose he ran away from a very negative world. He doesn't talk about his past... ever. We only know what he told us that first night he arrived. But I'm quite sure that he was very unhappy. It seems like people made him feel like he wasn't worth much, like he'd done something wrong. Now he's scared and confused. He's scared because he likes it here, and he's afraid we'll send him away. Still, good things are happening to him here and he's starting to wonder if maybe it's not such a terrible world after all. He loves farming; I can tell that already, and he's good at it. My suspicion is that he's real smart."

"I think you're right," Mary responded. "He's been so private that I haven't tried much but small talk with him. But the sentiments expressed in his card seem like a not-so-subtle invitation into his life. I think we need to do things to build his confidence and show him that he's worth something. He needs constant reassurance that he's safe and wanted here."

"Well we could start by getting some furnishings to make the trailer more like a home than a cheap motel. All he has in the living room is that chair. Maybe I can refinish the maple table and chairs that Joe and Mabel left here."

"I think we could get the television cable extended over there," Mary responded. "And maybe a phone line. We can tell him it's part of his salary. And we should have him eat dinner with us more often. Maybe he'll start to relax and open up to us."

* * *

Ben lay awake for hours reliving the events of the day. While he would continue to struggle with insecurity, and often need to be reassured, right now he felt relieved. He smiled as he thought of the terror he had felt from the sentiments expressed in the card to Slim and Mary, and then to find out that they had written almost the same exact words to him. He was wanted here and needed too. It wasn't a dream. It did not need to end. He would continue to work hard and learn the art of farming. He would be courteous and helpful. He would make life easier for Slim and Mary. He would also be a part of the community. Yes, he would attend the planning meeting for the clinic's fundraiser. He would do whatever they asked to help make it a success. He would help Nellie Zenger when she needed it. He would be a part of this new world where people saw the brighter side of life and were concerned for one another. What a great day it had been! He had hopes and dreams that he never would have considered before. He finally fell asleep thinking that he could not wait for tomorrow.

Chapter 12

The week between Christmas and New Year's was a vacation time for Mary. School would not be in session until January second. The weather that week was seasonably cold but not extreme. The forecast called for clear sunny days with no snow. On Wednesday night Slim told Ben that he was leaving early the next morning with Mary for a day on the Maine coast. He told Ben that it was a long drive and asked him if he thought that he could handle evening chores by himself. "I'm sure that I can," Ben responded adding, "Why don't you stay over for the night? I'll do the morning chores on Friday and you and Mary can have a real vacation." He waited silently while Slim stood deep in thought. Finally Slim said, "It's been a long time since Mary and I have had more than a day trip. You know what, Ben—I'm going to take you up on that offer."

* * *

The next morning at nine thirty Slim and Mary pulled out of the driveway and disappeared down the road. Ben took Anabel to the barn with him and let the cows loose in the barn yard where they began to eat from the large metal feeders. Ben scraped the barn floor clean, turned the switch to start the barn cleaner and as the machine ran its course he applied new bedding throughout the barn. The moderate weather meant that the milking cows could be left outside for the day and with a look of satisfaction Ben left the barn with Anabel and returned to the trailer for breakfast.

Slim had left instructions for Ben to load and deliver fire wood to one of his customers in town. After a big breakfast, Ben backed the dump truck up to the pile of wood and began loading. He worked quickly but noticed the job was much bigger without Slim's help. It was nearly eleven thirty when the truck was fully loaded. Ben put Anabel in the trailer and delivered the wood into town. "Slim sick?" the man asked when he saw Ben stacking the wood by himself.

"No," Ben replied. "He and Mary are over at the coast until tomorrow."

"It's about time Slim took some time off. I told my Mrs. he made a good move when he hired you. Slim's worked hard all his life and it's good to see he can relax a bit. Yes sir, it's a nice thing. Say, you want me to pay you?"

Ben told the man to wait until he saw Slim. And as he drove away the man was still saying, "Yes sir, it's good Slim can relax a bit. He's worked hard all his life."

* * *

Evening chores went smoothly. Ben started the process early but still didn't leave the barn until nearly eight o'clock. He double checked everything to make certain all switches were turned off, all calves securely tethered and all pails and buckets cleaned and stacked on the racks. He returned to his trailer very tired. His exhaustion was as much from the stress of not wanting to make any mistakes as from the physical labor. After a hot shower and a big meal he took the key that Slim had given him and with Anabel walked across the yard to the main house. It seemed cold inside. It was the first time that Ben had seen the large fireplace dark and cold. The electric heat, which Slim and Mary seldom used, kept the house a cool sixty degrees. At exactly nine thirty the expected call from Slim and Mary came. They were in York Beach, Maine in a motel overlooking the ocean. It had been a good day to walk the beach and they were surprised at how many people were there in the off season. They asked if things were going smoothly at the farm and Ben was pleased when Mary said that she knew he would have everything under control. Slim reminded him to check the water pipes before going to bed. He said that they would be home late the next day.

Ben was restless throughout the night. Several times he got up to look out the window. Each time Anabel would want him to play. Once he took her outside and while she took care of business he checked to see that the water pipes weren't frozen. He was tired when he got up for good at five thirty, but the desire to get the day started quickly invigorated him. He worked at morning chores and milking until nearly ten o'clock and was famished when he finally had breakfast. By eleven he was in the main house checking that everything was in order. He noticed that the message light was blinking on the answering machine and pushing the button he heard a man's voice say, "Slim—George Rogers here. I've got to get hay today. Is there any chance you could bring fifty bales over? I'm desperate." Taking the phone book from the shelf, Ben looked up the name and was happy to find only one George Rogers. He dialed the number and explained that Slim was away.

"If you give me directions, I'll bring the hay over," Ben said. It was about ten miles, the man explained, as he gave the directions to a place unfamiliar to Ben.

"If you get confused, ask at Jensen's Restaurant," the man said. "I'm about five miles on the other side of them but remember to turn left on Wilson Hill Road."

Ben loaded fifty bales into the back of the dump truck, checked the cows feeding in the barn yard and drove off. He missed the turn off to Wilson Hill Road and drove a few miles beyond before asking directions and turning back. When he finally spotted the road he noticed that the road sign had been hit by the plow and lay on its side in the ditch. Arriving at the Rogers place, he was met by a very elderly man who walked with a severe arthritic limp. The man talked as Ben unloaded and stacked the bales. "I shouldn't be farming anymore," he said "but I'd be dead in a month if I didn't have a few cows. I can't milk anymore and I can't do any haying. It makes me sick seeing my fields grow up with brush but there's nothing I can do. Thanks to Slim I can keep a few heifers. Since my wife died, they're what keeps me going."

Ben liked George Rogers immediately. He admired his desire to keep going when it would have been easy to give up. He could sense the devotion that George had for this land and the frustration of seeing it deteriorate. The old man thanked him for the hay and took out his worn wallet. "Why don't you wait until you see Slim," Ben said. "I'll tell him that I brought you fifty bales." They shook hands and Ben drove away. He looked at the two large fields, one on either side of the road. They weren't bad yet. Young saplings were beginning to take over but beneath the snow the fields were relatively open.

* * *

Ben was more than half done with milking when he heard the car in the driveway. Slim and Mary entered the barn and Anabel ran excitedly to them. They told Ben that they had a wonderful time. "It was good to get away," Mary said adding, "and it looks like you've really handled things well here."

"I was nervous," Ben responded, "but now I know I can do it and that feels good."

He told Slim about George Rogers and the hay. "Poor old George," Slim said. "He's a lost soul since Maggie died. He's in no shape to work but that's all that keeps him going. They have a son who is a total good-for-nothing. As soon as George is gone that place will be sold for building lots. Too bad, too. It's a small farm but it's a good one, the only level farm on Wilson Hill Road."

* * *

It was Saturday morning, two days before New Year's, and Ben was helping Slim finish morning chores. "You have plans for today?" Slim inquired. Ben said that he didn't, and Slim asked if he was interested in a table and two chairs for his living area. "They are solid maple and in good condition," Slim said. "They belonged to Joe and Mabel Thurston and never were moved out. They have been sitting in the basement for years."

* * *

Ben had never been in the basement of Slim and Mary's house. One end was an old-fashioned cellar with a dirt floor. It was very cold but always remained above freezing. Slim used the area to store vegetables for winter. In one section he had a large bin that held potatoes. He told Ben that they only bought potatoes in the late spring and early summer. The rest of the year they either dug them fresh from the garden or used the ones stored in the cold cellar. In another section of the cellar were several wooden crates filled with peat. Slim had placed chicory roots in these containers last fall. By keeping the peat moist and above freezing, the roots produced growth that made fresh winter salads. Ben had enjoyed one such salad during Christmas dinner. The south side of the cellar was lined with wooden shelves which contained the various vegetables and jams canned by Mary during the summer months. They also contained jars of honey from Slim's hives.

The other end of the cellar was an enclosed basement containing a long wooden work bench and Slim's wood working tools, including a wood lathe. His hand tools and machines were arranged on wooden shelves along one wall. The room was bright from fluorescent lights installed throughout. When they entered the basement Slim plugged in a large industrial electric heater which warmed the room in a few minutes.

For three hours Slim showed Ben how to strip the old varnish from the table and chairs. After a late lunch upstairs with Mary, they returned to the basement and began the process of applying fresh finish to the furniture. By afternoon chore time the furniture looked perfect to Ben, but Slim said that tomorrow he would lightly sand it and apply a second coat. The new furniture, along with the collage of Mary's photographs hanging on his wall, would really make his living area nice, Ben thought. He also felt pleased that he was beginning to learn how to use tools that until today he didn't know existed.

Chapter 13

January 1, 1996

So much has happened since I last wrote in this journal... I was in Florida and if my life had been described in one word, it would have been "DESPAIR." But I took a chance + headed towards a dream. I told no one because my trip north looked like an exercise in foolishness. I had a worn-out car, very little money, no specific destination + no job possibilities. I arrived in a small Vermont town almost by accident... it was a cold November night, and I had no place to stay. A minister gave me food + shelter in his church. The next day he found some warm clothing + directed me to a farm where I found employment + lodging. Someday I will tell him how he changed my life. Because of him, life can no longer be described by the word "DESPAIR." Rather, the word I can now use is "HOPE."

The couple who I work for are so wonderful. The man is teaching me to be a farmer – a real farmer who understands + loves the land. The woman is a teacher + a photographer. She is also a partner in the life of this farm. Together, they represent all the things I want life to be... More than anything, I want to be part of that life.

The first week of January remained seasonably cold, but there was no new snow. Mary returned to school while Slim and Ben continued with their winter work. Because the cattle were inside so much there was much barn work to do. Slim told Ben that it would be very different when warm weather came and the cows were turned out to pasture. The middle portion of their day was taken up with sharpening posts and delivering firewood. Soon, Slim said, they would take the crawler up the mountain on the other side of the stream and begin cutting wood for next season. Ben had never been up that mountain, and he looked forward with anticipation.

Wednesday morning, as they were milking, the door of the barn opened and Ben was surprised to see the minister, Jim Braxton, enter. After a few minutes of light conversation the minister became serious and said to Slim, "I received a call from Jane Hiller this morning. She is the woman with the three small children who you delivered some wood to last month. Her husband never came back. She thinks he's gone for good this time. At any rate, she has about a day's supply of wood left and is pretty desperate. She was unwilling to call you because, as you know, she hasn't been able to pay you for the last load. I told her that I would see what I could do. Listen Slim, I don't expect you to give firewood away. We have some money in our ministry of kindness fund, and I was hoping we could pay you to deliver her another load."

Slim answered immediately, "No need to pay me, Pastor. We've got plenty of wood out back, and I can spare another load or two. There's no way those kids can get by in this weather without heat." Pastor Braxton looked relieved and thanked Slim several times. He shook hands with Slim and Ben and then headed off to a morning meeting.

Slim was quiet and deep in thought as they loaded the wood into the dump truck. He had mixed emotions about this problem and divergent thoughts spun through his mind. On the one hand he knew he had to help those kids. They couldn't be left in a cold house while a big pile of wood sat behind his barn. But on the other hand, was he really helping them in the long run? Here was a woman who had three children, all younger than school age, with a man who was clearly an irresponsible bum. These parents, and they didn't deserve that title, had created an impossible situation unless others constantly came to their rescue. Slim believed that it was a terrible message to send to the children and still he had no choice but to bail them out.

When they arrived at the Hiller house, Slim backed up to the side door and they began to unload and stack the wood. Ben could see a small child, about two years old, peeking out the window at them. Slim told Ben to keep working while he went inside to check that the stove was working properly. Once inside he could tell from the fire in the stove that the pipe was open and clear of soot. Still he tapped on the pipe with the back of his pocket knife to assure himself that there was no build-up. Mrs. Hiller appeared nervous at first but relaxed when she realized that Slim was more concerned than irritated with her situation.

"I really appreciate you helping us out," she said. "I know that I owe you for two loads now. I won't forget it when we get back on our feet."

Slim was thinking of a proper response when he noticed the oldest child, a girl about five years old, curled up in a chair and crying softly.

"She's got a toothache," Mrs. Hiller explained. "I'm trying to doctor it, but I haven't had much luck yet."

"Where does it hurt?" Slim asked the little girl as he knelt down by the chair.

"Way in the back," the child answered and she opened her mouth to show a large cavity in the center of the tooth farthest in the back on the bottom. The gum around it appeared red and swollen. Slim stood up and looked at Mrs. Hiller.

"I'll see what I can do," he said simply. "You will hear from someone, either Dr. Taylor or Jim Braxton, in a couple of hours."

"I've got no phone," she responded. "They disconnected it when I couldn't pay the bill."

Slim told her that she would hear from someone, one way or another, and with that he returned to the truck. He said nothing to Ben as they drove from the Hiller place but instead of returning straight to the farm they drove to the clinic. Slim left the truck running and as he went inside he said to Ben, "I'll just be a minute."

* * *

That afternoon, while they were sharpening fence posts and then doing the milking, Slim was silent and thoughtful. It was a mood that Ben would often see in Slim and he knew well enough that Slim wished to be left to himself. Around five o'clock Mary arrived home from school and came straight to the barn. "I stopped to see Dad on my way home," she said. "It sounds like you had an interesting day." She told them that her father had asked Jim Braxton to bring the child to the clinic. She said that her father was able to clean out around the rotting tooth and relieve the pressure that was causing the pain.

She explained that Dr. Taylor was trying to arrange for the tooth to be removed but so far no dentist would accept the girl because she had no money or insurance. She said that situations like this just dramatized the need to add a part-time dentist to the clinic's staff and that Jean Taylor was already looking into grants that would fund such a project. Then Mary looked at Slim and said, "Anyway, thanks to you there is a little girl who is warm and free of a toothache tonight." Then looking at Ben she said, "Ziti for dinner. Plan on joining us around six thirty."

* * *

The John Deere crawler moved slowly across the open meadow toward the stream that ran along the base of the mountain. The large steel treads dug through the snow effortlessly. Slim had the blade on the front raised approximately one foot off the ground and angled to push the deepest of the snow to one side. They crossed the stream at a spot where the water ran shallow. Ben noticed the five piles of stones placed strategically across the stream just down from where they were crossing and asked Slim about them. "Poor man's bridge," Slim said above the noise of the crawler. "That's how Mary and I get across with dry feet. We'll have to do some rebuilding in the spring when the ice clears," he added. They started up the narrow wood road with Slim at the controls while Ben stood on the frame behind him holding on to the back of the seat. The ascent was steep but Slim had found a route that meandered up the side of the mountain in a way that appeared safe and secure.

The day was clear and cold. Ben wiggled his fingers and toes to keep the circulation going. Once they reached their destination the exercise of wood cutting would quickly warm their bodies. Along the way Ben could see evidence of trees that had been removed in previous years. Piles of branches were stacked neatly, many of them nearly decomposed. Ben noticed many newer young trees of various sizes and asked Slim if they reseeded themselves. Slim told him that in some cases they did but mostly the new trees had been planted by him and Mary over the years. "We come up with seedlings in the early spring," he said, "and plant a new one for each one cut in the winter. Old Joe Thurston taught me a lot about forest management. He didn't have any training in it—just used a lot of common sense." Slim told Ben that one of Joe's favorite expressions was "treat the land light." Slim added that Joe would often look down at him and say, "You've got to treat the land light, boy; treat it light."

Slim stopped the crawler near a stand of oak trees that looked dead or dying. He told Ben that periodically gypsy moths would hit the area and take a heavy toll on the young oaks. He said that it was from this stand of trees that most of the firewood was cut.

Ben had never seen a large tree cut down before. He watched as Slim located which one to cut first. It was a tall, completely dead oak about a foot and a half wide at the base. Slim cut a large notch in the tree on the side where he wanted it to fall. Then using the chainsaw on the opposite side he cut into the tree and toward the notch. Within seconds the tree fell into a small opening between several other trees. Once on the ground Slim took a smaller chainsaw from the crawler. He told Ben that using the smaller saw was better to remove the limbs from the tree. This would be Ben's job—to remove the limbs and stack them in a pile. Slim showed Ben the dangers when cutting the branches beneath the trunk. They could snap and kick up with a violent motion causing serious injury if you weren't careful. He also showed the technique to use that would avoid getting the bar of the saw bound up in the wood. He warned Ben to keep both hands on the saw's handle and never cut above shoulder height. When he was satisfied that Ben could use the saw safely, he began to locate a second tree to cut.

The morning went smoothly for the most part. Twice Ben's saw got stuck in a limb and Slim helped him dislodge it. By noon time more than a half a dozen trees were cut, de-limbed, and ready to be hauled down the mountain.

At lunch time they sat on a log and ate sandwiches. They took no more than a twenty minute break. Slim took Ben to a nearby spring where they drank the icy cold water. Ben couldn't remember ever drinking water as cold. After lunch Slim brought a long chain from the tool box and laid it on the ground by the first log. Then using a tool consisting of a stout wooden handle with a hinged metal hook and a strong sharp spike, he maneuvered the log onto the chain. Ben had never seen the hand tool before and asked Slim what it was. "It's called a cant hook," Slim responded, "but don't ask me why. I just know that it makes moving a heavy log real easy."

Once the chain was wrapped tightly around the log, Slim attached the other end of the chain to the crawler and pulled the log onto the wood road. He repeated the process until the logs lay beside each other in a straight line. The next maneuver, Ben learned, was entirely an invention of Slim's imagination. He had welded to the back of the crawler a piece of heavy steel that extended approximately a foot and a half behind the crawler. This flat piece of steel could be raised and lowered hydraulically. By lowering it to ground level Slim could back the crawler until the steel slid under the huge logs. Then by raising the steel up a few inches Slim could pull the logs down the mountain without the front ends digging into the ground. To keep the logs from sliding off the steel plate, Slim would attach large straps around each log and then fasten the hooks on the straps to the back of the crawler.

They moved slowly down the mountain, across the stream, through the meadow, across the county road and to the spot behind the barn where the logs would remain until they were sawed and split into firewood next fall. Slim and Ben would repeat this process many times during January and February. Mostly they cut firewood, but Slim also thinned out some live trees which he sold to an acquaintance who owned a lumber yard. "There's good money in lumber," Slim explained to Ben, "especially if it's hard wood that can be used to make furniture."

Ben loved these excursions onto the mountain. Slim worked hard but he never seemed rushed. By the time they were finished logging for the season Ben could identify nearly every variety of tree on the mountain. He was also learning about conservation and wise forest management. Once, Slim spent ten minutes deciding whether or not to cut a large tree, finally deciding to leave it based on the fact that they had already taken a tree nearby. He chuckled out loud when he heard Ben say, "Treat the land light, boy; treat it light."

Chapter 14

The last Saturday of January saw the temperature reach a high of forty-five degrees. The sky was a cloudless blue, and there was no wind. Ben finished washing his lunch dishes and, looking at the beautiful day outside his kitchen window, decided to hike to the upper pasture. The ascent was difficult as the snow was deep and no trail had been cut. When he reached the summit Ben was warm and wiped perspiration from his forehead. He went to a protected spot by the stone wall and lay down on a large, flat rock. The sun felt good on his face, and he nearly fell asleep. After a few minutes he sat up and looked around. How he loved this spot. Looking northward he could see the beauty of the Green Mountains, range after range until they disappeared in the distance. Down the mountain trail he could see the shiny tin roof of Slim's barn. Beside him was the upper pasture, clear in many places, but also rich with endless numbers of cedar trees, ranging in size from tiny seedlings to trees that were over a foot in diameter at the base. Ben looked at the neat pile of branches that he had stacked when they had cut fence posts a few weeks ago. He watched as a rabbit ran across the snow and into one of the large piles.

Resting in this place, the place that had already become Ben's favorite spot on earth, his mind curiously returned to his senior year of high school and a class he had taken in economics. He recalled his teacher, Mr. Weaver, a quiet gentle man who, for some reason, seldom had discipline problems in his class. It had always intrigued Ben that this man of average size and calm demeanor could command respect even from students who were unruly in other classes. Ben had always suspected that his obvious love for things academic, coupled with a sincere desire to help his students, were the secrets of his success as a teacher. And so, on this quiet Saturday afternoon on a beautiful mountain top in Vermont Ben recalled a specific lesson from his economics class. Mr. Weaver was teaching a unit on poverty in America, and he spent several days discussing the impact of poverty on human development. He had introduced the students to a theory formulated by Abraham Maslow.

Maslow had created a hierarchy of needs that he saw as universal for all people of all cultures. On the bottom of the pyramid were man's physiological needs identified by Maslow as the necessities of life—food, water, and shelter. Mr. Weaver explained that many people spent their entire lives striving to meet these basic elemental needs, never having the opportunity to advance beyond them. However, if a society was capable of seeing that these needs were adequately met, then man could proceed to a new level that Maslow called the need for safety. This level represented a person's need for some sort of order and predictability in life. It also included the need to feel safe and protected from physical harm. Mr. Weaver had pointed out that all people, even young teenagers who might not admit it, longed for things that could be counted on. Ben remembered that he had used his own classroom rules as an example.

"Suppose that I told you," he had said, "that there will be a test on chapters nine through eleven this Friday. Now you know you can count on that happening, and you also know that by studying those chapters you will successfully pass the exam. But suppose that you arrive to class on Friday prepared for the exam, and I announce that I didn't get the test prepared. Or worse yet suppose that you take the exam and discover that I have included different chapters than those originally announced."

Ben remembered that someone had said, "Sounds like McNulty's English class," and the students broke into a sarcastic laughter. He also recalled how Mr. Weaver had calmly directed the conversation away from the attack on his colleague and continued the discussion. He explained that if the need for safety, order and predictability could be provided, then a person could advance to Maslow's next level—the need for intimacy. The best word to describe this need was "belongingness". Ben recalled how that word had resonated in his mind. Belongingness. How wonderful it must be, he had thought, to feel that you really belong. To have friends and family who wanted you around. This had a special meaning for Ben because the class had taken place less than a year after his mother's death, a time when he had felt completely alone. It seemed almost like Maslow was describing him.

Next Mr. Weaver had explained that if a person's need for intimacy could be provided, he then was capable of advancing to the next level which was referred to as the need for esteem. Esteem meant achieving self-respect, recognition, and respect from others. Put another way it meant to feel good about yourself and to know that others respected you also. Mr. Weaver pointed out that as one advanced through Maslow's hierarchy the needs became more complex and intangible. Finally there was the highest level of need, referred to as the need for self-actualization which meant the need to reach your highest potential in whatever pursuit you might choose. Mr. Weaver had used music as his example explaining that a concert pianist would never, according to Maslow, have reached that level if the needs below it on the pyramid had not been met first. He finished his series of lessons by opening this provocative theory up to the class for discussion. Some agreed with Maslow and some disagreed, but all had thought deeply. Ben recalled that, as was his custom, he had said nothing. But the lesson had made a lasting impact on his seventeen-year-old mind because he knew that, at best, he was on level two. He had wondered if he would ever advance beyond it.

Lying on the rock in the upper pasture Ben marveled at the vividness of those lessons in his mind. So much had happened to him since then and still he could see Mr. Weaver standing there at his lectern. He could hear the sound of his voice and even remember specific lines and quotes. How they had made him think deeply. How they had called him to action. Mr. Weaver would never know that it was his lessons on Maslow that had given Ben the courage to escape from his prison. The plan to come north, to find work, to seek a place where he belonged, to find people who didn't view him as nothing more than the result of a mistake, and to discover what it was he had potential for—these possibilities were before him because a teacher had done a good job in his classroom. And as all this went through Ben's mind, Nellie Zenger's words also rang out. "Ben," she had said, "it wasn't an accident that you ended up here. I'm sure of that."

* * *

The meeting to plan the clinic's April fund-raiser was held on the last Sunday of January. Ben arrived at the clinic at exactly one o'clock and joined those already gathered for a light luncheon. He knew many of the people present and found that conversation came more easily for him than in the past. He talked with David Burnham, who had recently returned from his semester break. David introduced him to three nursing students who worked part time as interns at the clinic. Dr. Taylor walked to the microphone at one thirty and the meeting began. He started off by reminding the group that last year's fund-raiser had brought in excess of twenty-five thousand dollars to the clinic. It was mainly from this money that people without insurance or private resources could be served, he said, adding that with increased costs it was his hope to raise thirty thousand dollars this year. Using the dry board he began to list the activities for this year's event to be held on the last Saturday of April. In the clinic's community room the auxiliary would have their bake sale and bazaar. Items including Nellie Zenger's famous quilts would be sold. The president of the auxiliary reported that the group had met on a regular basis throughout the year and she estimated more items for the sale than ever before. Dr. Taylor also announced that for the first time autographed photographs from his daughter Mary's collection would be on sale. He said that announcements of this new feature would be placed in newspapers throughout the state.

Next Dr. Taylor talked about the activities on the village green. Two large tents would be raised on that site. Tables and chairs would be arranged for the chicken barbeque that would be served with the usual baked potatoes, coleslaw, and fresh made rolls. The barbeque usually served over one thousand meals throughout the day. Dr. Taylor said that David Burnham had volunteered to raise the tents, set up tables and serve the meals. "He'll need lots of help with this," Dr. Taylor added, and looking at Ben said, "Ben, I'm hoping that you will consider co-chairing this project with Dave."

Dr. Taylor announced that the Methodist church would host a petting zoo with pony rides at the church's playground located behind the parsonage. He said that members of the youth group would run this activity, adding that members of the high school honor society would also have a booth to paint faces on the children.

Mary was asked to speak about the library book sale. She explained that this year, for the first time, the library would hold its annual book sale on the same Saturday as the clinic's fund-raiser. Proceeds from the sale would go to the library, however; a section of the lawn in front of the library would be reserved for the clinic. Any books donated to the sale by the public would be put in this section with fifty percent of the proceeds going to the clinic. She urged people to spread the word for donations of books, adding that the project would also be advertised in area papers.

The final event of the day's activities was to be the band concert on the village green. The jazz band from the college would perform from eight to nine o'clock, followed by the college orchestra from nine thirty to eleven. As was traditional, the concert would culminate with the "1812 Overture". Tickets would be sold for seating under the tents and collections would be taken from those who brought lawn chairs or blankets and sat elsewhere.

Ben had no idea that the fund-raiser was so large and involved. When Dr. Taylor had asked him to consider co-chairing the barbeque with David, his first inclination was to accept immediately. He decided quickly, however, to check with Slim first. He was, after all, employed on a large farm, and he knew that spring was a busy time. When the meeting ended he immediately went to Slim and asked his advice. Slim said that the daylight savings time was in effect by then and usually the set up times were in the evenings of the week before the event. Slim added that they would do only necessary chores on the Saturday of the event so much of Ben's day would be available. With that information Ben went to Dr. Taylor and volunteered to help evenings before the event and all day Saturday except for chore time. A smiling Dr. Taylor shook Ben's hand and thanked him with sincerity.

Conversation followed the meeting, with people enjoying each other's company over coffee. Dr. Taylor was talking with Slim and Mary about the Hiller children. Ben was sitting nearby and heard Dr. Taylor say, "We brought all three children into the clinic and gave them a good physical. They have had their childhood shots and, except for their teeth, are in good health. Mrs. Hiller seems like a good mother who is in a helpless situation right now." Mary inquired as to the mother's maiden name and expressed surprise to find that she was a former student.

"She was a bright young girl with no guidance from home," Mary recalled. "I wonder if there isn't some way to help her get on her feet." Dr. Taylor responded that the town desperately needed a daycare center for preschoolers. He said that looking for employment was an impossibility until she could solve that problem.

Ben listened to the conversation with interest. "People working together to solve problems," he thought. "And they are enjoying themselves at the same time." It was a simple concept that until recently was completely foreign to him. Dr. Taylor's final comment surprised Ben even more. Looking at Slim he said, "The girl's tooth came out easily but the dentist still charged a hundred dollars. Thanks for taking care of that bill."

Chapter 15

February was a month of accomplishments for Ben. To most people they would have seemed mundane, but for Ben they further solidified his position in the place that he wanted to be. He changed his driver's license from Florida to Vermont. It was at the motor vehicle bureau that he encountered the first nasty person since moving to the area. The clerk demanded a copy of his birth certificate, a document that Ben was quite certain remained at his grandparents' home in Florida. After several minutes of bickering, the clerk's superior gave Ben a waiver on the condition that he locate the document as soon as possible.

Things went much smoother at the local bank where Ben opened a savings and checking account. The woman at the desk had been friendly from the start, but when Ben gave his name and address she said, "Oh, Mr. Thomas— Mr. Johnson will want to see you before you leave." When the paper work was completed she buzzed Mr. Johnson's office and he came out immediately to greet his newest client. He told Ben to be sure to see him if he needed any financial advice.

"You will want to start an investment program as soon as possible," he said.

* * *

Slim had strung both television and telephone lines to Ben's trailer and loaned Ben a phone and television that he said they were not using. The hook ups were Slim's own concoctions and probably not legal, but Slim had said that they were already paying too much for the services. The television cable came from the main house using what Slim called a "splitter" that he had bought at the electronics store in the mall. On the phone Slim had rigged up

97

a light that flashed if the call was for Ben. When Mary saw the set up she simply shook her head and said to Ben, "We'll probably all end up in jail."

* * *

The television was nice, but Ben watched it sparingly. Books were his passion; they always had been. As a small child it had been comic books. Ben had fond childhood memories of hours spent with Spider-Man, Batman, and Superman. He would read the stories over and over until the pages literally wore out. Still today there were scenes from those books vivid in Ben's mind. Some dialogue was so ingrained that he could recite it from memory. Many experts in education criticized the time children spend with comics, but Ben would always disagree. It was from those books of his very early life that Ben had developed his life long love of reading.

It was at an early age that Ben's mother began to take him to the public library. How he looked forward to those visits! Surrounded by hundreds of books, Ben would become lost in learning, completely losing track of time. He felt safe in the library. It was a place of peaceful security. The routine was always the same. They would go after lunch on Saturdays. His mother would read newspapers and magazines for two hours while Ben would take books from the shelves and read at the large round table. Before leaving, Ben would be allowed to sign out three books for the week ahead. By the following Saturday he would have read them several times. As the years passed, he advanced from young children's books to the Hardy Boys. By the time he had reached age ten he was reading classics like *Treasure Island*, *Swiss Family Robinson*, and *Tom Sawyer*. He loved *Heidi* and *Little Women*, but he read them in the library, standing up between the high shelves because he didn't want anyone to see him reading "girls' books." As he grew older, Ben's interests turned more to non-fiction. He loved travel books with colored pictures. He learned the climate, geography and animals for all areas of the country. It was in these books that he fell in love with seasons, not the kind in Florida but real seasons where it changed from very hot to very cold. He spent much time looking at pictures of snow and always told himself that one day he would see it for himself.

By the time he finished high school Ben had read hundreds of books. No one would know that he was the best-read student in the class. He never talked about the books. They were his private world and his best friend in a lonely existence. Years later Ben would look back with gratitude for the books of his youth. He was certain that books saved his life until almost by accident he found himself in a small Vermont community.

* * *

"Hello Ben," Meg said, looking up from her place behind the counter. "How are you doing?" After a minute or two of light conversation, he left the books he was returning and headed into the main part of the library to find some new ones. It was only a few minutes until he decided on a long biography of Franklin D. Roosevelt. There were several on the shelf but this particular one contained a multitude of photographs that added appeal for Ben. It also contained a large appendix featuring many documents and speeches from the Roosevelt era. Back at the counter Meg said, "So you're going to immerse yourself in a biography this week."

"Yes," Ben replied. "I remember that I enjoyed studying the Great Depression and World War II when I was in high school, but I don't know much about Roosevelt himself."

"He was very controversial," Meg responded. "Most people either loved him or hated him. There weren't many people neutral about FDR."

* * *

That evening Ben started the book, and for the next several days he read whenever time would permit. He was surprised at how much he actually remembered about Roosevelt—the pampered youth, his Harvard education, the contraction of polio, the strange relationship with his wife Eleanor and his famous home at Hyde Park. He also recognized many aspects of Roosevelt's New Deal program. Ben smiled as he recalled learning the multitude of programs designed to deal with the economic crisis. There was the CCC, WPA, PWA, AAA, FERA, and TVA. He saw familiar terms—the Brain Trust, the Hundred Days, Pump Priming, Fireside Chats, and the three R's. As he read, Ben wondered how Slim felt about Roosevelt. His guess was that Slim would be skeptical about all those big government programs.

The World War II era fascinated Ben. It always had. He felt that it was a clear cut war: Hitler was bad; we were good. The conflict was about justice and freedom. It seemed to Ben that today's conflicts were different—more vague in terms of right and wrong. It was more difficult to determine who the good guys were. Motives were often economic rather than moral. This troubling thought kept a place on Ben's mind as he read first of Roosevelt's involvement in the European strategy and then later against the Japanese in the Pacific theater.

The book ended with the death of Roosevelt in the spring of 1945. Ben had not realized that Roosevelt had been elected president four times. He was amazed to think that people who were his age at that time would probably remember no other president. How different from his own experience in which he had a distinct recollection of three different presidents and had been an infant for a fourth.

It had been a wonderful book, one that had captured the attention of Ben's curious mind. He was about to set it aside when he absently turned to the appendix in the back and saw Roosevelt's first inaugural address, delivered in March of 1933, when the Great Depression was at its worst. Ben read FDR's bleak description of the nation's situation. It was blunt and honest, so different from the rhetoric of most politicians. "Values have shrunken, the withered leaves of industrial enterprise lie on every side, farmers find no markets for their products, the savings in thousands of families are gone, a host of unemployed citizens face the grim problem of existence." Roosevelt ended his long litany of problems with the words, "Only a foolish optimist can deny the dark realities of the moment." Then the president went on the attack. Never popular with big business, he attacked the "rulers of the exchange" as stubborn, incompetent and self-seeking. He condemned their lack of vision and obsession with profits. And then came the line that leaped from the page and into Ben's mind. It would remain a conscious part of his memory forever and become a guiding principle for his life. Roosevelt said, "The joy and moral stimulation of work no longer must be forgotten in the mad chase of evanescent profits." These words hit Ben like a hammer, for he had come from a world where people worked because they craved money. Nearly everyone he knew had hated their job and lived for the weekend. Indeed most of the people Ben had known would have mocked Roosevelt's statement. The joy of work—moral stimulation—who was this guy kidding? People work because they want money. There is no joy in work.

Ben leaned back in his chair and smiled. How different things were in this place. Slim and Mary Smith were living examples of Roosevelt's affirmation. They believed in what they did. Their work had meaning. It did stimulate them morally and in other ways as well. Ben thought of Dr. Taylor and his wife Jean. He thought of Pastor Jim Braxton and Nellie Zenger. These people led lives that meant something Monday through Friday, not just on weekends. The word profit wasn't heard much around here. It was clearly far down on their list of priorities.

He looked further into the appendix, stopping at the Atlantic Charter. Drafted by Roosevelt and Churchill on a ship in the North Atlantic in August of 1941; it was a statement of democratic principles delivered when fascism was running rampant in Europe and the Pacific. The two men declared that they sought no territory. They called for respect of the rights of people to choose their governments. They asked for fairness in trade and freedom on the seas. They said that for realistic and spiritual reasons the use of force should be abandoned. What a ray of light, Ben thought, these words must have been to a world where concentration camps, civilian bombings, forced regimentation and death marches were the order of the day. He was reminded of a film he had once seen entitled *The Dictator and the Democrat*, which contrasted the lives and beliefs of Hitler and Roosevelt.

He looked further into the appendix, stopping to read Roosevelt's "Four Freedoms" speech delivered in January 1941. The profound words came near the end of the speech and as Ben read them chills went up his spine. "In the future days," Roosevelt began, "which we seek to make secure, we look forward to a world founded upon four essential human freedoms. The first is freedom of speech and expression—everywhere in the world. The second is the freedom of every person to worship God in his own way—everywhere in the world. The third is the freedom from want—which, translated into world terms, means economic understandings which will secure to every nation a healthy peace time life for its inhabitants—everywhere in the world. The fourth is the freedom from fear—which, translated into world terms, means a world wide reduction of armaments to such a point and in such a thorough fashion that no nation will be in a position to commit an act of physical aggression against any neighbor—anywhere in the world."

As Ben thought about the four freedoms his mind returned to a classroom in his high school where one teacher had a permanent display of Norman Rockwell's portraits that were inspired by the speech. How little they had meant to Ben then, but now they became rich with meaning.

Near the end of the appendix there was a speech delivered by Roosevelt at the end of his life. Spoken by a sick and dying man, Ben read several lines that he thought should be Roosevelt's legacy. For Roosevelt had said, "I have seen war on land and sea. I have seen blood running from the wounded. I have seen men coughing out their gassed lungs. I have seen the dead in the mud. I have seen cities destroyed. I have seen children starving. I have seen the agony of mothers and wives. I hate war."

Ben was glad that he had discovered the appendix. What a gold mine he had almost missed! Several things had touched him. Foremost was the importance of living a noble life in which service outweighed profits. He was also motivated to live each day to the fullest, to find work that brought meaning and joy; to never find himself trapped in a world dedicated to weekends. Finally, Ben knew, in a way that he had never considered before, the power of language. Language was Roosevelt's great gift. He used it so effectively that he could not only explain events, but he could actually alter events through the power of his delivery. And his words had lasting power. They were spoken at a specific time in history, but they echoed down through the generations with meaning for Ben more than a half a century later.

Chapter 16

February had been kind by Vermont standards. The thermometer hovered around zero each morning, but there were no dangerously cold spells such as there had been a few weeks back. The month's first significant snowfall came during the third week, and Ben rode in the truck beside Slim as they returned to the farm after a day of plowing and shoveling. Looking across the truck at Ben, Slim said, "We need to talk. George Rogers up on Wilson Hill called last night. He took quite a liking to you when you delivered that load of hay to his place. He asked if you might be interested in working at his farm for a few days in March. He wants all the saplings in his two hay fields cut and hauled away. It's driving him crazy seeing those fields disappear. He is willing to pay you ten dollars an hour to do the job. When you get the fields cleared he wants me to mow them with his brush hog and spread the piles of manure from his heifers. He has offered me the hay from the two fields in exchange for enough bales to feed his stock next winter. I figure if we could get two cuttings from those fields I could turn a good profit selling that hay. I want you to think it over. We can't do any haying until those saplings are cut."

"How many days would it take me?" Ben asked.

Slim answered, "I need you to help with morning and evening chores. That gives you five or six hours in the middle of the day to work over there. I figure it would take about a week. By the way, I would still pay you your regular salary. This is strictly an extra project that might pay off well for both of us—and make old George happy in the bargain."

"I think I would like to try it," Ben said.

"Me too," Slim responded. "It's quite an undertaking and we will be real busy for a few months from April until the end of June but after that things will ease up. Now I guess I have to convince Mary. She's afraid that we'll be working too hard."

* * *

Ben heard the phone ring and then saw his light begin to blink. He picked up the phone and heard David Burnham's voice on the other end. "You have plans for Friday night?" David asked. Before Ben could answer Dave told him about the college hockey game and invited him over to see it. "The game starts at eight o'clock and we'll go out for wings after." Ben said that he was interested and David told him to be at the rink's ticket window at seven thirty. Later when Ben mentioned his plans to Slim and Mary, they insisted that he leave evening chores to them so that he wouldn't have to rush. Ben could see the look of satisfaction on Mary's face. Later she told Slim, "He really needs to do things with people his own age."

* * *

Ben found the hockey rink with no problem and had waited nearly fifteen minutes when David arrived. Ben had never been to a hockey game and found the rules confusing. David explained "off sides," "icing," and "cross checking" as best he could. Despite the confusion over terms and rules, Ben enjoyed the excitement of the game and was impressed with the players' skills of skating while handling a puck at the same time. The game ended around ten o'clock and before going out for wings they stopped at the student union where David made a long-distance call to his parents. It was while Ben waited for David to complete the call that he noticed the bulletin board and casually began to read the posted announcements. One poster caught his eye. It advertised an upcoming event sponsored by the university's business department. An expert from the United States Department of Agriculture was speaking on the topic "Agribusiness in the Twenty-First Century." Ben took a pencil that was attached to the bulletin board with a thin chain and on a scrap of paper wrote the words, "May 1, eight p.m., Becker lecture hall." He put the paper in his wallet and looked up to see his friend David Burnham approaching.

* * *

Slim and Ben scrubbed the metal buckets and lids in the sink at the milk house. They carefully cleaned the spouts that would be inserted into the maple trees. Slim had Ben bring the small tractor with the front end loader to the shed where he stored a one hundred gallon tank. Ben watched as Slim took two heavy pieces of metal approximately an inch thick, six inches wide and three feet long from the shed. Holes had been drilled in the metal strips which lined up with holes drilled in the bottom of the bucket on the front of the tractor. By attaching the metal strips to the bucket with large bolts, Slim could use the front end loader as a fork lift. Ben was continually amazed at Slim's ability to improvise. Heavy work was made lighter, time was more productive and, in the end, the farm was more successful because of Slim's ingenuity. Slim noticed the look on Ben's face and said, "I priced fork lifts one time and decided to make my own." Gently Slim slid the two metal strips under the large tank and lifted it onto the sled that he and Ben had used to haul fence posts. "There," he said with satisfaction. "We're ready to go into the maple syrup business."

The following morning they loaded twenty-five buckets into the dump truck and drove to the adjoining farm. They parked in the driveway of the deserted home and began the task of carrying buckets across the field to a grove of maples beside the creek. It took three trips and the walk was difficult. The warm, late February sun had softened the snow just enough that they broke through with every step. When the third trip across the field was done both men were warm with perspiration. For several minutes they sat silently on two large rocks and watched the water flow beneath the ice-covered stream.

Slim took the drill from his back pack and inserted a large wood bit. Locating a smooth area of bark he drilled a hole into the tree. He inserted a spout and tapped it with his hammer until it was secure. He attached the bucket to the spout and said to Ben, "That's all there is to it. Twenty-four to go." As they worked Slim told Ben that some people would put on as many as three spouts in a large tree, but he felt that more than one would drain too much of the tree's life blood. He said that people weren't using buckets much anymore but rather used a plastic tube that ran from tree to tree. He told Ben that they would not boil the sap into syrup but would sell it bulk to an acquaintance who had a large operation. Slim explained that the man would pay mostly cash for the raw sap but that he would also give them a few gallons of the finished product. He said that he and Mary loved the syrup on pancakes and that she also liked to package some in fancy bottles to give as gifts.

When the twenty-five buckets were attached Slim said, "Now all we need are some warm days. I think you will like collecting sap."

* * *

The final few days of February and the first few weeks of March were busy ones. In addition to their usual work, Slim and Ben would use the crawler to pull the sled along the creek. They would stop at each tree and empty the sap into the large tank. Each time the tank was filled, Slim would use the forklift to transfer the tank from the sled to the truck. He would then deliver the sap to his friend, where it would be processed. Ben learned quickly that spring tapping would become one of his favorite activities. He especially enjoyed Saturdays when Mary would join them and they would have their lunch by the creek. Anabel was now big enough to come along and enjoy the fun.

* * *

The ground was bare of snow by mid March. Several times before the end of April it would snow again but there would be no measurable accumulations. They were completing Sunday night milking when Slim told Ben that tomorrow he could begin clearing the saplings from George Rogers' fields.

Slim taught more by example than by word, and he was effective. First he made certain that Ben knew how to safely handle George's old gray Ford tractor. He showed him the safe distance to keep from the steep bank where he would discard the cut trees. He demonstrated how to clear the stubble from the base of each sapling so that the cut could be made close to the ground. Next he showed him how to hold the bar of the chainsaw parallel to the ground to prevent dirt from dulling the chain. Then Slim attached the long rope to the hitch on the back of the tractor and laid the rope in a straight line on the ground. He stacked the saplings in the middle of the rope with the butts extending approximately fifteen inches. Finally he showed how many saplings to stack before wrapping the rope around them and tying it off securely. Not until he was certain that Ben understood the job and could do it safely did he leave him to work alone. "I'll be back at three thirty," he said as he climbed into the truck and drove away.

The work was difficult. Ben worked steadily, taking only a twenty minute lunch break. He found that he could cut for about ten minutes before accumulating enough trees to haul away. Throwing them over the bank was strenuous work because Ben wanted them as far off the field as possible. At first it seemed he was making little progress but as the day wore on his efficiency improved and by the time Slim returned he had made a good start on the first of the two fields. Ben's back ached and he had a bad blister on the side of the finger that pulled the trigger of the chainsaw. His shirt was soaked with sweat and his face was flushed. Slim looked at the field and said, "Good start—I'll bet you sleep tonight."

* * *

Evening chores were done by six forty-five. Ben returned to his trailer, made a large sandwich, drank a quart of milk, showered and fell into bed. He slept deeply and was startled by his alarm when it rang at five thirty. He helped with morning chores, made a lunch and drove the pick up to the Rogers farm, arriving at nine thirty. His work progressed more quickly as he developed an understanding of the machines and the techniques. At two o'clock he saw George park his truck on the road's edge and hobble across the field. He looked pleased with the progress and said, "You're doing a good job, boy." Ben found that George would always call him "boy," but did so in a way that was complimentary. Reaching into his pocket George removed a candy bar and a can of soda. He told Ben to take a break. "I've been watching you from the kitchen window," he said. "I know you're young but you're going to kill yourself. This is hard work and I know it." For the next ten minutes Ben listened as the old man told him how much he missed farming but his legs just wouldn't go anymore. He said it would be good to see the fields clear again. "You've got no idea how much this means to me," he said. "I kept these fields in good shape for over sixty years and it's about done me in seeing them go to the dogs."

* * *

The week went on and by Thursday Ben was well into the second field. After lunch he noticed Slim's truck pull into George's driveway. He saw the two men stand by the truck and visit for a few minutes. Soon Slim drove George's tractor into the first field. A brush hog was attached behind. When the large blade was engaged it cut and ground the dead hay and briars into small pieces. By three thirty, when they returned home, Slim had cut about a third of the field. They both returned the next day and while Slim continued with the brush hog, Ben finished cutting the saplings in the second field. They ate lunch together in the field and Slim asked if Ben minded working on Saturday. "I can brush hog the second field and you can spread manure," Slim said.

The next morning Ben noticed that George had attached a bucket loader to the Ford tractor. There was a spreader parked beside the huge pile of manure near the barn. Ben used the bucket to load the manure in the spreader. He would then attach the spreader to the tractor and take it to the field. By mid afternoon both fields were clear and the manure was spread as far as it would go. "Too bad we didn't have enough for both fields," George said. "You'll see a smaller hay crop on the field we didn't get to."

Ben had worked a total of thirty-six hours for George Rogers. It seemed incredible that he would receive three hundred sixty dollars in addition to his regular wages. He was even more surprised when George shook his hand and gave him four one-hundred dollar bills. "You're some worker, boy," he said. "I'm looking forward to seeing those fields get hayed in June."

Ben felt good as he rode with Slim back to the farm. It had been a positive experience and a profitable one too. Next week he would add the four hundred dollars to his growing bank account. He knew that he would have nearly two thousand dollars, more than he had ever imagined, and he felt like a millionaire. "You did a nice job this week," Slim said as they drove along. "I haven't seen old George look this good in a long time. He feels like he's got his farm back." And Ben realized once more that it wasn't so much the money that was important to Slim. More than that, it was the satisfaction of helping a neighbor and friend.

Chapter 17

Ten rows of oak pews filled the sanctuary of the Methodist church. Wine colored cushions lined the seats. A wide aisle ran down the middle with smaller ones on either side. The altar rail extended across the front with a kneeling pad, also wine colored. Immediately behind the rail sat a large oak table with the words "In Remembrance of Me" carved across the front. On the table rested an open Bible, a gold cross and candles. The platform behind the table was raised approximately two feet. In the center of the platform stood the pulpit and three chairs, all made of oak. To the right sat a large organ with pipes extending to the ceiling. The left hand side held three rows of chairs for the choir. Throughout the church were stained glass windows, each depicting a theme. One was devoted to music; another clearly represented the sacraments of baptism and communion; others showed scenes from the life of Christ ranging from a picture of him surrounded by children, to images of His birth, crucifixion and resurrection. The walls on either side of the church held cloth banners clearly made by the children. The banner made by the youngest group contained a flower, a dove, a fish, and a cross. Banners made by the older children were more detailed. One showed a picture of Christ surrounded by lambs with the words "The Good Shepherd." Another showed a man bending over to help an injured person with the words "Who is your neighbor?" Still another showed children playing ball, riding bikes, swinging and playing tag. Beneath it were the words "Love one another." All of the banners were bright and colorful.

Ben stood alone in the back of the church observing these things. It was the first time he had ever been inside a church sanctuary. He was surprised at its peacefulness but more so by its warmth and friendliness. It was nothing like the dark, dreary place designed to make you feel frightened and guilty that his mental image had always suggested.

Ben had just helped David Burnham erect two large tents on the village green. They would be used for Saturday's fund-raiser, first for the chicken barbeque, and later for the band concert. Once the tents were erected, David began to assemble the large grill on which nearly a thousand chicken breasts would be barbequed. While he worked on the grill he asked Ben to haul tables and chairs from the church to the green. To reach the area where the tables and chairs were stored, it was necessary to pass through the sanctuary. This accounted for Ben's presence in the church.

Ben, deep in thought, did not hear Pastor Braxton approach from behind and was startled when the pastor said, "Well, what do you think?"

"It's nice," Ben replied. "Not like I expected." Realizing immediately how inappropriate the remark sounded, Ben said, "I mean, it's warm and friendly, not what I think of when I think of churches." Ben quickly recognized that this statement was no better than the first but his mind eased when the pastor smiled and asked simply, "What do churches make you think of?"

Ben answered honestly, "Dark, scary places that make you feel guilty."

"I'm afraid that in many cases you are right," the pastor replied, adding quickly, "but not here."

The conversation ended and the two began loading tables into the truck. The pastor talked about Saturday's fund-raiser and the importance of the event. He spoke of Dr. Taylor's dedication to the clinic and the important role it played in the community. He talked about the Hiller children and how so many people like them had no other medical options. Ben was surprised when the pastor climbed into the truck and rode to the village green to help set up the tables. Together the two men made five trips to the church hauling and setting up tables and chairs.

Ben went home that night very tired and confused. How could things be so different from his life long perceptions? Had he been wrong all these years or was this place just an exception to the norm? He fell asleep wondering.

* * *

Saturday was sunny but cool. Slim and Ben drove to town as soon as morning chores were completed. Mary had gone very early to set up her photography display. As Ben approached the village green the smell of barbequed chicken greeted him. Members of the Knights of Columbus, as always, had volunteered to cook the chicken. The technique was to cook it

110

slowly, high above the coals, basting it constantly with their famous barbeque sauce. People came from several states to enjoy the meal that included coleslaw provided by the women of the Lutheran church, and rolls baked by Nellie Zenger and several others from the Methodist church. From eleven o'clock until three thirty, when he returned to the farm for evening chores, Ben cleared tables and emptied garbage cans. He could see large groups of people on the library lawn. He could hear that the other activities were experiencing similar crowds.

When he returned to town at seven thirty the streets were filled with people arriving for the concert. By eight the tents were full and along the streets hundreds of people sat in lawn chairs or on blankets. Ben had never heard a jazz band before and he loved it at once. They were loud and enthusiastic, playing mostly famous numbers including Gershwin's "Rhapsody in Blue." A half hour break following the jazz concert allowed time for the college orchestra to set up. During this time Ben and several others walked up and down the streets carrying large buckets into which donations were placed. The orchestra played for an hour and a half with an emphasis on marches by Sousa. They ended the concert with the "1812 Overture," a rendition that concluded with a cannon blast from a nearby knoll and ten minutes of fireworks. The crowd broke up slowly as many people stood around discussing the events of the day. Ben was, as usual, contemplative. By modern standards the day had not been exciting. Bake sales, book sales, photography exhibits, pony rides, chicken barbeques and band concerts could hardly be considered an extravaganza. Still, for these people in this place, it was enough. Ben could not recall a bored face all day. Tomorrow he would learn that this community effort had raised in excess of thirty thousand dollars for the clinic's budget. Orders for Mary's photographs alone had raised nearly five thousand dollars.

Chapter 18

Daylight savings time pleased Ben. It was the very end of April, and Ben sat on the steps of Slim and Mary's porch throwing a tennis ball across the lawn. Endlessly Anabel would fetch the ball and return it to his feet. The rapidly growing puppy was completely house broken and while she was full of energy and mischief, her goal in life seemed to be to please Slim, Mary and Ben. She would not go near the road. Twice Slim had caught her there and his stern voice, along with the rolled up newspaper that he used across her backside, had solved the problem in short order. When Mary took her on a walk through the lower field she had to carry the whining pup across the road.

Slim was out for the evening. He rarely went out during the week but he loved clams and Mary had convinced him to go to the Elks' annual bake. Mary, whose stomach turned at the very sight of clams, was doing school work at the kitchen table.

Anabel finally used up her energy and lay down on the grass next to Ben's feet. Ben sat looking across the lawn at the fields beyond. Quickly they were turning green, and he could see the early signs of yellow dandelion blossoms. He heard the door behind him open and Mary came to the steps and sat down beside him. They were silent for a few minutes and when Mary finally spoke she said, "Would you tell me about your mother?"

Ben was surprised that he was not taken aback by the question. From most people it would have been an intrusion but from Mary it seemed more like an act of caring. It was as though she knew he needed to talk—that he needed to get things out in the open before he could move forward. And so, quietly, he began.

"She was very alone except for me—actually, because of me. Her parents basically disowned her when I was born. The rest of the people in their world did the same. She moved to a city far from them because she felt that staying there she might as well call herself 'Hester' and sew an 'A' on her shirt. We lived in a small bungalow near the grocery store where she worked. It was a poor-paying job but they had health insurance so she stayed. She never made any new friends because she said, 'They would just turn on you when things went wrong.' I stayed in a daycare center while she worked. When I started school our finances improved because she no longer had to pay for daycare. If school wasn't in session I stayed home alone. I never played with kids except at school. We had no television so mostly I read books. My mother loved the library and so did I. We went there every week. Our other recreation was riding bikes to a nearby lake. It was a three-mile ride from our home. It was a beautiful lake with lots of islands. We would rent a boat and ride all day from island to island. My mother always packed a lunch and we would have a picnic where I could play in the sand by the shore. I loved those days. We went all year even when the weather was cool."

Ben stopped a moment—deep in thought and then he continued. "She was very nervous; always afraid that something bad was about to happen. She smoked constantly even though she knew it was bad for her. But she always went outside to protect my lungs. She told me that it was a terrible habit and I must never start. I listened to her and obeyed. I always obeyed. I never caused her trouble because I knew everyone else did. I never asked to play with other kids because I knew she didn't want me to. I was what my high school psychology teacher called passively compliant. I don't know why. Somehow, even as a small child, I knew how terrified she was of the world, and I didn't want to make things worse. Maybe it was my personality. I just don't know. When I started high school she got sick. For over a year she kept going and never missed work, but she was losing weight and was very pale. On Christmas vacation during my second year of high school she got so sick that she passed out. I was so scared that I called 911 and they took her to the hospital. A few days after that, we found out about the cancer. The doctor said she had maybe a year, but she died nine months later. Before she died she called her parents and asked if they would take me in. She said it was the hardest thing she'd ever done except when she had to tell them she was pregnant with me. She took care of everything before she died—even bought a cemetery plot and paid for the burial. There was no funeral. The funeral director read a Psalm at the cemetery. She doesn't even have a marker. Someday I want to get her one."

He stopped. They sat together silently on the porch steps. It had felt good to talk it out, especially to Mary. He knew that she wasn't being pushy—just

113

wanted to know more about him. And maybe she also knew he needed to talk. She was right.

Slim drove into the yard and put the car in the garage. Before he came to the porch, Ben looked at Mary and said, "Thank you. That helped." Mary said nothing but smiled softly with a mother's smile.

* * *

When it came to farming, Slim Smith was a paradox. He could, with some accuracy, be labeled both progressive and old-fashioned. He read the journals issued by agricultural experts and was very scientific on such issues as soil testing and crop rotation. He was an expert on farm equipment, spending hours poring over catalogs that showed the latest technology. His barn was state-of-the-art, especially in the area of cleanliness. He even had learned how to manage some of his records using computer software. He was very conscious about the environment, greatly influenced by Mary, and was careful about the use of pesticides and chemicals. Still, in many ways he was a throw back to another era. For one thing, all he wanted chopped as ensilage was field corn. Hay he wanted cut, cured and baled dry. "Cows need high-quality dry hay," Slim said. "Their systems aren't designed for a steady diet of green chopped haylage."

And when it came to hay Slim was a near fanatic about quality. The first crop was harvested in late May and early June. The prominent grasses were timothy and clover. Slim's hay field produced timothy that rose nearly to his shoulders. At its base grew a thick crop of clover approximately one foot in height. For Slim harvesting hay was nearly an art form. Watching the weather forecasts carefully, he would cut a section of hay when there was a forecast of sun and no rain for two days. He liked to cut early in the day to ensure a full first day of curing. On the second day he would fluff the hay using a machine called a hay tedder. Few farmers used a tedder any more but Slim was convinced that it speeded up the curing process by several hours. If there had been full sun, Slim could bale and collect the hay mid afternoon of the second day. Partly cloudy days often meant that the hay would be harvested on the third day. As soon as the first crop was off the field a new growth of alfalfa would sprout. By late July and early August Slim would harvest this second crop. It was much easier to manage as it was neither as tall nor as dense as the first crop. Many years, if there was adequate moisture, he would harvest a third crop of alfalfa in mid to late September. All of Slim's hay was stored inside where it was dry. He always knew where hay from each cutting was stored and used his own formula for feeding. Any hay that had gotten wet from a surprise rain or sudden thunderstorm was stored in a separate barn and sold. Slim also mowed the swamp areas of his farm in late August and stored it loose and unbaled near the main barn. It was this hay that he used for bedding under the cows.

Slim's ideas about hay were becoming more and more out of date. Most farmers were chopping the hay green and storing it in huge concrete pits. This new method eliminated the worry of bad weather and was quick and efficient. Still, Slim knew he was right and smiled when he read articles about the supplements that farmers now had to buy, and feed to replace what the cows lost from having no hay. And most important, Slim loved haying season. It was one of his favorite parts of farming. Good equipment had made the job less strenuous and now with Ben around it was even easier. Mary loved to be a part of the process, especially after the school term ended, but it pleased Slim that Ben's presence made her role in the process lighter.

Slim was also from the old school when it came to pasturing. Many farmers no longer let their cows out to pasture, preferring to feed them inside year round. Slim's herd was turned loose from mid May until mid October where they roamed and grazed the large hill sides behind the house and barns. At milking time, both morning and evening, the cows would obediently meander down the mountain where they would be milked, grained and sent back to the pasture. Near their watering hole on the mountain Slim kept a feeder with hay to supplement their grazing. Nearby he had a large block of salt attached to a stake driven in the ground.

For three days each spring, Slim would check and repair the pasture fence in anticipation of the upcoming season. The entire experience was new to Ben and he loved it. The spring days were warm and pleasant. The mountains were turning shades of red and green as buds began to swell and open. He especially enjoyed the Saturday they spent fixing the fence because Mary and Anabel came along. The job was hard but they did not rush and often stopped their work to talk. Mary had packed a lunch which they ate as a picnic on a stone wall in the most remote part of the pasture.

The fence consisted of four strands of barbed wire attached with staples to sharpened cedar posts. Slim checked each post by taking hold with his huge hands and moving it back and forth. To some of the posts he did nothing; others he drove more securely in the ground using a heavy maul. Others had rotted and needed to be replaced. Ben learned to remove the staples from the rotted posts by driving the pointed end of the staple remover behind the staple with a hammer. Once removed, the old staples were placed in an old honey pail so that they wouldn't end up in a cow's foot. Once the old post was removed, a new one was driven into the ground and the barbed wire reattached with new staples. Occasionally a section of wire itself would be broken or rusty and need to be replaced. After removing the old or broken section, new wire would be used to replace it. For this job they put on heavy work gloves. The necessary length of new barbed wire would be unrolled and cut. Then it would be attached to the first post and strung along the ground until it reached the post at the other end. Slim would staple the wire to the first post after which Ben would use a wire stretcher to keep the wire taut until Slim attached it to the remaining posts. The wire stretcher consisted of an old pickaxe handle that had been planed flat on one end. To the planed end the guard from an old sickle bar had been loosely attached. Slim showed Ben how to hook the burrs from the barbed wire into the guard. Then by placing the flat end of the handle behind the cedar post the wire could be stretched tight. "It's homemade," Slim said as he saw Ben examine the primitive-looking tool. "It was Joe Thurston's, actually probably belonged to his father. You know what they say about necessity being the mother of invention."

* * *

Early on a Sunday morning in mid May Slim turned the cows out to pasture. When he opened the swinging steel gate the animals knowingly walked through and began to graze. Slim, Mary and Ben leaned against the fence and for a half hour silently watched as the cows slowly worked their way up the mountain path. It was a scene that would become a favorite for Ben. There was a serenity to it to which he could find no equal. Perhaps Mary put it best when, after watching the grazing animals for a few minutes, she said, "They think they have died and gone to heaven."

Chapter 19

It was lunch time on Wednesday, the first day of May. Ben sat at the table in his trailer eating a lunch consisting of a tuna sandwich, milk and cookies. He took the wallet from his pocket and began to search for the slip of paper that he knew was in there somewhere. After nearly giving up he found it between his driver's license and library card. Unfolding the paper he found that he was right about the date: Tonight at eight the speaker from the Department of Agriculture would be at the college. Ben read the date with mixed emotions. He really wanted to go; he had learned so much about farming in the past six months and had truly fallen in love with the profession. He wanted to know more and this speaker offered an opportunity to do so. Still, the college made him nervous. He somehow felt inferior to the confident-looking students who roamed the campus. And even though he now had a decent wardrobe he couldn't shake the belief that he looked different and stood out like a sore thumb. Several times during the afternoon he decided to go and then not to go. Then, while milking he asked Slim if it would be all right to use the truck that evening. He didn't say why and as usual Slim didn't ask.

When evening chores were completed, Ben showered and dressed quickly. He gobbled down a can of pasta with meatballs, brushed his teeth and was on the road towards campus by seven. He parked the truck in a large parking lot located on the very edge of the college. From there he began the nearly quarter-mile walk to the lecture hall where the speaker was to appear. On the way he noticed the well-worn path that was clearly a short cut to his destination. Taking the path, he crossed green, neatly cut lawns accented with large old maple trees as well as with smaller shrubbery including forsythia which was currently in full bloom. As he neared the lecture hall he crossed a small foot bridge above a brook that was about ten feet wide. Ben stopped for a few moments and looked over the railing at the brook below. Then, noticing people entering the lecture hall and seeing on his watch that it was seven fifty-five, he hurried up the concrete steps and entered the building. The large room was nearly two-thirds full and Ben found a seat on the end of an aisle six rows from the back. As soon as he was safely in his seat, Ben began to feel relaxed.

The room filled up quickly, mostly with students who clearly wanted to be elsewhere. Ben noticed adults, probably professors, taking attendance and he realized that this was, for the most part, a captive audience of students who were there only because it was a course requirement. The room was warm. An inadequate air conditioner failed to keep up with the demands created by a room full of body temperatures. Later in the evening one of the professors would turn off the unit and open the windows, bringing instant relief as the cool May breeze entered the room.

At precisely eight o'clock two men entered the room and went to the front. One was the professor who would introduce the featured speaker. The speaker himself was a young man in his early thirties. He wore a stylish dark blue suit with a well coordinated shirt and tie. His cordovan shoes were polished to perfection. Ben noticed the expensive looking gold watch on his wrist and the extraordinarily large ring on his right hand. His manner exuded confidence—even arrogance. Before he spoke his first word Ben took a dislike to him.

"It is my pleasure," the professor said, "to introduce tonight's speaker, Mr. Michael Catler, who comes to us from the United States Department of Agriculture." The professor said that the title of his lecture was "Agribusiness in the Twenty-First Century." He went on to give the man's credentials and accomplishments, which included the fact that he was an economist with advanced degrees from two large urban universities. Ben thought it strange that nowhere in the speaker's resume was there any indication that he had ever spent time on a farm.

The introduction completed, the audience applauded politely as the speaker walked to the podium. He opened a manila folder and took out his prepared notes. After some opening remarks that included a humorous anecdote he looked at his audience and said, "Tonight I want to discuss with you some agricultural truths for the twenty-first century. Let me warn that what I say is not popular with those enamored by nostalgia. But happily your government is more concerned about the continued economic growth of our nation and a high standard of living for its citizens than it is about a naive nostalgia. The first truth is that agriculture needs to be understood and dealt with as an industry. Like any business its major concerns are productivity and efficiency that translate themselves into profits. Without profits no business deserves to exist and agriculture is no exception. Too often we have allowed, even endorsed, behavior from our farmers that would never be tolerated in other industries. Pastoral scenes on calenders look nice but frankly, they are museum scenes for the next century. We must see the farm of the twenty-first century as a work place rather than a home. You will never hear that line from an elected official because in politics it is suicide to separate the words family and farm. So the politicians say what they have to say. Fortunately the real policy makers in this country are the technical experts, not the politicians. Now let's return to the issues of productivity and efficiency. The new global economy puts never before felt pressures on these concepts. No longer are they economic advantages. Rather they are economic necessities. To ensure that the United States be on the cutting edge of agribusiness, your government is accelerating its research into the areas of high technology and genetic engineering of both crops and animals. There is no reason to think that with the proper use of science and technology that productivity can't be increased several fold. Even today many dairy farmers are milking three times daily rather than twice and that is only the beginning of the agricultural revolution you are about to see."

The speaker continued on this theme for several more minutes. He praised the agribusinessmen, as he called them, who had already seen the light and were pioneering the revolution. He told of one such person who told him that he had produced a five hundred acre crop of corn without ever getting his hands dirty.

"Now let us move forward to another agricultural truth," the speaker said. "With increased production it is vital that we dramatically increase our exports of agricultural products. This, of course, will be a major challenge to our national government. We need to play hardball with our trading partners to force easier access to their markets. Now, once again, the politicians have to walk softly on this issue so as not to appear callous or impersonal. But the fact is we must use our superiority in such areas as computer technology and health care to coerce countries, desperate for these services, to also purchase our food. I believe that there is also a huge opportunity for us in third world and developing nations. True they have no money to purchase our products but many have valuable untapped resources to which we must gain access. To some this may sound like economic exploitation. I have even been accused by some extremists of advocating economic imperialism. However, I view it as a healthy aspect of capitalism. If we have advantages in certain areas, we need to use those advantages as leverage in developing trade agreements."

The speaker then embarked on his final agricultural truth. He said that we were currently on the door step of a new frontier in biotechnology. He spent several minutes explaining the research into the cloning of animals. It would, he believed, lead to new breeds of "super animals" engineered to whatever need the economy demanded. The same would be true for crops such as corn, hay and grain. This area of science was clearly a favorite of the speaker for he became even more dynamic and enthusiastic than he had been in discussing his earlier truths.

As the speaker concluded and entered the portion of the meeting reserved for questions, Ben found his head spinning. His mind was combined with feelings of confusion, anxiety and anger. Essentially the speaker had rejected, even poked fun at, Slim Smith's way of life and all that he believed in. Slim's method of farming was local, not global. Except for his milk, which went to Boston, all his earnings were derived from the local economy. And Slim's farm was far more than a work place. It was indeed his home. He knew his land as an old friend. The contours of his hills, the meandering of his stream, every stone wall and hedgerow were a part of him. Slim wanted to get dirty when he raised his crops. He craved the soil. He hungered and thirsted for the land. All these things Ben had grown to love and admire. Slim's brand of farming was a way of life, a kinship with the earth. And yet this speaker referred to it as obsolete—an irrelevant nostalgia for the new age.

These thoughts raced randomly through Ben's mind. He was totally unprepared to be coherent but when the professor asked for questions he felt his hand go up. There were other raised hands as well. In the short term it seemed like the worst of fortunes. Years later, looking back at it, Ben felt it to be the opposite. But for whatever reason the professor saw him first and pointed at Ben. "Please stand and ask your question," he said.

When Ben spoke his voice sounded weak, almost squeaky. Immediately he wished that his hand had gone unnoticed, but it was too late—and so he said, "I was wondering if you have ever lived or worked on a farm?"

The speaker looked irritated as he responded, "Your question is irrelevant to this discussion. One need not clean the stables to understand the business of agriculture." He looked for another question but Ben felt himself continue.

"It just doesn't make sense to me to say there is no difference between a farm and a factory. How can..."

"Excuse me," the speaker interrupted. "What is your major here at the college, young man? And what year are you currently enrolled in?"

"Actually, I am not a student here," Ben replied.

The speaker smiled and said, "Oh, we've got one of the locals here, and he's upset that I have exposed the flaws in his daddy's farm." There was laughter throughout the room as Ben sat down. Immediately he felt beads of perspiration form on his upper lip and forehead. He knew that his face was red and his ears burned. His eyes blurred and he thought to himself, "Don't cry, you've made a big enough fool of yourself already." Mercifully there were other questions and the focus of the audience went elsewhere. Still, for Ben the final twenty minutes of the question and answer period were pure agony. He wanted to leave his seat and run from the room but chose instead to wait until the end and then escape in the sea of faces.

Ben barely heard the remainder of the discussion but he was conscious of the professor thanking the speaker, and as the students rushed from the hall he slipped out among them. As the crowd moved down the sidewalk Ben noticed very little talk of the lecture. The students appeared anxious to head down town to the local watering hole, and the only comment Ben picked up concerning the lecture was from a student who said to the group he was with, "That was the most boring hour of my entire life."

Ben came to the place of the short cut path that led to the parking lot and seeing the path deserted, he quickly moved into its shadows. The isolation of the path and the cool night air revived him and his mind began to clear. When he reached the foot bridge he stopped and looked over the railing into the brook below. He watched a leaf as it circled slowly in a small eddy and disappeared under the bridge. It was then that he heard the voice say, "Have you ever read Schumacher?" Thinking that two people were passing by, Ben did not look up. But then he heard the voice again, "Have you ever read Schumacher?" Ben turned around slowly and saw her standing at the end of the bridge looking directly at him. She was wearing brown sandals and baggy jeans with a large hole in one knee. The gray sweatshirt she wore inside out and cut off above the elbows. Her wavy brown hair was cut short and fell gracefully around her face. She was very thin - almost too thin, and she stood approximately five feet five inches tall. Her most outstanding feature was her eyes, large and brown and full of wonder. Long black lashes accented them.

"I don't know what you mean," Ben said hesitantly.

She replied, "Schumacher, E.F. Schumacher, I think you would like him."

Ben looked embarrassed as he said, "So I guess you saw me make a fool of myself in there."

Her expression changed from one of wonder to one of determination and she replied, "He was an arrogant, rude moron speaking to a roomful of immature idiots only there because it was a course requirement. You were the only one to question his stupid remarks so don't be embarrassed. I'm the one who should be embarrassed for sitting there in silence. Anyway, I have one of Schumacher's books in my dorm if you want to borrow it."

"That would be nice," Ben answered.

"Come on," she said. "I'll get it for you. My dorm isn't far from here." And she started back up the path towards campus. They walked in silence until she reached the dormitory. "Wait here," she said, "I'll get it for you."

It was only a minute or two before she returned with the book. "Here you go," she said. "I have to run." And she was gone.

As he walked to the truck Ben realized that he had borrowed a book from someone and didn't know her name. He stopped under a street light and looked down at the book. Its title read *Small Is Beautiful*. The subtitle was *Economics as if people mattered*. Ben opened the cover and on the inside in ink barely dry was written: Reeta Sorvino—Room 210—Molly Stark Hall.

Chapter 20

Anthony Sorvino was a second generation American, born in New York City to parents of Italian descent. Early on it was evident that Anthony was a bright, motivated and compliant young man. His parents' dream was that he would be the first Sorvino to attend college, and he did not disappoint them. He earned a bachelor's degree in history and government from a state university and immediately thereafter applied and was accepted into law school. There he met and fell in love with Judith Butterfield, who was the daughter of John and Marie Butterfield, both of English descent whose families had lived in America since colonial times. Anthony and Judith were married upon completion of law school. Anthony accepted a position with a prominent firm that specialized in corporate law. Judith, whose background was psychology and sociology, joined an equally prominent firm where she specialized in divorce law and estate planning. Within a few years Anthony and Judith were both established in their professions and enjoyed an affluent lifestyle on Long Island. They were blessed with two beautiful children, a son and a daughter, who from infancy were given every possible opportunity. They were the perfect family. Both children took full advantage of life, delighting their parents as they excelled both academically and in their extracurricular activities. When both children were well into college, the lives of Anthony and Judith Sorvino were turned upside down when Judith discovered that she was pregnant. It was with a sense of alarm and regret that they entered middle age with the unexpected responsibility of raising a little girl whom they named Reeta.

From the beginning it was obvious that Reeta was different from her older siblings. She preferred mud puddles to ballet slippers, and climbing trees to playing the flute. She was always coming home with an assortment of "live" things ranging from crickets to spiders and snakes—all to the horror of her mother. Her parents tried, unsuccessfully, to send her to private school, but she insisted on returning to public school to be with her friends. Inherently bright, she maintained high grades throughout her elementary years. Still her report cards always included such comments as "needs to apply herself" or "lacks organizational skills."

Middle school saw a decline in Reeta's grades and appearance. Her parents were beside themselves. Increasingly they disapproved of her choice of friends and worried that she would become involved in the drug culture and sexual activity. The truth was that when Reeta entered high school she was involved in neither—but she was curious.

Reeta's high school was in walking distance from her home. She soon discovered that by exiting school from a back door she could cross the athletic complex, enter a jogging trail, and walk home absent from the noise and fumes of residential traffic. It was on a warm September day that she was walking near the track when she happened to see an acquaintance named Jenna sitting on the grass stretching. "What's going on?" Reeta asked as she walked by.

"Just track practice," Jenna replied getting to her feet to begin running. Impulsively Reeta dropped her backpack and joined her friend jogging around the track. Several trips around, the girls stopped running and sat down on the grass. "You must be in good shape," Jenna commented. "I'm breathing heavier than you, and I do this every day."

As they talked a man approached them. He was tall and thin—a man in his forties. His sleeves were rolled up and his tie was loose. He carried a clipboard. Looking at Reeta he said, "Are you a student here?"

Reeta, with her usual dislike for authority said, "Don't worry, I'm leaving."

"You don't have to leave," he said calmly. "I noticed how easily you ran around the track, and I thought you might like to join us."

"Thanks, but I don't think so," Reeta answered as she picked up her pack and started home.

"If you change your mind, stop and see me." he called after her. "I'm Mr. Brink, Room 105." Reeta did not look back.

* * *

That evening Reeta lay in her room listening to music when her mother came in. "Phone for you, honey," she said. Reeta picked up the phone and was surprised to hear the voice of her friend Jenna.

"I was hoping you would change your mind about joining the track team," Jenna said.

"I don't think so," Reeta answered. "I've never thought much of the jocks."

She could hear Jenna laughing as she said, "We're not jocks. The jocks don't even consider us athletes. We frustrate them because we ignore them—plus we almost always win and they can't stand that. By the way, the preps don't like us much either. Actually most of us don't fit in anywhere. That's why we call ourselves Brink's misfits."

"What's he like?" Reeta questioned. Jenna told her that he was a great teacher and a great coach.

"He's really good at what he does," she said. "Plus, he cares about things—including us. We try hard in his class and on his team because we don't want to let him down."

"You sound like a commercial," Reeta said sarcastically.

"Only one way to tell," Jenna answered, and added with equal sarcasm, "Just don't get me wrong; I'm not begging you to join us. We are doing fine without you. I just thought you might enjoy running."

Reeta spent a night of restless sleep. Twice she woke for over an hour and lay thinking of the events of the past day. Several times she decided to join the team and then each time decided against it. By morning her decision was not to join, but she stuffed sneakers, shorts and a tee shirt into her pack in case she changed her mind. Classes that day were a blur. Reeta paid little attention to the events that took place, even turning in an earth-science quiz completely blank except for her name at the top. When the final bell rang, she walked by herself to the girls' locker room and changed into her running clothes. Years later Reeta would look back on that day and try to determine what finally had led to her decision. She was never able to come up with a rational answer. She only knew that it was the most life-changing decision she had ever made.

* * *

She loved it from the start. Running exhilarated her. In the track area she loved the one hundred meter sprint, the fifteen hundred meter run and the fifteen hundred meter relay. In field events she would come to excel in both the high jump and the long jump. She found Jenna's description of Coach Brink to be correct. He knew how to give a person space and yet show concern. She was fascinated by his talks about track and the proper way to prepare the body for it. He was an expert on fitness and training and often emphasized the differences between training for strength as opposed to training for endurance. She loved his demeanor as he moved from group to group, always with his sleeves rolled up above the elbows, his tie loosened, and one shoulder appearing to be slightly higher than the other. And so it was difficult when he came to her midway through the first marking period and told her that she was failing most of her courses. "If your grades have not improved when the marking period ends," he said, "you won't be able to remain on the team."

Reeta gave him the cold look of steel that would become her trademark and said, "My grades will improve."

* * *

When the marking period ended, Reeta's report card showed three C's and two B's. Her response to Coach Brink's congratulations was simply, "They will be even better from now on." And they were. Her natural intelligence coupled with her desire to remain on the track team manifested themselves in honor roll grades that delighted her parents and were a slight source of embarrassment to her.

"What do you know about this track business?" Reeta's mother asked her husband.

Looking up from his reading Anthony Sorvino replied, "I know that we spent a lot of money on ballet lessons when all we needed to do was get her a good pair of running shoes." Then smiling he added quickly, "I want to meet this Brink guy sometime. He must be something special."

* * *

One thing Reeta discovered as her involvement with the track team intensified was that many of her teammates would assemble in Coach Brink's room each morning for the half hour before the start of classes. As she began to join them on a regular basis she discovered that the team was involved in a variety of service projects. Coach Brink believed that it was the right thing to do, with the added benefit of unifying the team members. Reeta learned that each month team members contributed money to support a young girl from a third world country. Many wrote notes and sent pictures so that the child would experience them as people rather than faceless entities who contributed to her welfare. On a bulletin board behind his desk, Coach Brink posted return letters and pictures from the little girl. The team also conducted a food drive for the poor at Thanksgiving time, an event that for over a month made Coach Brink's room appear more like a grocery than a classroom. At Christmas time volunteers from the team helped the local branch of the Salvation Army wrap gifts for distribution to poor children. Reeta remained a curious observer of these projects for over a year, offering no direct involvement. Coach Brink never pushed her in that direction.

It was early in Reeta's second year of high school that Coach Brink posted the notice of an inner city Catholic mission's need for volunteers to help serve meals in its soup kitchen. Reeta had grown up traveling into New York City from her suburban home and had no fears or anxieties about directions or dealing with mass transit. And so one Saturday morning in October she found herself and two track teammates entering the mission to help with the noon day meal. Reeta was teamed with a young sister of mercy named Sarah. Together, for nearly two hours they served soup, bread, and coffee to mostly ragged homeless men. Then for two more hours they washed dishes in the small kitchen in the rear of the building.

Sister Sarah was a woman of about thirty years of age, petite in stature, with an angelic face and dancing eyes. Her personality was intriguing because she seemed both shy and outgoing. She had an appealing sense of play that bordered on mischief, and at the same time she maintained an attitude of caring and concern for those under her watch. The men who came through the soup line clearly saw this and treated her with a respect that was not normally part of their characters.

Work at the mission was difficult and it was not long before Reeta's teammates found reasons to prevent them from coming back. But Reeta continued. Soon she developed a friendship with Sister Sarah and found herself calling during the week just to visit. One conversation somehow led to the subject of Acquired Immune Deficiency Syndrome and Reeta learned that one of Sarah's ministries was to visit dying AIDS patients at a local hospital. Surprising herself, Reeta asked if it would be possible to attend one of these sessions. And so one Sunday afternoon Reeta found herself sitting beside the bed of a young man who was clearly near death. His appearance shocked Reeta and at first she was unsure if she could remain in the room. But as she watched Sarah talk calmly to the young man she saw a smile form on his gaunt face. "This is my friend Reeta," she told him, adding, "I knew that you wouldn't mind if she came with me."

They talked for a long time, Sarah carrying the bulk of the conversation, the young man responding briefly, and Reeta remaining silent. After a while, seeing that he was tired, Sarah asked if he would like her to read before she left. He nodded, and she took from her purse a small book of "Reflections on the Psalms" and read a poem written by Dag Hammarskjold:

> Have mercy
> Upon us.
> Have mercy
> Upon our efforts,
> That we
> Before thee,
> In love and in faith,
> Righteousness and humility,
> May follow thee,
> With self denial, steadfastness, and courage,
> And meet thee
> In the silence.
>
> Give us
> A pure heart
> That we may see thee,
> A humble heart,
> That we may hear thee,
> A heart of love,
> That we may serve thee,
> A heart of faith
> That we may live thee
>
> Thou
> Whom I do not know
> But whose I am.

In the silence of the room, the clear soft voice of Sister Sarah reading those words touched Reeta in a way she had never before felt. She looked at the face of the sick young man and saw the tears well up in his eyes. And in the quiet of that place, Reeta reached out and took his hand.

It was only two days later that Sarah called to say that he had died. They talked only briefly and when she hung up the phone, for the first time since she was a little girl, Reeta cried.

* * *

Increasingly Reeta discovered that she lived in three different worlds. There was the world of her parents—a world of status and influence. Their beautiful suburban home sat in the best of neighborhoods. A lawn service kept the yard and shrubbery looking like something from the pages of *Better Homes and Gardens*. In the three bay garage sat her father's BMW, her mother's Lexus, and a bright red Honda Civic for her to drive. Reeta loved her parents, but increasingly their world seemed foreign to her. She felt, in many ways, an alien in familiar surroundings.

Then there was the world of track. Here Reeta felt more comfortable. She loved the competition, a trait that she would possess for a lifetime. She loved the idea of being physically fit and was acutely conscious, not only of the need for exercise, but also for a healthy diet. She grew close to Coach Brink and her teammates, always enjoying the comradery that developed among them. Still, in some ways, she felt like an outsider. Her teammates were interested in "teen" things. Theirs was a world of consumption. The mall was the place to be. Reeta had moved beyond that world. She was interested in intangible things. What ought to be was more important than what was. To be truthful, she found the worlds of her parents and teammates boring and insignificant. It was not so much that she felt superior to them—just different. And so Reeta found herself spending more and more time in her third world, the world of Sister Sarah.

* * *

Nearly every Friday afternoon Reeta would hurry from school, pack her bag, and take the train into the city where she would spend the weekend with Sarah. Friday evenings were a favorite time. In Sarah's tiny apartment they would cook the evening meal and then talk endlessly over it. While much of their conversation was serious and often philosophical, there was also much laughing and teasing. The thirteen years difference in their ages seemed irrelevant. They were simply what they were—the best of friends. Saturdays were always busy. The work at the mission took much of their time, and then later in the day they went to the hospital that housed the AIDS patients. Normally they were exhausted by the time they arrived back at the apartment. Sarah rose early on Sundays and attended mass. Reeta never joined her and appreciated the fact that Sarah didn't pressed the issue. Sundays were special. By eight o'clock Sarah would be back from mass and after breakfast they would go out for the day. Often they walked, skated, or rode their bikes in Central Park. Sometimes they would take the bus to a place called "The Cloisters," a restored medieval monastery brought to this country by the Rockefeller family and placed beautifully in a spot that allowed a person to forget that the world's largest city surrounded them. Sunday brunch was always Reeta's treat, and she often took Sarah to places that were beyond the budget of a sister of mercy.

* * *

Reeta's parents were bewildered and concerned. They had met Sarah and found her charming, but somehow the relationship seemed strange to them. "I hope she's not turning into a religious nut," her father said one evening. "I just don't understand her motivations at all. Maybe we should get her to talk with a professional."

Her mother answered, "Maybe the best thing to do right now is nothing. She still has two more years of high school. She may have moved into a new phase by the time she graduates." She thought to herself a moment and smiled as she continued. "It's strange—a few years ago we were worried that she was hanging with the wrong crowd. Now she gets all 'A's,' hangs out with a nun, and we are still worrying."

To which Reeta's father replied, "That's the problem. She never does anything normal. Sometimes I think she was switched in the hospital."

* * *

The spring of Reeta's junior year in high school found her thinking about the future. One day she remained at school long after classes had ended and the other students had left. Hesitantly she went into Coach Brink's room and was relieved to find him there alone working at his desk. "Do you have a minute to spare?" she asked from the doorway.

"Sure do, come on in," he replied. "What's on your mind?"

Reeta was honest and to the point. It was a trait that she admired in Sarah.

"I want to find a college and get accepted before my parents start pressuring me with one of their choices."

"And what would be their choice?" Coach Brink asked.

"Something big, expensive, urban and elite," Reeta answered, adding, "Everything I don't want."

"So what do you want?" he inquired further.

"I want a small four-year college with a good reputation. I want to major in nursing, but I also want courses in philosophy, religion, and literature. I want a school with a good track team, and I want to be in the country, where I can see trees and mountains." She paused and then said, "Please don't tell me that it doesn't exist."

Coach Brink smiled as he looked across his desk. "Have you ever been to Vermont?" he asked. Reeta shook her head. "I know a very good school up there that might interest you. The track coach is a friend of mine. With your grades and SAT scores, I am certain that you could gain early acceptance status." He dug through the bottom drawer of his desk and pulled out a catalog. "Take this along with you and look through it," he said. "If it looks interesting to you, let me know and I'll help you get started." Then he added, "Your parents need to be a part of this, you know."

Reeta replied, "I have to do this on my own. It's the only way I won't be pressured into something I don't want."

* * *

That night, alone in her room, she pored over the catalog. She read every page and before she fell asleep Reeta knew that she would apply to this school, and that she would be accepted. She also knew that her parents would willingly agree and breathe a sigh of relief when she left for her first semester.

And it had happened. Here she was in Vermont, nearly finished with her first year of college. Coach Brink was right. She loved it here even though she found most of her classmates boring and immature. She sat in her room looking at the Green Mountains that she had already grown to love. In two weeks finals would be over, and she would leave for the summer. She looked forward to seeing Sarah again, but dreaded the three week vacation to Europe that her parents had planned for her. As she sat there in the quiet of her room, she thought of the young man she had just met. It seemed strange that the most challenging questions that she had heard at college had come, not from a classmate, but a non student who lived on a nearby farm. She wondered if he would read the Schumacher book, if he would be inspired by it as she had been, if he would return the book to her. And she wondered what his name was.

* * *

The ride from campus back to the farm was a blur. Sleep that night was fretful and restless. Ben rose earlier than usual and was preparing the machines for milking when Slim entered the barn. Morning chores were easier now that the herd spent much of its time in the pasture. The barn needed cleaning only every other day and less hay and ensilage was required since fresh grass was now the cows' main diet. Ben had become completely proficient at the milking process and Slim noticed that the operation from start to finish had been cut by one-half to three-quarters of an hour. This morning, as had become their practice, Slim worked his way down one side of the barn while Ben took the other. While the automatic machines did their job, the two men would stand in the center of the barn and visit.

"I went over to the college last night and heard a speaker from the Department of Agriculture," Ben said casually.

"Good speaker?" Slim inquired.

"Oh he knew how to speak," Ben answered. "I just didn't agree with what he had to say."

"And why was that?" Slim asked with a wry smile.

"Basically he said that you are doing this farming thing all wrong. He thinks everything has to be big. He thinks that a farm is like a factory—not a home. He was real big on technology and cloning and genetically engineered plants and animals. I thought it was interesting that he never called it farming—always agribusiness. Oh, and by the way, you are not supposed to enjoy getting your hands dirty."

Slim laughed, as much as Slim ever laughed, and noticing that his milking machines were ready to be moved to the next two cows, he walked towards them. But as he walked, Ben was amazed to hear Slim say to himself, "I'll bet he's never read Schumacher."

Chapter 21

The fields were dry enough for planting. This year Slim would plant enough field corn to fill the two large silos attached to the milking barn. The other fields were left for hay, three cuttings if all went well. This particular spring no plowing would be necessary. Slim only used his plows when rotating his fields from hay to corn and that process would not be done until next season. Instead he used huge discs to break up the soil. Additionally the discs broke down the roots from last year's corn crop and also mixed the manure that had been spread on the fields during the winter with the soil beneath it. Some years Slim would spread lime on the corn fields but, using a soil testing kit, he found the acidity level of the soil acceptable without doing so. Slim explained to Ben that when the sod from a new field was turned over it was necessary to work the field level with harrows. This year, however, once given a thorough discing, the fields were ready to plant. The corn was planted by a machine called a drill that was pulled behind the tractor. The drill planted many rows at one time and was designed to insert each seed at the appropriate depth. Slim planted corn on some of his own fields as well as some on the farm next to his. Combined with normal farm work, the planting process took about two weeks. This included time lost on rainy days and a day to clean up the equipment once the process was completed. Slim never put equipment away for the season until it had been thoroughly cleaned and all the fittings freshly greased.

Ben enjoyed the two weeks of planting. It was all new to him, and he absorbed it like a sponge. Slim was a natural teacher doing most of his instruction by example but explaining things when necessary. Ben found the work rigorous. Slim was anxious to get the planting done for soon haying season would be upon them and securing a quality crop of hay was one of Slim's highest priorities as a farmer.

After these long days of spring work, Ben found himself exhausted. His inclination was to eat a large evening meal and go to bed; instead he pushed himself to read for an hour from the Schumacher book. As he read he took notes in a tablet. He found the book interesting but difficult for his youthful and undisciplined mind. For him it was a book that required discussion and instruction. He felt intellectually unprepared to deal with it alone. He was also distracted by his own motivations. He was sincerely interested in the book and its contents, but he was also anxious to complete it so that he could return it to Reeta Sorvino before she left campus for the summer. As he read the book, his mind was prone to wander from the contents of the pages to the mysterious girl who had loaned it to him. If he should see her when he returned the book, what would he say if she asked him about it? Would he know enough to say something coherent and worthwhile? Would she even remember him?

Ben decided to choose a chapter from the book that he found interesting and somewhat understandable and then prepare some hopefully interesting comments about it. What else could he do? Convinced that he was in a situation intellectually "out of his league," the series of events from the past week had left him with extremely low self esteem. He leafed through the chapters many times before deciding to focus on the one entitled "Buddhist Economics."

"Economists suffer from a sort of metaphysical blindness," Schumacher wrote. Ben read the line several times. He knew from context that the thought reflected negatively on economists, but what did it mean? Looking up the words metaphysical, metaphysics, and metaphysician in his dictionary, he concluded that economists refused to consider anything that wasn't rational or explainable in natural terms. He read on, "Some go so far as to say that economic laws are free from metaphysics." Again Ben found himself confused but concluded finally that economists felt no obligation even to consider the spiritual and supernatural when discussing their theories and principles. Could it be that they considered the work of philosophers, theologians and even many writers and poets to be irrelevant to the real world—completely divorced from the idea of work? Schumacher continued by saying that modern economists view labor as nothing more than a necessary evil—an item of cost. Ben was confused, at first, by the word labor but concluded that it did not refer to work itself, but rather to the workers specifically. If he was right, then Schumacher's view was that modern economists saw people as no different than a piece of machinery—actually lower than that, for he continued by saying that in their eyes the role of labor should be reduced to a minimum if it could not be eliminated all together. Ben was conscious of the fact that, as he considered these words, the voice and face of the speaker he had heard at the college kept coming into his thoughts. He could actually hear the man saying these exact words.

Schumacher then explored the issue of work from the Buddhist perspective. Ben saw that he broke their view of work into three parts. First they believed that work should give a person the chance to utilize and develop their faculties. Looking the world faculty up in his dictionary, Ben decided that the correct application of the word in this context was "natural aptitude." He immediately thought of Mary. Things people had said about her made him sure that she was a superb teacher. He knew from his own observations that she was a gifted photographer and a person very adept in agriculture. He also knew that her work was a joy and inspiration to her. It was, to use his new word, metaphysical. He was certain that Mary Smith would never see her work as an item of cost or something to be eliminated all together if possible.

The second point of Buddhist economics was that work enabled a person to overcome the tendency of ego centeredness by joining with other people in a common task. Ben felt comfortable that the term "ego centeredness" referred to a person thinking only of himself. He was sure that this selfishness was a negative trait, but he had never thought of work as a remedy for overcoming it. Ben found himself thinking of Mary's father, John Taylor, and also of Jim Braxton. He thought of the clinic and how its work was indeed a common task performed by so many members of the community. He thought of the huge fund-raiser held recently and how the minister had helped him load and unload several truckloads of tables and chairs. He thought of Nellie Zenger sitting in her home sewing quilts that would be sold to help with the clinic's finances. And he thought of Slim delivering wood to a poor family— wood for which he knew no money could be paid, and then paying to have a small child's aching tooth removed. Ben was perplexed as he thought, "These people do these things, but they aren't Buddhists."

Schumacher's final view of work from a Buddhist perspective was that work was necessary "to bring forth goods and services needed for a becoming existence." The terms "goods" and "services" presented no problem for Ben but he was confused by the expression "needed for a becoming existence." He went once more to the dictionary and discovered that the word "becoming" made sense in this context using the words "appropriate" or "suitable." In other words, Ben speculated, Buddhists thought it acceptable to have goods and services in order to live a pleasant and comfortable life. It was neither evil nor selfish to seek these things as long as one's life was not consumed by material belongings. Ben found that as he pondered this idea, Slim and Mary's home came to mind. It was not a mansion but it was a sturdy, comfortable, well-equipped and pleasant place to live out one's life.

Ben read on and learned that in Buddhist thought it was possible to turn the concept of work into something evil and dehumanizing. Work could be made to be boring, meaningless, stultifying or nerve-racking. These words reminded Ben of so many people he had known growing up in the South. Most, including his mother, had hated their jobs. Work was something to be endured, made necessary by the need for money. He remembered a man who lived in his apartment complex saying, "I exist from Monday to Friday so that I can live on Saturday and Sunday."

Schumacher continued by issuing a scathing indictment of employers who created these kinds of working environments. He said that they had an evil lack of compassion, and that their tactics were soul-destroying. According to him, Buddhists believed that when work became degraded, people began to strive for leisure as an alternative. This, the Buddhists believed, was a complete misunderstanding of one of life's basic truths; namely that work and leisure were complementary parts of the same living process and could not be separated without destroying the joy of work and the bliss of leisure. As Ben looked at the words written in his tablet, he said out loud several times, "The joy of work—the bliss of leisure." And both phrases were deep and meaningful to him.

* * *

Ben stopped at the car wash and cleaned the truck inside and out. Periodically as he drove toward campus he glanced down at the book lying on the seat beside him. He was nervous and apprehensive, hoping that she hadn't left for the summer and yet not knowing what to say if he should see her. Embarrassed by the pick up truck, he parked on the edge of campus and walked the nearly quarter mile to her dorm. He noticed that many students were still on campus although some were carrying boxes and clothing to waiting cars. When he entered the foyer of the dormitory Ben saw a girl sitting behind an official looking desk. She was talking on the phone, so Ben waited nervously until she hung up and looked at him. "I have a book for Reeta Sorvino," he said. "Could you check to see if she is in?"

Without answering, the girl picked up the phone and pressed two digits. After waiting what seemed an eternity Ben heard the girl say, "Reeta, someone here to return a book." Then without looking up the girl said, "She will be down in five minutes."

Ben leafed aimlessly through a magazine while he waited. "Hi," she said, and Ben looked up. She looked as he remembered except that she was more neatly dressed, wearing brown sandals and yellow shorts with a white top.

Ben stood up and handed her the book. "I wanted to return this before you left for the semester," he said.

"You just made it," she replied. "My last two finals were today. I'm leaving in the morning."

"How did they go?" Ben asked.

"They weren't bad at all. I'm pretty sure that I did all right."

Ben's mind went completely blank and he could not think of a single word to continue the conversation. He was about to say goodbye and leave when she said, "Where are you parked? I'll walk to your car."

"It's quite a way," Ben said. "I wasn't sure if there would be spaces up here."

"Good," she replied. "I need a break from packing," and she walked to the door. After a moment of silence she said, "So how did you like the book?"

"I liked it a lot," Ben answered. And then surprising himself he added, "Parts of it were hard for me. I spent a lot of time with the dictionary." Surprising himself again he said, "I don't think Schumacher and that speaker we heard would agree on much."

Reeta laughed and said, "You've got that right."

Ben was nervous and embarrassed as they approached the truck so he said, "Thanks for loaning me the book."

But as he reached for the door Reeta said, "Gee, I loan you this really good book and you don't even offer to buy me a soda."

"I'm sorry," Ben answered. "I guess being here on campus intimidates me. Where can we get a soda?"

Reeta replied, "Well we could walk over to the student union, but if you take me downtown I could fulfill a lifelong dream."

"And what is that?"

"To ride in a pickup truck."

* * *

The ride to the snack bar went easily. Reeta was curious about the truck and asked a multitude of questions. She wanted to know how the clutch worked, how you knew if you were in the right gear, when to use four wheel drive, why there were two gas tanks and what kinds of things could be carried in the back. Just as they were arriving Reeta asked casually, "By the way, what is your name?"

When Ben answered, "Ben Thomas," she repeated out loud, "Benjamin Thomas."

* * *

Ben asked what she would like and she said a small soda. As he was walking toward the window she added, "How about we celebrate the end of finals with some nachos and cheese? Get a large order and we'll share it. I'll find a picnic table." When he returned she was sitting at a table on the lawn near the driveway. It was an unusually warm May evening and most of the other places were already occupied. Several small children were running among the tables playing tag. An elderly couple sitting nearby seemed to enjoy watching the children more than eating their ice cream cones.

"So you work on your parents' farm," Reeta said.

"Actually, they aren't my parents. I grew up in Florida. When my mother died three years ago, I stayed with her parents until I finished high school. Last November I came up here."

"Why Vermont?" Reeta inquired.

Ben smiled and said, "When I was a little kid my Mom took me to the library every Saturday. I always wanted to look at the big picture book of New England. I loved the mountains and the snow. Even back then I knew that someday I would come here."

"Did your grandparents bring you?" she asked.

"I drove to New Jersey, where my car died. The rest of the way I hitched a ride in a trailer truck." Reeta asked how he knew about the farm job. "I didn't," Ben said. "I stopped in a town mainly because it was getting dark. A minister let me sleep in his church. I told him that I was looking for work and he took me to the Smith farm. He knew they were looking for a hired hand."

"Had you done farm work before?" she asked.

"No," Ben answered, "but the Smiths are really good people and I have learned on the job. I love farming. It's what I want to do. Just not the way the speaker last week said it should be done." They sat silently for a few moments and then Ben asked, "What about you?"

"Not much to tell," Reeta answered. "I live on Long Island. I love track. I came here because my track coach said they had a good program, plus he knew I needed to escape from suburbia. It was a good choice. I'm glad I came."

There was another moment of silence until Ben said, "How did you get interested in the book by Schumacher?"

"I was on a retreat. We read the book and then discussed it. My best friend Sarah, was the group leader. I mostly listened. I was the youngest one there and the only one that wasn't a nun." Reeta stopped talking and Ben could see that she was deep in thought. Finally she said, "Sarah loves that book. She thinks everything has gotten too big and impersonal—like there's no sense of community. She says that money rules the world. People don't find satisfaction in their work—just in the money that results from the work."

"That's kind of what I got from the chapter on Buddhist economics," Ben said.

Reeta smiled, "Sarah loves that chapter but she always says it could just as easily be titled 'Judeo-Christian economics.' She quotes passages from Ecclesiastes and Proverbs and the Psalms and the gospels that have the exact same sentiments. I wish I could remember them all. You would be amazed. Sarah says the problem is that most people who call themselves Christians don't follow these ideas. They chase after the money instead."

Ben responded, "Maybe most people who call themselves Buddhists don't follow them either."

Dusk was approaching and Reeta told Ben she had better get back to her packing. When they reached the dorm she said, "I'm leaving tomorrow. I will spend most of June in New York City with my friend Sarah. For three weeks in July I will be in Europe on vacation with my parents. I will be back here in mid August when track practice begins. If you give me your address, I'll send you a postcard from Europe."

Ben wrote his address on a scrap of paper and handed it to Reeta. She took his pen, asked for his phone number, and wrote it down. Then getting out of the truck she said, "I'll see you, Benjamin Thomas." She smiled at him as she left. And with that smile a feeling went through Ben's body that he had never felt before.

Chapter 22

Ben remembered back to that cold November day when he had first looked from the window of his trailer and seen the garden. It was seventy-five feet wide and two hundred feet in length. Around its perimeter at ten foot intervals Slim had placed cedar posts, each inserted two and one half feet deep and extending nine feet high from ground level. Along the bottom was small-gauge rabbit fencing buried six inches into the ground to prevent animals from digging beneath it. Above the rabbit fencing a five foot high chicken wire fence kept larger animals from jumping over. Together, the rabbit fence and the chicken wire enclosed the garden to a height of nearly eight feet. Just to be certain that deer got the message, Slim had added a strand of barbed wire to the top of each post. The Smith garden was secure.

Snow covered the garden the day that Ben first saw it and so he was unaware that a strip of lawn was maintained inside that fence approximately six feet wide down each side and double that at both ends. The grassy area nearest the house included a red brick patio on which, during the warm weather months, sat a picnic table with a large umbrella, several chairs and a chaise lounge. The opposite end of the garden housed a row of bee hives wrapped in black tar paper to keep out the winter winds. The garden itself contained a deep rich soil with very few stones. Each spring Slim applied a thick layer of composted manure which he worked into the soil with a large rear-end tiller.

Planting, maintaining and harvesting the garden was a joint effort for Slim and Mary. Still, in Ben's mind, except for the bees, the garden seemed more as belonging to Mary. Perhaps it was because Slim's time there was limited to evenings and Sunday afternoons while Mary, as soon as the school semester ended, was there almost constantly. Crops were a blend of flowers, fruits and vegetables. Ben would learn that the variety of flowers was chosen not only for color but also so that blooms for the bees to work would be available from early spring to late fall. Some of the plants were perennials while others were planted yearly, with Mary always including a long row of Slim's favorite, zinnias.

One section of the vegetable garden was known as the salad bed. It contained several varieties of lettuce as well as endive, mustard, spinach, radishes and scallions. The salad bed was planted very early in the season, often the last week of April. It did well until the heat of summer arrived and warmer weather crops took center stage. Near the end of August a late crop of salad greens would be planted which normally could be enjoyed well into October.

Another section of the garden was reserved for berries. Slim always planted twenty-five strawberry plants in the early part of May. The young plants were carefully weeded throughout the summer in a manner that allowed the runners to spread in all directions. Mary was careful to remove blossoms to ensure that all strength could go into the plants themselves. She also "trained" the runners in a way that by September the twenty-five plants resembled a continuous two foot wide row that ran nearly fifty feet in length. Before the first snows of November, Slim covered the berries with straw beneath which they would lie dormant and protected throughout the winter. The following spring the straw was loosened to allow the plants to grow and develop. A bed of straw left beneath the plants served the three fold purpose of holding moisture, preventing weed growth and keeping soil off the fruit itself. By June first the strawberry bed was covered with blossoms and honey bees. During this delicate stage Slim often covered the entire row at night with old blankets to protect the crop from destruction by a late Vermont frost. The crop arrived around mid June usually, when Mary was finishing school. One of her first summer tasks was to harvest the strawberries, which she used for jams and jellies, or froze for the following winter. And for the approximate two weeks when they were producing fruit, Slim ate them every night over hot buttered biscuits. Some of the jams and jellies were preserved in fancy jars and given as gifts throughout the year. Usually, at their peak, the plants produced more than could be consumed. These surpluses were picked in quart baskets which Slim sold at the local market.

The raspberry bed consisted of three short rows, each between two and three feet across. The path between each row was narrow, with just enough space for a person to squeeze through. Raspberries began to produce fruit about the time the strawberries were done. These delicate berries were placed in pint boxes rather than the quart size used for the strawberries. Ben would learn that too many raspberries piled on each other could actually damage the fruit from its own weight. Once again Mary took charge of harvesting the fruit. Much was squeezed and strained into juice, which when mixed with the juice of red currants, made a tart jelly that was one of Slim and Mary's favorites. Again some of the jelly was used as gifts. Once or twice Mary would make fresh raspberry pies, another of their favorites. And she always made one in a smaller pan for Nellie Zenger. Excess berries were taken to the local store for sale. Each fall Slim removed all the dead canes from the raspberries and cut back the stalks on which next year's fruit was grown. Then he mulched the bed with a layer of leaves followed by another layer of manure. He did this procedure because Joe Thurston had done it before him. Years later he would learn from Mary that this mulch prevented iron deficiency in the plants. Slim often wondered if old Joe had known the science behind the mulch or if he simply knew that it worked.

Beside the raspberry patch stood six red currant bushes. Except for mulching with leaves and manure, they required little care. Mostly Mary used the juice for jelly, but she would also mash some in a bowl, add sugar, and chill them for Slim to eat as a dessert. While they were a favorite of Slim's, Mary didn't care much for them herself. "Too much sugar to make them edible," she would say and add, "then you spend the evening picking the seeds from your teeth."

The only other bed in the garden was reserved for asparagus. Slim said that asparagus required more work than the rest of the garden put together, which was an exaggeration, but not by much. This bed Slim took care of by himself, except for the harvesting which Mary did by cutting the stalks at ground level with a sharp knife. Asparagus had to be weeded often and carefully so as not to disturb the roots. It was a sensitive plant that did not react well to neglect. Despite the effort Slim said that it was his absolute favorite vegetable in the garden. As a child Ben had always hated asparagus, but he soon discovered it was wonderfully different when cut fresh from Slim and Mary's garden.

The remainder of the garden was planted in rows. It contained all the usual varieties including peas, string beans, corn, cucumbers, carrots, cabbage, cauliflower, Brussels sprouts, shell beans and potatoes. Slim planted the corn at three different times so that when one lot ended another began. He did the same with string beans. He planted both red and brown potatoes, enough to last through the winter. Mary took charge of most of the garden's maintenance. Early in the season much hoeing and cultivating was required. Once the rows were well established she would carefully lay newspaper, six sheets thick, in the rows between the plants. To keep the sheets from blowing away she would put dirt along the edges and moisten the paper with a garden hose. As the season progressed, Slim would place grass clippings from the lawn on top of the newspaper but there was never enough to complete every row.

The most unusual plant in the garden was chicory. Slim planted the variety that grew throughout the summer and was dug up in the fall. Once it was dug up, Slim trimmed back the leaves to one half inch from the root and lay them in a box of moist peat. Then every three to four weeks he would plunge some of the roots into a container filled with peat which he packed tightly around the roots. This process ensured nice firm chicons. After placing the container in a warm place for four to five weeks, the chicons would have grown six to eight inches in length and made delicious fresh winter salads. Mary's Christmas dinner always included one of these salads.

Ben saw that it was in this garden that Slim and Mary spent much of their time on summer evenings. Often he would see them have their evening meal on the garden patio and then proceed to work among the flowers and vegetables until nearly dark. He loved to see them there. It was a sort of reassurance to him that things were all right. It was a picture of harmony between people and nature. It was a place of peace. One night as he saw them working among the flowers Ben thought to himself that wars would cease if people had gardens.

And so it was a special event when on a warm Sunday afternoon in May Slim and Mary asked Ben to join them for lunch on the garden patio. When they finished eating, Ben was given a tour of the life emerging from the earth. He asked many questions, for he knew next to nothing about gardening. They delighted in his interest. When they reached the garden's end Ben asked about the bees. "One of the most interesting creatures on earth," Slim said of the honey bee, and added, "The best run communities in the world are being lived out in those hives."

Ben looked confused and said, "I would like to know what that means."

Mary laughed and said, "Ben, I hope you didn't say that to be polite because I have a feeling you will hear a lot about bees from now on."

That evening Ben sat in the living room of his trailer thinking of the day's events. It seemed strange but the day was sort of a milestone for him. In a sense, being invited inside the garden fence was almost like becoming part of the family. He reminded himself that he was a hired hand living in a trailer but, try as he might, the word family kept entering his thoughts.

* * *

Some things were easier for Reeta than most college students. She observed classmates as they spent hours packing for the summer break. Many parents came with multiple vehicles to handle the cargo. Reeta packed her clothes into two large pieces of soft luggage and put them in the trunk of her Honda Civic. She placed the books that she wanted to keep in a cardboard box. The rest were taken to the college bookstore to be sold. The few that neither she nor the bookstore wanted were taken to the recycling center. Her toiletries, shampoos, hair dryer and bedding were packed in two large Rubbermaid tubs and placed in the back seat. There wasn't much else. She had a Discman, a radio and a small television. Everything was packed and she was ready to go when she thought of her skis, one pair for cross country and another for downhill. Her parents had brought them last fall. She had no ski racks on her car, and they wouldn't fit inside. After a few minutes of thought, she took Ben's phone number from her bag and made the call. Mary heard the phone ring as she was walking out the door on her way to school. "He's in the barn milking," Mary said. "If you hold on, I'll take the portable phone to him."

"Thank you, if it's not too much trouble," Reeta answered.

Ben was surprised to hear her voice. She asked him if it would be possible to leave her skis with him. She would leave them in the lobby of the dorm behind the desk. Could he possibly pick them up before the week's end when the dorm closed for the summer? She told him that she really appreciated the favor and that she would see him in August. That was it—a simple two minute phone call. But for Ben it was a confirmation that he really would see her again. He was pleased that when she needed a favor she had thought of him. For the next three and a half months, whenever he saw the skis leaning against the wall in the corner of his bedroom, Ben would be reminded of the girl who had approached him out of the shadows on the footbridge. Through that wonderful summer, the best of his life, she was often in his thoughts.

* * *

Reeta noticed at once that things were different at home. It was as though she and her parents had reached a meeting of the minds. They asked her about school, complimented her high grades and looked with interest at a highlight film from the past track season. It seemed they had made a conscious decision that she was very different from them but that it was all right. They had begun to realize that there was nothing to be done about it anyway. Their youngest daughter had a determined mind of her own, and a very good mind at that. The change pleased Reeta and she found herself actually enjoying her parents. At dinner a few days after her arrival home, she told them that she was going to spend the month of June in the city with Sarah. She said that she would be back in time for the July vacation to Europe. They offered no opposition to her plans and told her how pleased they were that she would be with them for the three week European holiday. They would travel first to England, Scotland and Ireland, then on to Italy and finally they would spend a week in Germany. Reeta was pleased that they recognized her interest in things rural, and thus had planned the trip with an emphasis on the European countryside.

For the rest of May, Reeta remained at her home on Long Island. She saw old friends from her high school track team and spent some time with Coach Brink. It was a relaxing time for her but by June she was anxious to be with Sarah and help with her work. She arrived in New York City on the first Friday night in June. Using the key Sarah had given her, Reeta let herself into the apartment. By the time Sarah returned from the mission, Reeta had unpacked her things and was settled in for a month's visit. That first night they talked until well past midnight. Sarah talked much about the mission. She told Reeta of a new program with which she was involved to help homeless high school drop-outs earn their GED's. Many people would start the program and disappear before completion, but Sarah was excited about those who were successful. Sarah said that she loved teaching and was making inquiries about taking some college courses.

"Enough about me," Sarah said, "I want to know all about your college."

Reeta began, "I love Vermont. It is the most beautiful place; especially the mountains. The track team is great. It is very challenging and I know our coach wasn't pleased with our ten and ten record, but we had very few seniors and lots of freshman like me. Hopefully we will be really strong the next three years. My classmates—most of them are pretty dull intellectually and mostly want to party. I would say that is the biggest disappointment so far. There aren't too many people there who are motivated towards anything except maybe making money. To be honest, I haven't made any close friends. I find them dull."

"What about your professors?" Sarah asked.

"For the most part," Reeta answered, "they are very good. Sometimes I think maybe I'm the only one who enjoys class. Face it Sarah, I'm a misfit."

There was a pause in the conversation and after a few moments Sarah said, "But you have met someone."

Looking a bit embarrassed, Reeta replied, "And what makes you think that?"

"Because I know you, and there is something different about you. You have someone on your mind."

"It's probably nothing," Reeta said. "I went to a lecture given by some disgusting man from the Department of Agriculture. He was really into cloning and genetic engineering and lots of other stuff I hate. Anyway, when he finished, a guy who is not even a student at the school tried to question him. The speaker totally humiliated him in front of the whole group. The guy was so embarrassed he practically ran out of the place. I saw him go down a path across campus where he could be alone so I followed him." Sarah smiled but said nothing and Reeta continued. "I told him that he shouldn't feel embarrassed—I should for just sitting there like an idiot. I asked if he had read Schumacher's book *Small Is Beautiful*. He hadn't heard of it so I loaned him the copy you gave me. When he returned it we had a discussion, better than any I ever had with a classmate. I think he is real smart—I think he's an orphan. He works on a farm near the college. That's it." Sarah remained silent and after some time Reeta said, "He is really good-looking, but so shy. In some ways he is very much like a little boy. I think he's had a tough life."

Sarah finally spoke. "What is his name?"

"Benjamin Thomas," Reeta answered.

And Sarah said, "I doubt that I've heard the end of Benjamin Thomas."

Chapter 23

Ben had grown up in a world where money ruled. His mother had lived in perpetual fear that there would not be enough. Ben could see her in his mind, sitting at the kitchen table in their small apartment writing figures on a piece of paper. He recalled the wrinkles that had come too soon to her forehead, and he remembered the look in her eyes, a mixture of worry and terror as she worked on the monthly budget. Ben felt bad for her. She had lived such a difficult life and had suffered such a painful death. How he wished that she could see him now. Things were different here. There was a sense of security that he never knew existed. Here money did not seem to rule. It played a role in their lives, but it was not the controlling factor. And the irony of it was that here where money did not seem to rule people's lives, Ben found that he had more of it than ever before. He almost felt rich. He kept a few hundred dollars in the trailer to use for general expenses. His checking account at the bank had a balance of over five hundred dollars, and recently his savings account reached two thousand dollars. Mr. Johnson encouraged Ben to take one thousand from the account and open a six month certificate of deposit. "It earns much better interest," he had said, "and you are not tying the money up for long if you should need it."

Ben's expenses were few. Increasingly he ate his meals with Slim and Mary so his grocery bill was actually decreasing. The electricity bill for his trailer, which had not been a major expense, disappeared altogether in March. When he reminded Slim about the March bill, the response, accompanied with a wry smile, had been, "St. Patrick's Day bonus." The same thing happened in April with Slim saying, "Easter bonus."

Ben knew that he should have health insurance and was troubled that he could not yet afford it. Still he only thought about it occasionally. He had never felt so good and was confident he could take a chance without it for a while. What other option did he have anyway?

These thoughts passed through Ben's mind as he sat in the living room of his trailer on a warm evening during the last week of May. He heard the knock on his door and Slim entered the trailer with Anabel close behind. "Got a minute?" Slim asked. When Ben nodded, Slim pulled out a kitchen chair and sat down. "If the weather cooperates, we'll have the corn in by week's end. Tomorrow I want to disc the fields over on the neighbor's place and get it planted the next day. I can do it if I work late. Do you think that you could handle the evening chores by yourself?" Without hesitation Ben answered that he could. Slim continued. "I will probably need you to do that most of the time for the next month or so. We'll be starting the haying next week, and on days when the weather is good I like to keep going until dark. Haying season is always my busiest time and this year we've got the fields over at George Rogers' place that you cleared in March." He paused for a moment and then continued. "I'm hoping to get three good crops of hay this season. We will if there is enough moisture. I would like to have plenty for our own herd with a lot left over to sell. I could have sold more this year if I'd have had it."

Ben listened as Slim talked. When it was time for him to speak he said, "I will do whatever I can to help. I have no other plans, so if you need me to work it's no problem. Remember I've never done haying before, but I'm anxious to learn. I just hope that I don't mess up."

Slim smiled as he rose from the table. "You'll be fine," he said. "I'll show you the ropes. I just want you to know what you're in for the next few weeks. You will sleep at night, I guarantee. Mary has always helped with the haying. This year she will be able to spend more time with her camera and less time baling hay." He paused and then added, "You have made things easier for her, Ben. I appreciate it. She has always worked too hard."

* * *

They could begin baling by noon time if the day was sunny. Preceding the baling operation Slim would have facilitated the curing process by going over the mowed hay with the tedder and then raking it into the windrows. Ben sat on the John Deere tractor and watched as Slim circled the field on the big International, pulling the baler with the wagon behind it. Every few seconds a bale sprang from the back of the baler into the wagon. When the wagon was full Slim released its hitch and hooked on to a second wagon. Ben then hauled the full wagon to the barn where he unloaded the bales and stacked them. Slim had showed him the method for stacking bales that utilized every possible

148

space. Ben could normally have the wagon unloaded and about a third of the load stacked when he would hear Slim arrive with a second load. Slim helped Ben complete stacking the first load before taking the empty wagon back to the field to resume baling. Try as he might, Ben could not keep up. Before he could complete unloading and stacking the second load, Slim arrived with a third. Usually on a good afternoon four loads could be baled and put away. Ben helped with the first three loads but by then it would be four thirty and Slim kept haying while Ben got started with the evening milking. He usually had the milking approximately one third complete when Slim returned with the fourth load of hay. When Mary's school was finished with the spring semester in mid June she continued the milking while Ben helped unload and stack the final load. Once completed Ben returned to the barn to finish the milking while Slim quickly hooked the tractor up to the mower and returned to the fields to cut a new section of hay.

Most of June saw this hectic schedule continue. The days were hot and the work was hard, but Ben seemed to thrive on it. Hay production was not only strenuous work, it was also more complex than most other farming techniques that Ben had learned. There were so many variables. Hay cured faster with full sun than with partial sun. Some fields had thicker growth than others, which meant a longer curing time. Moist hay made for poor quality to say nothing of the possible fire hazards it could create in the barns. Overly cured hay lost some of its quality and was unacceptable to Slim. Ben would run the hay through his hands and attempt to predict Slim's evaluation of it, but he knew it would take him more than one season to become competent. He found himself jotting ideas in a journal to help him remember, not just about the hay itself but also the equipment. He noted the frequency with which Slim greased the fittings on the equipment. He tried to be very detailed, even making sketches of the baler, rake, tedder and mower with arrows pointed at each fitting. He even noted that Slim gave three shots of grease to some fittings, and only two to others. Slim noticed Ben's attention to these things with satisfaction.

One morning in the third week of June, Slim told Ben that they were on schedule, maybe even a bit ahead. "Maybe you can imagine what this was like with just the two of us," Slim said. "Mary did most of the baling and I did your job. We wouldn't even start evening chores until six o'clock and were lucky if we got to the house by nine. We wouldn't have survived if it had gone on too long. We usually finished first cutting by July fourth and then things got back to normal. Second and third cuttings are easier—you will see. The bales don't add up as fast with alfalfa and the curing time is much shorter."

Haying wasn't the only job in June. There was also the corn. Most farmers sprayed their fields with weedkiller, but Mary was opposed to pesticides and over the years had convinced Slim to feel likewise. This organic approach to farming was environmentally sound, but it did require that the huge corn fields be cultivated twice while the corn was in its early stages of growth. Ben was fascinated by the procedure. Slim planted the corn in rows that accommodated the wheels of his tractor. When the corn was approximately six inches high he attached small metal cultivators to the tractor, and by driving up and down the rows he cultivated out the small weeds that were competing with the young corn. When the corn was higher but still fit under the tractor's axles the process was repeated. By then the corn was tall enough that the foliage could block the sun from the ground and prevent a serious growth of weeds later in the season. But it was extra work in a time when there were already too few hours in the day.

The job of cultivating the corn, which in the past had almost always gone to Mary, now was given to Ben. Usually in the morning when Slim was mowing new hay to be baled later in the week, Ben went to the corn fields to cultivate. It was a job he enjoyed, requiring only the ability to drive in a straight line. Ben loved to look back at the freshly cultivated fields and see the straight green rows of corn among the deep brown soil.

* * *

Nearly every night in June Ben went swimming. Around eight o'clock, with still an hour of daylight, he would call for Anabel and head for the creek. Once across the county road he released the dog from her leash and started across the field. Nearly one hundred feet upstream from the location of Slim's "poor man's bridge" was a place referred to by Slim and Mary as "The Deep Hole." It was a pool of water about thirty feet in length. Near the middle of the stream the water was between four and five feet deep, perfect for swimming on a hot summer night. The water was much cooler than what Ben was used to in Florida but as his body adjusted to Vermont he found it more refreshing. While he swam in the cool water, Anabel played along the shore, sometimes wading into the stream up to her belly. By nine o'clock they would be back in Ben's trailer where, more and more, Anabel spent the night. Before falling asleep Ben read at least one chapter from Wallace Stegner's book *Angle of Repose*. It was the first of many Stegner books he would eventually read, an author he would come to admire as much for his powerful use of words as for the story itself.

Even during the hectic month of June, Sundays remained a day of leisure except for morning and evening chores. Typically, once Slim and Mary had left for church Ben took Anabel to the upper pasture. On their way the herd of milking cows would approach them and Ben would scratch their heads between their ears as they gently nudged him. By now they were so familiar with Anabel that they barely acknowledged her sniffing at their feet. Ben always took a book with him and after sitting on the huge flat rock and looking off into the mountains he would read for a while and then fall sound asleep. His love for this spot grew with each visit and he knew that whatever lay in his future he could never stray for very long from this place.

* * *

The cutting of the first crop of hay on their farm and the neighboring farm was completed during the final week of June. Ben felt good. He could see the look of relief and satisfaction on Slim's face now that the huge crop of hay was harvested and safely stored away. And it was quality hay. Only once during the past month had a surprise shower prevented them from baling on schedule, and it came in the late afternoon, leaving just two loads in the field to be redried and baled the following day. Ben had learned a great deal about the art of producing hay. He had thrived on the rigorous schedule, viewing it as a challenge rather than a problem. He had tried hard to meet Slim's high standards and for the most part he felt that he had succeeded. Ben thought of these things one evening as he looked out upon the freshly mowed fields. Somehow they appeared larger than before the hay was mowed. He was surprised at how quickly the short brown stubble of the harvested fields was being replaced with the deep green carpet of young alfalfa. Already the fields first cut had new growth of two or three inches. He knew from listening to Slim that harvesting the second and third crop would be easier. For one thing, the alfalfa did not grow tall so curing time was quicker. He also knew that alfalfa did not produce as many bales, so there would be fewer loads to store away. And as he stood looking at the fields Ben's mind was also on a girl who, in just a few days, would board a plane bound for Europe.

Chapter 24

Ben saw the sparkle in George Rogers' eyes when he and Slim pulled into the driveway. George hobbled along beside them as they walked to the edge of his nearest field. "It's not bad hay considering it hasn't been cut in several years," he told Slim. "There's still a lot of clover in there amongst the timothy. You won't want this hay for your milkers—too many weeds mixed in—but it will be good for heifers. They are growing so fast they'll eat anything."

"We'll get the equipment over here tomorrow," Slim said. "If the weather cooperates I hope to have you finished by the Fourth of July." They walked to the two big barns where the hay would be stored.

"There's plenty of room," George said, adding, "It's going to be good to see these barns full of hay again."

Moving the equipment to the Rogers place was a day-long job. The morning phase consisted of Slim on the tractor pulling the baler and a large wagon. Ben followed in the truck with the hazard lights flashing. Behind the truck he towed the mowing machine. Traffic was light but whenever possible Slim pulled onto the shoulder so that cars could pass by. That afternoon Slim took the smaller tractor with the rake. Again Ben followed with the truck, this time towing the tedder. George had sold most of his farm equipment, but he did have a good wagon which eliminated the need for a third trip. It was nearly three thirty when they arrived at the Rogers place with the second load. Slim sent Ben home to begin evening chores while he hooked up the tractor to the mower and got started cutting the first field.

* * *

They spent most of the following week on the Rogers place. As George watched the process unfold he could hardly contain his excitement. He went

152

to the barn each time Ben came with a load of bales, and as Ben stacked the hay, George talked. At first he mostly talked about the hay, explaining how he used to mow with a horse-drawn rig and gathered it loose with a hay loader. He said that hay didn't grow so thick back then. Whatever came up, came up. "These fields were mostly June grass and orchard grass," he said, adding, "Clover, timothy and alfalfa seed changed haying around here completely." The more George talked the more Ben could see a connection between the man and his fields. It was as though the man's life itself was a part of this land. Ben began to see that when arthritis had separated him from the farming process it was as though the life blood had been drained from his body. With each load of hay going into his barn some of that life blood was returning. The fields that had almost become like foreign land now belonged to him again. Ben also sensed that the old man liked him and approved of his work. "You're a big help to Slim, boy," he said. "He's lucky you came around. There ain't many boys who want to farm anymore—especially dairy. Too much work. Yes, boy, he's lucky to have you."

* * *

The process was the same as it had been back home. Ben would unload and stack a load of hay while Slim continued to bale. The difference was that now Ben could keep up. Since the hay in George's fields was not as thick, it took Slim longer to bale a load. This gave Ben more time to unload and stack. But there was more to it than that! Ben had also increased his speed and efficiency. He had learned simple techniques to make the job go quicker and with more ease. Slim had shown him, for example, how to use the bales themselves as steps to transport other bales to the highest reaches of the barn, thus avoiding much of the exhaustive work of hoisting them up with brute strength.

The barns filled quickly. The last day of June saw two of George's four large fields completed. July first was rainy, and they were unable to work. It cleared in mid afternoon, and Slim was able to mow a large portion of the third field. When he returned to the barn that evening Ben had the milking nearly completed. As they finished cleaning up the milk house, Slim told Ben that they would not be able to finish by the Fourth. "We will have about half of the third field to finish and all of the fourth." Still he said that he was pleased with the progress and if they could finish by July tenth they would yet have a couple of weeks' break until they began the second cutting. Slim said that except for morning and evening chores they were taking the Fourth of July off. He told Ben that the town always joined with two nearby communities for a morning parade. He said that Mary had a picnic planned for later in the day, and Mary hoped that Ben could join them for the day's activities. Ben found himself looking forward to the holiday.

* * *

July Fourth was hot and sunny. Slim hated to lose a day of haying, but he put the thought of working out of his mind and enjoyed the time off. They picked up Nellie Zenger on the way to the parade. Mary found a level spot with plenty of shade and set up lawn chairs along the parade route. By nine thirty the four of them sat among the gathering crowd awaiting the ten o'clock parade. Shortly after ten the siren of the police car that headed the parade blasted its beginning. For the next hour a menagerie of groups passed their viewing area. Fire trucks and police cars represented the three communities. The high school band played and later in the procession there was a group of bagpipers from Rutland. There were horseback riders from the local riding club, several antique tractors and automobiles, as well as groups of Scouts and 4-H-ers marching en masse. The Elks and Rotary had floats, as did the Senior Citizens Club and several churches, including one constructed by the youth group of Slim and Mary's congregation.

The parade ended at a local park. Awards were presented and speeches given. Many people walked to the park for the festivities, but Slim brought the car to where they were sitting, and they returned to the farm, taking Nellie with them.

The afternoon picnic was held on Slim and Mary's screened-in porch. Mary had wanted to have it on the garden patio, but the sun was extremely hot, making the porch more comfortable. The usual group attended, each bringing food to share. Mary's parents were there as well as Slim's sister and her husband. The group also included the families of the nurses at the clinic as well as the receptionist. There were no people of Ben's age group in attendance, but he didn't mind. Slim had two charcoal grills under a maple tree near the porch and while he grilled hamburgers on one, Ben took charge of hot dogs on the other. Later in the afternoon Ben toasted marshmallows for the children and also used the hot coals to ignite Fourth of July sparklers. Slim also convinced Ben to join in a game of horseshoes, a game that Ben had never before played. Slim explained the rules as they played and Ben immediately fell in love with the game. From that day on Slim and Mary would often hear the clang of horseshoes late in the evening as Ben practiced his skills. Usually Slim would join him for a quick game. By summer's end, Ben's skill had increased, but he was still looking for his first victory over Slim. One evening while watching Slim win another match Mary remarked to Ben, "Slim's a wonderful man but when it comes to horseshoes he has no mercy." To which Ben replied, "I've found that out."

The evening of July Fourth as they were finishing milking, Ben told Slim that he felt more tired from the holiday than he did from a day in the hay field. "Playing is always harder than working," Slim agreed. "Especially if you like what you are working at."

* * *

They finished haying the Rogers place on July ninth. The fields had produced well and the final three loads had to be stacked outside. Slim had laid boards on the ground to keep the bottom layer of bales from direct contact with the dirt. Then he had stopped at the local lumber yard and collected a dozen large plastic covers that protected plywood when it was delivered. "They throw these away by the hundreds," Slim had told Ben. "They will be good to cover the bales we are stacking next to George's barn, and I think they are actually as thick as the tarps from the store. And better yet, they're free," he added, smiling.

When Slim brought the final load of hay from George's field, he left Ben to unload it alone and went to the porch where George was waiting. Ben could see them talking intently for several minutes. Then they walked to a nearby shed and went inside. Ben had finished the final load by the time they emerged from shed, still talking. Slim helped Ben cover the final load of hay and anchor the plastic down with several large stones. "We'll be back for the equipment in the morning," Slim told George. "I would take the baler home now, but it's already past chore time." As they rode back in the truck, Slim was silently thinking. Ben had learned this expression on Slim's face and knew it was best to keep quiet and let him think. When they arrived home, not a single word had been spoken, and the silence continued while they did the evening chores.

* * *

Mary just let him talk. She knew it was how he sorted things out. She also knew it was a big issue for him—and for her—and for Ben. "The easy thing," Slim said, "would be to sell the hay. I could sell two trailer loads, make a nice profit and be done with it. I don't want to expand. I want to work less, not more. I don't need more money, we both know that. Still, what about the boy? What if he wants to stay? He'll be nineteen years old in November. He's got no car. He's got no insurance. He needs to make more than twenty-five dollars a day." Slim sipped his tea and sat in silence.

After a minute Mary leaned across the table and said, "Let me think out loud for a few minutes. Then you react to my thoughts. Let's see, you have thirty-some calves born each year. You keep about five to replace your older milkers. The rest you either sell as calves or a few months later as young heifers. Now George is suggesting that you keep about twenty heifers at his place until they are old enough to breed. They would feed on his hay, and from mid summer through fall use his fields for grazing. Ben would drive over once a day to feed them. Besides feeding he would need to go over at least once a week to clean the barn. Now about you. What role would you play in this project?"

Slim answered, "Not too much. It would take two of us to transport the calves over there. Then there is the haying, of course. That's about ten days to two weeks depending on the weather. Then I would probably have to help Ben with the electric fence at least until he learned to do it himself. That's about it."

"What about expenses?" Mary asked.

Slim replied, "I figure it's a few hundred dollars to do the haying—gas and wear on the machines. It's hard to say. Three or four hundred tops, I would say."

"What else?" Mary asked.

"Not much," Slim answered. "George doesn't want anything out of it except to see the farm worked again. He's got a shed full of posts and electric fence wire and insulators. I don't think we would need anything else—a block of salt once in a while."

Mary continued, "How profitable would it be?"

"It would turn a real profit," Slim answered. "Much more than just selling the hay. A healthy registered Holstein ready to breed and milk brings several thousand dollars.

"What are the risks?" Mary asked.

"Hopefully we wouldn't get too many bulls. For this to work we need heifers. Other than that there's not much risk as long as people keep drinking milk and eating cheese."

They sat silent for a few minutes and finally Mary spoke. "Why don't you explain the whole thing to Ben and see what he thinks? If he is interested, I think you should do it. It doesn't appear that your work load would increase much, and he would have a much better income." After a pause she added, "Part of this is selfish. I don't want him to go. He needs us and, more and more, we need him. Not just to help with the work. We need him because we just need him."

Slim waited for a few minutes and then said, "We'll have him eat with us tomorrow night. I think this is a conversation I want you in on. There is too much at stake for me to do this alone."

* * *

Transporting the equipment back to the farm was an all day job. As he had two weeks earlier, Ben followed in the truck with the hazard lights flashing while Slim led the way with the tractor. The slow pace gave Ben time to think and, as usual, his mind played its negative games. Something was clearly troubling Slim. Perhaps, Ben thought, his performance during the busy haying season had been inadequate. Perhaps Slim had discovered that a full-time hired hand was too costly. Perhaps Slim and Mary missed their privacy. Whatever the problem, Ben was certain that his days in this place he had grown to love were numbered, and he found himself doing math in his mind as he tried to determine how long he could survive on the money he had saved. The doubts grew as he went about evening chores. Again there was silence as Slim was absorbed in thought. When they left the barn Slim said to Ben, "Eat with us tonight, Ben. Come over as soon as you've cleaned up." And as they parted Ben went to his trailer feeling about as low as a person could feel.

* * *

Despite his mental state Ben was hungry and the meal was like a feast to him. There was chicken, cooked soft and tender all day in the crock pot. It was served as a stew surrounded by a variety of vegetables fresh from the garden, including potatoes dug that morning, green beans and carrots also harvested that day. With the stew Mary served hot biscuits, and for dessert, a raspberry pie still warm from the oven. The conversation during dinner had consisted of small talk ranging from the weather to the fact that Mary had dug out the two hills of potatoes a bit early but that she couldn't wait any longer for fresh ones. When the meal was over, but before the pie was served, Slim removed the dishes from the table, scraped them clean and loaded the dishwasher. Then, while Mary remained at the table talking to Ben, he made a pot of coffee and brought three mugs to the table. With the coffee and pie in front of them, Slim glanced at Mary and she said to Ben, "Slim and I have a proposal we would like to make to you, and we hope that you will think about it and tell us how you feel." She paused for a moment and then she began. And from her first words Ben felt his spirit begin to soar.

"Ben, Slim and I can't imagine how we got along without you. You are doing a terrific job. Slim says that you have a natural inclination towards farming. He says that you learn things so quickly. More importantly than that, we are very fond of you. You are a special young man, and in less than a year you seem like a part of our family. It is important to us that you have a more secure future than you currently enjoy. Your salary is inadequate, and you really need to have health insurance. These things have been on our minds for some time and last week, out of the blue, George Rogers made Slim a proposal that might resolve some of our concerns. I hope you will listen carefully to what he asked Slim and let us know your thoughts on the subject." With that Mary stopped talking and looked toward Slim, who took a swallow of coffee from his mug and began.

"George Rogers' family goes back in this area longer than anyone I know. They have farmed that land over there since the 1700s. George and his late wife, Alice, had one son who has been no good since he was a teenager. George and Alice probably made a mistake of trying to make a farmer out of him when he never cared a thing about it. All he wanted to do was hang out with other kids—usually the wrong kids. First it was drugs, and then later he turned to alcohol. Either way, he has turned into a hopeless bum. George only sees him when he is in trouble or needs money. At any rate, since George lost his wife and his arthritis has kept getting worse, he has about gone crazy watching the brush take over his land. Last March when he asked if you would clear his fields I agreed more as a favor than anything else. Truthfully, I didn't want to get involved. But now that the fields are cleared he has offered me free use of the land. So here is what I am considering. I have thirty-some calves born each year—all registered. Usually I raise four or five to replace milkers that are getting old. The rest I sell either as calves or as young heifers. I haven't had the time or the space to keep them. Now with George's hay and space I could keep all the heifers until they are full grown and ready to breed. They increase dramatically in value at that point. The problem is that a great deal more time and effort would be required, and that is where you come in. If you were interested in the project, and by that I mean basically doing the work, I could increase your income by several thousand dollars a year if all went well. This is a big decision for you, one that you should only agree to if you are really interested. I won't mislead you. This would be extra work because I wouldn't want you to decrease what you are currently doing here. I don't want Mary doing all the farm work that she did before you came. She has enough on her agenda already with school and her photography business." Slim stopped for a minute before adding, "I guess that's about all I have to say."

Ben sat in silence for a few seconds and then he spoke, hesitantly at first and then with more confidence. "I have been really worried the past few days. I knew you had something on your mind and, as usual, I expected the worst. I really don't need to think about this. I want to do it. Naturally I'm nervous and I need to know specifically what the job entails, but if you show me what to do I'll get started. I hope you know how much I like it here. If I am needed, I want to stay and learn more. I love farming—your kind of farming."

A sense of relief filled the room as Ben finished talking. Even Anabel sensed the change, and she stood up and wagged her tail. Mary poured more coffee and Slim talked of posts, electric fencing and registered cows. Within an hour Ben had a general understanding of the job he was about to undertake, and he wished it were morning so he could get started. When he left for his trailer it was nearly nine o'clock. Slim shook his hand and Mary gave him a hug. Outside it was very dark. Thick clouds foretold the heavy rain that tomorrow would bring. But no clouds could dampen Ben's spirits. He stood in the yard for several minutes thinking of the evening's revelations. He was needed and wanted. He could stay in this place. He would have security physically, emotionally, financially and spiritually. He entered his trailer thinking that sleep would not come easily this night. He was wrong. As soon as he lay down on his bed he fell into a deep and peaceful sleep. He did not dream and he heard nothing until his alarm rang at five thirty. He awoke instantly, surprised that the night had passed. He lay quietly for five minutes listening to the rain as it hit the roof of his trailer.

The rain continued throughout the next day. While doing morning chores, Slim talked of the new project. He told Ben that if the rain ended by tomorrow they could go to the Rogers place and begin to install the electric fencing. He said they would wait a couple of weeks before transporting any heifers. That would allow the freshly hayed fields a chance to start new growth. He said that the heifers would be able to graze well into the fall at which time they would begin feeding them hay. He told Ben that the watering trough needed a good cleaning—that it was filled with leaves and mud. He said that it should be cleaned as soon as possible so that if any leaks were discovered they would have time to patch them before any heifers arrived. Ben listened intently as Slim talked, and he sensed that Slim was as excited about the project as he was. Slim said that he had called George last evening and told him of the plans to go ahead with the project. He said that old George had sounded as excited as a kid on Christmas morning.

The rains came heavier as they left the barn. Slim said that Mary had a meeting with some people who wanted to use her photographs in an upcoming magazine feature. He was going with her since it was too wet to work outside. "So you have the day off," he told Ben. "Have a good day and I'll see you for evening chores at four o'clock."

Chapter 25

July 10, 1996

    I hope that someday I will be more secure. Maybe it is a part of my personality or perhaps it is because of my life's experiences, but, whatever the reason, I tend to fear that the worst rather than the best is about to happen to me. For the past 2 days Slim has been very quiet — deep in thought. Naturally, I assumed that he was unhappy with my work, or sick of having me around, or both... I became certain that my time here was over. I was so sure that I actually figured my finances to see how long I could survive without a job or a place to live. Yesterday afternoon when he invited me over for dinner I became even more convinced that my fears were true, & they were going to give me the bad news over dinner. The opposite has happened — they like my work. They want me to stay. Slim was quiet because he was planning a way for me to make a better salary. He is going to raise all his heifers to maturity rather than sell most of them as calves. They will be kept at George Rogers' farm. It will be mainly my duty to take care of them. It will mean much more work for me because I will still need to do my chores here at the farm. But my salary should increase by several thousand dollars a year. I am very excited & happy... I wish there was someone to share my news with.

Ben replaced his journal in the cardboard file box that sat next to his bed. He looked out at the heavy rains. Streams of water ran down the driveway and into the country road. He watched as Mary hurried to the waiting car, closed the large umbrella and entered the front seat beside Slim. He watched the car ease from the driveway and disappear up the road. Ben was famished and went to the kitchen to prepare breakfast. Within minutes he had made coffee, poured a large glass of orange juice and another large glass of milk. Two frying pans sat on his stove, one cooking home fried potatoes while he scrambled four eggs in the other. Four pieces of bread were toasting and on the table sat fresh strawberry jam that Mary had given him. When the meal was prepared Ben ate slowly and in the silence of his trailer he began to think. His mind returned to Florida and his final months there.

From the time he graduated high school in May until November when he turned eighteen he had worked in a fast food restaurant. The manager had liked him and continually told him that in a year he would recommend full-time employment with benefits. Ben recalled the turmoil this situation had created in his mind. He hated the hot and tedious job, he hated the South and he hated living with his grandparents. Throughout that summer he was planning his trip North—his "escape," he used to call it. But in the midst of his planning he often thought that he should stay. It was the safe thing to do. He would have a steady income and eventually be able to find an apartment of his own. Many times he had made the decision to leave and then to stay. Looking back to that time, Ben was astonished that eventually he had mustered the courage to leave. It was against his nature to take such a risk. He had left a place he hated, although it was one of relative security, for an unknown destination with no job and no place to stay. Often as Ben recalled this time he felt a sense of terror come over him. What if he had chosen to stay? What a different life he would be leading. He was frightened by the thought that except for a decision he could not explain, he would know nothing of this place, this job, these people. Usually Ben's thought process ended at this point, but today he found his mind moving further. He began to think about the freedom he had to make the decision. The only obstacle had been his own personal fears. He had to ask no person or government for permission to leave. Once he found the courage within himself he simply packed his few belongings into the worn out car and left. Ben thought this was remarkable and it created a feeling of warmth, almost patriotism, for the land where he lived. He realized how few nations existed where a person could simply go from one place to another without permission from anyone. This idea of personal freedom intrigued him and so on a rainy July day Ben decided to go to his favorite indoor place, the public library, and find out more about freedom.

* * *

Ben's arrival at the library coincided with that of a group of children who had come for a session of storytelling and crafts in the upstairs children's room. One of the volunteers for the children's program was Judy Braxton and, upon seeing Ben she came over to say hello. As they talked, they watched the young children climbing the stairs to the activity room. Ben remarked that one small child looked familiar to him, but he could not remember from where.

"That's the little Hiller girl," Mrs. Braxton told him, and then Ben remembered her as the little girl with the toothache at the home where they had delivered firewood.

"How are they doing?" Ben asked.

"Not very well, I'm afraid," Judy replied. "The father never came back and the mother has no job—not that she could work anyway with the children to care for. We need a daycare so badly but it is difficult to find funding. Dr. Taylor has tried all kinds of grants but to no avail so far."

The children had entered the upstairs room and Mrs. Braxton said goodbye to Ben and joined them. Ben walked down the corridor of the library still thinking of the Hiller children. There was nothing he could do for them now, but maybe someday. He knew that he would often think of the Hillers and others like them—children without fathers and without much hope. Children, he thought, like himself until he found Slim and Mary Smith.

* * *

Ben sat in front of the computer and typed in the word freedom. There were many entries. After some time Ben came upon a book about Greece and the birth of freedom. He jotted down the book's location and headed toward the shelves that held books on ancient history. The book was there and Ben smiled as he noted that it had not been signed out in over four years. He walked to the end of the aisle where he knew a soft leather chair sat by a window. Ben could see the rain still falling steadily outside. He sat down in the comfortable chair and turned to the book's flyleaf, for he had discovered that he could introduce himself to a new book by reading the comments and statements printed on it. This particular book contained several such remarks. Some were inside the front cover while others continued on the back.

One remark stated that the very concepts of political and personal freedom came from the Greeks. Another said that the concept of freedom itself was unique to Greece and had spread to other civilizations from there. One statement commented that freedom was so alien to places like ancient Egypt that their language had no word for it. A remark that struck Ben said that only civilizations somehow touched by the Greeks had developed such political and personal freedom. Ben wondered if that could possibly be true, and he sat for several minutes thinking of that notion before he read on. A final statement that intrigued Ben was made by a British thinker named James Mill who declared that the Battle of Marathon was more important to English history than the Battle of Hastings. Ben was embarrassed that he knew so little about either event and so decided that he would begin with them. That afternoon and for the next several evenings Ben would read of the birth, development and spread of freedom. He would marvel at how the "thread of freedom," as the author called it, weaved its way from Greece to the Roman Empire and from there to Britain and finally to the United States Constitution. How could it be, he thought, that actions of Greek soldiers on the field at Marathon in 490 B.C. had in a large way been responsible for his right to leave Florida with no one's permission and make a new life for himself on a farm in Vermont?

* * *

The big coastal storm moved on to Canada and by Saturday morning the sky was blue. The temperature was already over eighty when morning chores were completed. "We are in for a hot spell," Slim said as they left the barn. "Next week we'll start cutting on the lower fields." Then looking at Ben he said, "I'm taking it easy today—what about you?"

Ben said that he would like to build fence at George Rogers' place but he needed help getting started.

"It won't take much to show you the ropes," Slim said, adding, "I'll go over with you after breakfast if you want."

It was less than a half hour later that Ben heard Slim loading a small maul, an iron bar and a tool box that doubled as a step stool. Ben joined him, carrying his lunch and a gallon jug of ice water. Ben drove the truck and Slim followed in the car. By nine thirty they had arrived at the Rogers place. Slim showed Ben where the posts were stored. He took two from the shed and carried them to the field. He showed Ben the perimeter where the fence should be built. Then, taking the iron bar, he started a hole of approximately one and a half feet deep. Placing a post in the hole he stood on the tool box and drove it securely into the ground. He pointed out the two insulators on the post and told Ben to make certain they were facing inward toward the field. He showed the distance of the lower insulator from the ground and explained that it was important for each post to be the same. "If it's any lower," he said, "the grass will soon reach the wire and short out the electricity. Any higher and the heifers will try to reach under."

Next Slim paced off the distance to where the second post should be placed and repeated the process. "Just follow this pattern around the field," he told Ben. "If you hit a big rock, just try a new spot a few inches left or right. They don't have to be exact as long as they are close."

Slim was about to leave when George arrived back at the farm from his daily breakfast at Jensen's. While they talked Ben carried a dozen posts from the shed to the field and got started. It was more difficult than it appeared when Slim had done it. The Vermont fields were stony and Ben had to learn to maneuver the bar among them to get the hole started. Setting the posts was tricky. At first his aim was bad, and he had trouble hitting the top of the post squarely with the maul. Often the post would twist as he drove it into the ground, and he would discover that the insulators were not facing inward. Then he would have to remove the post and repeat the process. Within minutes he was sweating profusely. He removed his shirt and took the time to spread sun screen on his back and chest. (His mother had always insisted on sun screen, and he discovered that Mary was equally insistent.) He had installed five posts when he saw George come through the field on the old golf cart he used to get around.

"How's it going, boy?" he said as he approached.

Ben said that it was going poorly and was much more difficult than he had expected.

"Building fence is hard work, especially among these Vermont stones," George said. "Keep at it. It will get easier as you get the hang of it."

Ben replied, "I wish my aim was better. I can't seem to hit the post with the maul."

George laughed and said, "Practice makes perfect, boy. Just keep at it. By the way, don't try and do the whole field today. It's too hot. Slim doesn't want the heifers here for another week or so anyway. He wants more time for the new grass to get started. Oh and don't carry those posts down here by hand. Use your truck. You won't hurt the fields any."

George was right. Ben began to get a feel for the work. He learned quickly how to maneuver the bar between the stones, or if the rock proved too big, to avoid it all together. His aim remained poor but by lunch time he could see a slight improvement. He worked until two in the afternoon and had posts set from the barn to the road and about one third of the second side of the field. When he stopped, he estimated that with two more sessions the posts would be in. Then Slim could show him how to string the wire.

* * *

Ben arrived back at the farm to find Slim, Mary and Anabel coming across the field from the swimming hole. "You look worn out," Mary said as Slim looked on smiling.

"Yes, and I have the blisters to show for it," Ben replied, holding his palms out.

"So how did it go?" Slim inquired.

"Not as good as I wanted," Ben answered. "It's much harder for me than it looked when you did it. My aim isn't very good yet. I figure I'll need two more sessions like that to finish the posts."

Slim said that Ben had time for a swim before milking but Ben decided to wait until chores were done and then take an evening swim. "Just as well," Slim said. "By then Anabel will be ready to go back for another dip."

* * *

Ben's sleep was restless that night. The heat was intense and the trailer never cooled down from a day of baking in the sun. His muscles ached from the day's work. Several times he awoke thirsty and went to the kitchen for ice water. Around four he fell asleep and was startled when the alarm rang at five thirty. He dragged himself from bed, pleased that it was Sunday and, except for chores, he could relax. Little did he know what the afternoon would bring.

While Slim and Mary attended church services, Ben took Anabel to the swimming hole, the only cool place he could find. Just walking across the field to the creek drew heavy perspiration and Ben knew that today would be even warmer than yesterday. He swam, then sat under a huge maple, then swam some more. He saw their car when they returned from church and started up the path towards the house. They had lunch together as had become their custom recently. Slim made cold chicken sandwiches and added fresh lettuce from the garden. Mary mixed lemonade in a large pitcher and took a jar of pickles from the refrigerator. "There are chips in the cupboard," she told Ben, and he got them for her.

When lunch was over, Slim took a book he was reading and went to the porch. Mary joined him with the Sunday paper. Ben sat on the steps while Anabel stood by his feet waiting to play. "It's too hot," Ben told her. "You lay down and sleep. I'll take you swimming again later."

For quite a while they sat in silence, Slim and Mary reading and Ben just gazing across the fields. He watched as a car came slowly down the county road, and all three of them saw it stop by the mailbox. It sat there a for few seconds before it cautiously pulled into the driveway. The man who emerged was probably not much older than Slim and Mary, but the years had taken a heavy toll on him. He was medium height and very thin—almost gaunt. His hair was completely gray and his forehead had deep wrinkles. Still, it was obvious that he had once been a handsome man and his features—even the gait with which he carried himself made it clear to all three of them that Ben was about to meet his father.

Ben sat in stunned silence. He could not move. The man's voice was blurry to him, but he still heard the words distinctly. "Hello Ben, I am your father, and I hope that you will give me just a few minutes of your time."

Next Ben heard Mary's voice as she said, "We will go inside and give you some time alone."

Ben looked quickly back at her and said, "No, I want you to stay, both of you."

The man standing before them said, "That will make this more difficult for me, but I realize that I am in no position to make demands." He paused for a moment and when he realized that Ben was not about to change his mind he began.

"My wife died a few months ago. She went to her grave never knowing you existed. Now that she has gone I find that I cannot go on without purging my soul of a nightmare that has gone on for nearly twenty years. I am an English professor at a small university in Florida. I have taught there for my entire career. I was young and happily married with two children when I met your mother. She was one of my students. The scholarship she had required that she work several hours each week for the university, and she was assigned to be my assistant. We got along from the start. She was young and excited about life. She loved my literature classes and while she worked we would talk. It was as innocent as that for a long time—almost two years. I was asked to give a presentation at an educational conference. I wanted it to go well. There were so many details to arrange—hand outs, flip charts, sample tests. Your mother was assigned to travel with me to the conference. She was so efficient. Everything was exactly as I wanted it. The presentation went very well. I was extremely pleased.

"I took her to dinner to celebrate. I don't know how it happened exactly. Things just got out of hand that night. We both knew immediately that we had made a terrible mistake. We vowed ourselves to secrecy and when we returned to campus your mother quietly dropped out of school. I didn't see her for several weeks until she stopped at my office to tell me that she was expecting. I was terrified. I didn't know what to do. I had never been unfaithful to my wife before and I never was again, but I didn't know what to do. My salary was small and my wife ran our finances completely. I hadn't signed a check in years. I couldn't have provided ten dollars a month for your support without her noticing it." He stopped for a minute and looked down at the ground. Then with his voice noticeably softer he continued. "I was such a coward. For nearly twenty years I have known that. Your mother let me off easy. She didn't get angry or bitter. She told me not to worry—that she would disappear to another place—that no one, including you, would ever know the truth.

"She kept her word. But it was at a terrible price as I am sure you know. Your grandparents never forgave her. You lived in relative poverty. She never fulfilled her intellectual potential. Worst of all she never trusted anyone again and lived a very lonely life. And it was my fault. I accept the blame. While your mother lived in isolation my career went on. I lived in a nice house in a nice neighborhood. We took vacations. I received promotions. Still today I chair the English department. We had another child. Yes, I faked it well. My wife never knew. My children don't know that I ruined another person's life and lacked the courage to do anything about it. It has been a nightmare for me, but a nightmare that I truly deserved. And now it is too late for me to do anything about it. Your mother is gone. My wife is gone. And the thing I feel worst about is knowing that if they came back I probably still wouldn't have the courage to face them." He stopped again and there was silence for what seemed forever. When he finally spoke he said, "Well anyway, I am sorry for what I have done to you. I am sorry that you are so alone. I know how much you must despise me for what I did to you and your mother. I feel worse knowing that you could never respect me—that I could never deserve your respect." His voice trailed off as he said, "I will go now and leave you alone."

Ben was surprised when he heard his own voice. He was surprised that it sounded firm and strong. "How did you find me?" he asked.

"Motor vehicle records," his father answered. "When you changed your license from Florida to Vermont."

"What is your name?" Ben asked.

"Paul Wilkes."

"What about your children?"

"Linda, Susan and Paul. Susan looks like you."

Ben paused and then he said, "You are wrong about me being alone. I do have a family. This is my family." And he looked back toward Slim and Mary.

"That is good," his father said, and he repeated absently, "That is good."

Slowly he walked back to the car and soon it disappeared down the road. The three sat on the porch in silence. Ben stared straight ahead into the field. The green alfalfa seemed out of focus, and he realized that he was crying. The tears flowed more rapidly, and he buried his face in his arms. Mary started from her chair, but Slim put his hand on her arm and said quietly, "Let him get it out." And so she sat for nearly ten minutes and let him cry away the pain of a lifetime. His arms were soaked with tears when suddenly his mind began to clear and his eyes focused again. He stood up and felt Mary's arm across his shoulders as she stroked the back of his head. He turned toward her, and she held him like a child. Then he felt Slim's strong yet gentle arms enclose both him and Mary. The three stood like that for what seemed to be a very long time. Finally he heard Slim's voice. "We have a big job ahead of us, Ben. We had better get started."

Ben looked up at him with a look of confusion and said, "I don't know what you mean."

Slim spoke again with more emotion than even Mary had heard before and he said, "Mary has waited a long time for her child to sleep in that big room upstairs, and I don't want her to wait any longer. Let's get your things moved over from the trailer. You are home now, Ben. You are finally home."

Chapter 26

His world had been transformed completely. He realized, as he lay in the queen-sized bed that night, that never in his life had he slept on anything larger than a cot. Never had he been in a bed with both a mattress and box springs. And despite the intense heat outside he was cooled by the air conditioner that extended from his window. Even in the heat of Florida he had never had air conditioning. He could still recall the roar of the two huge fans that his mother would place in the windows on opposite sides of the room. Other things impressed him as well—things that would seem normal to so many people. There were the huge soft towels in his bathroom. He had never owned a towel that you could wrap yourself in. His mother had always bought the thinner, smaller ones at the discount store. And there were curtains on the windows; and blinds that worked; nice soap with a manly scent; a soft terrycloth bathrobe—his first bathrobe; pajamas that Mary had gotten from the mall while he and Slim had cleared out the trailer.

There was a walk-in closet with sturdy hangers for his clothes; a large dresser which Mary had already filled with underwear and socks. There was a large wooden bookcase against the wall, completely empty. Ben looked at it and dreamed of a time when it would be filled. Perhaps most special was the large desk that sat in front of his window overlooking the fields to the South. Ben looked forward to the hours he would spend at the desk reading and writing and thinking. But best of all was the knowledge that under this same roof, in the large bedroom downstairs, lay Slim and Mary. They had stopped in his room a few minutes before to see that he was settled. Slim stood at the end of the bed while Mary sat on the edge beside him. Slim told him that he would call to him in the morning when it was time to get up. Mary kissed his forehead and before leaving asked if he might consider calling them Mom and Dad. When they left the room and were about to close the door Ben said, "Please leave it open. I like it better open." Then in the darkness of the room

170

Ben said a prayer to the God he was still not sure of. First he said a prayer of thanks and then he prayed that he might never take these things for granted. That he might always know the joy of what he felt tonight. And with that he fell asleep on the softest pillow he had ever felt.

* * *

The news traveled quickly. Some said simply that the young man who worked for Slim and Mary Smith had moved in with them. Others reacted positively. "Isn't it nice," they would say, "that Slim and Mary have taken in that young man as if he was their own." Then there were the critics. One man sitting in Jensen's Restaurant was heard to say, "Why that kid ain't been here a year yet. He ain't proved himself. I hope Slim and Mary know what they are doing. This ain't like them."

George Rogers was sitting in the next booth, and he found that silence was impossible for him. "I know that boy," he said. "He does work over at my place. What a worker he is. It's been a while since I seen a kid with his ambition. And he'll make a good farmer someday, I'm telling you. He has a knack for it. Don't you worry about Slim and Mary. They know what they're doing. I'm telling you, that kid is a good boy."

At the Methodist women's sewing circle one lady remarked, "I can't imagine Slim and Mary taking that boy right into their home. Why, they barely know him. He'll probably rob them blind. I notice that he hasn't been to church with them."

Nellie Zenger was unable to restrain her feelings. And so she told the story that she vowed she would never tell. "Last fall I walked to the bank and took out enough cash to get through the winter. It was the first cold day and I wore my heavy coat for the first time. I had forgotten about the tear in my pocket and the pouch with all my money fell out. I went back several times to look for it but with the leaves coming down it was impossible. Besides, I assumed that someone had probably found it anyway. Well, a few weeks later Pastor Braxton came to me with the pouch. It seems that young Ben, the boy you are so critical of, found the pouch with my initials on it and took it to the pastor. And I want you to know that every penny was in the pouch just the way it was when I lost it. So I think that you should get your facts straight before saying things that will hurt that young man's reputation." Silence fell over the sewing circle until one of the ladies broke the tension of the moment by raising a new topic for discussion.

The truth of the matter was that the change that had taken place in the home of Mary and Slim had been remarkably smooth. Ben became a natural part of the family. He appeared wise beyond his years in his approach to the new situation. Taking Slim's lead, he joined in the process of helping with the household chores. Most nights he set the table before the evening meal and helped with the clean up at the end. He kept his room and bath sparkling clean although sometimes Mary insisted on helping. He did his own laundry but often found it folded and put back in his dresser before he could do it himself. He loved the times together in the living room, on the porch or in the garden and found that conversation, and best of all laughter, came easily. Still, he made certain that Slim and Mary had time alone. He learned quickly of their devotion to each other, and he knew that they shared a very private passion that the years had not diminished. And so he would often go to his room to read or write. Often he would take Anabel to the mountain or the creek. And he still took frequent trips to his favorite place in town—the library. Slim and Mary observed all of this. They saw how much Ben enjoyed being a part of their lives. They recognized how much he tried to be a useful member of the family. They appreciated his conscious effort to give them time alone. And through it all they found their love for him growing day by day.

* * *

The heat continued. Through the next week they mowed and harvested alfalfa. Ben found the process easier than the heavy timothy and clover of the first crop. Often, with the intense heat, hay cut one morning could be harvested the following afternoon. "It's beautiful stuff," Slim said as he checked the texture of the hay. "But if we don't get rain soon we can forget about a third cutting in September."

Ben had time every morning of that week to work on the fence posts at George's place. There was a two hour space between morning chores and haying time when he could set posts. When he returned home on Wednesday he told Slim that he would finish the field tomorrow. "Good," Slim said. "Friday I'll show you how to string the wire, and we'll start hauling heifers over next week."

That afternoon they baled and stored away two more loads of hay. By Saturday, if the dry weather continued, they would nearly finish Slim's fields. Next week they would move the operation to the farm next to theirs and begin those fields.

The work and intense heat of the day had exhausted them. Mary suggested that they eat at Jensen's. By six o'clock they had showered and changed and were ready to leave. At the bottom of the driveway Slim pulled up close to the mailbox and Mary reached in to retrieve the day's mail. They started up the road toward Jensen's. Mary read the headlines from the daily paper and then sorted through the envelopes. "One for you, Ben," she said, handing the envelope to him in the back seat. He felt a sense of excitement when he saw a postmark from Germany. He laid the envelope on the seat beside him. He would open it later when they returned home.

That evening in the quiet of his room, sitting at his desk, Ben took his pocket knife and carefully opened the letter. It was dated July twentieth and it began simply, "Hi Benjamin. We are in our final week of our trip to Europe. I didn't want to come here, but I must admit that it has been nice. My parents have gone out of their way to do things that I enjoy—mainly spending more time in the country side than in the cities—even though I know that their preference would be the opposite. Our first week was spent in Britain. After two days in London we traveled by car through England and Scotland for five days. Next we flew to Italy for a week where we spent time in Rome before traveling on to Florence. This week we are in Germany, and I love it here. We are in the Bavarian Alps, and they are just breathtaking. The land is very green with many small farms. The villages are small and well kept. They all have a church with a tower and a clock. All the roofs are brown. As we traveled higher, the mountains became snow capped which seemed strange since it was sunny and nearly sixty degrees. We visited Neuschwanstein Castle which looks into the valley on one side and up at the mountains on the other. It was just beautiful there, if only a few of the annoying tourists could have been pushed over the edge. We are now back at our hotel, a really nice old one in a quaint village where we will rest for a day. On Friday we will fly back to New York where I plan to collapse for a few days. Then I'm going to the city for two weeks to be with my friend Sarah (the nun). I will be back in Vermont the third week of August for a two week track clinic before classes start. I will call you to make arrangements to pick up my skis which I am sure you will be glad to get out of your way. I hope that you are having a nice summer. See you soon." And the letter was signed simply, "Reeta."

Ben read the letter and then read it again. Carefully he placed it back in the envelope and into the desk drawer. He was pleased. She had said that she would send him a postcard and, not only had she remembered, but it was a letter instead. Somehow that seemed more significant and more personal.

Better still she said she would call, and it was only three weeks away. Ben turned off the lamp on his desk and went to bed. He lay awake for a long time, and he thought about Reeta Sorvino. The thought of seeing her again both excited and frightened him. It seemed so long since May when she had left. Sometimes he couldn't remember her face clearly, nor was he sure of the sound of her voice. There were even times when he wasn't really certain that she was real. He fell asleep thinking these things.

* * *

It was a long flight home. While her parents slept peacefully, Reeta found herself restless. She didn't like planes—never had. It wasn't really fear, more like a situation completely out of her control. And Reeta had never and would never like to find herself in that state of affairs. She often thought to herself that she hoped she was not a control freak of some sort. She had talked to Sarah about it once and, as usual, Sarah had given her reassurance by saying that there was a world of difference between someone being a control freak and someone who had confidence in herself to manage her life safely and effectively. At any rate, she would be glad when they were safely home, and she could move forward with her life. She looked out of the window of the plane and thought of the young man thousands of miles away on a Vermont farm. She knew that her relationship with him was uncertain. First, what did she actually know about him? He was good looking, very shy, nervous but still courageous enough to challenge a guest speaker. She was quite sure that he had no family, that he worked on a farm—and it was clear to her that he was bright. Other than that what did she know? She didn't even know if she would like him when she got to know him better. Sometimes she thought it would be best to retrieve her skis, say thank you and move on. Still, she knew herself well enough to know that she would want to be certain before taking such a course. He interested her. He seemed different than most young men his age. There was a depth in him that was absent from most of her classmates. These thoughts raced randomly through her mind as she stared down toward the Atlantic thousands of feet below, and she knew that when it came to the matter of Benjamin Thomas she would need to proceed carefully.

* * *

The hot dry weather continued during the first week of August. By late afternoon the leaves on the field corn drooped from the intense heat and lack of moisture. Slim was concerned that the ears would not develop fully. He hoped that the crop would be large enough to fill the two silos. They continued haying alfalfa on the neighboring farm. It was a good crop, but Slim had already decided against a third cutting. "Even if we get rain soon," he said, "the third growth won't be thick enough to bother with."

That same week Ben strung the two rows of electric fence wire around George Rogers' field. Slim had showed him how to connect the wire to each insulator so that the power running through it would not short out. He had learned how to splice the wire from one roll to the next in a way that was strong, made a good electrical connection and had the correct tension. When he finished the job he watched Slim run a wire from the top row of fencing to the bottom. Then a second wire ran from the bottom row of fencing to the solar-powered condenser. Still a third wire was attached to a metal pipe driven deep into the ground. "That's your ground wire," Slim explained. When everything was connected Slim flipped a switch on the condenser, and Ben heard a clicking sound about once per second. Slim took a blade of grass placed it on the fence. Ben saw Slim's body flinch as he felt the electric shock. "Want to try it?" Slim asked. Ben took the blade and held it to the wire. The feeling that passed through his body was alarming. It wasn't really pain; rather it was the most uncomfortable feeling that Ben had ever experienced.

"I can see why the cows don't like it," he said.

"They are terrified of it," Slim said adding, "and it's a stronger shock for them. If you don't think so take off those rubber-soled shoes and stick your nose on the wire."

Ben smiled and said, "I'll pass on that one."

* * *

Slim backed the pickup truck to the large sliding door of the machine shed and hooked on to a small trailer just large enough for one heifer. "It's really a horse trailer," Slim told Ben. "I bought it used several years ago and have never taken it out of the shed. I don't have it licensed but I'll keep to the county road where I know all the officers." The young heifer resisted as they loaded it into the trailer and delivered it to George Rogers' place. Once there the heifer was tethered inside the barn and given some hay. Slim said that it wasn't a good idea to let the heifer loose in the field by herself. "She might get spooked and run right through the fence," he said.

When they arrived with a second heifer both were let loose in the field and the three men watched while the frightened animals adjusted to their new home. Within minutes they had discovered the water trough and the salt lick. Soon they moved into the open field and began to graze. By the end of the next day Slim and Ben had delivered ten young heifers to their new home. At one point Ben watched as one approached the fence and touched her nose to the wire. After leaping away and letting out a blat, she moved away from the fence and continued eating. "She's learned her lesson," George commented. "They sure hate the feeling of getting shocked."

As Slim and Ben returned home, Slim commented on how excited George seemed to be having cows back on his place. "I haven't seen George look this good in years," he said. "I just wish his good-for-nothing son would learn to behave himself."

The next day marked the midpoint of August. The heat and dry spell continued. If the dry weather kept up they would complete the second cutting of alfalfa on the neighboring farm by early next week. Slim told Ben that they would then cut the hay in the swampy areas of the farm and gather it loose for bedding. "As soon as we finish haying," he told Ben, "I have to extract the honey from my hives. Then we'll see if you are as good around bees as you are around cows."

Chapter 27

Never in her life could Reeta recall being so exhausted. She had slept little on the flight back from Europe, and that combined with jet lag and three weeks of travel had drained her completely. That evening, back in her Long Island home, she walked down the hallway to her parents' room and knocked softly. She entered to find her father sitting in his recliner reading a copy of *Barrons*. Her mother sat at her desk working on a schedule for the upcoming work week. They both stopped their activities when Reeta entered and listened as she said, "I want to thank you for the nice vacation. I really enjoyed the itinerary you arranged. I know that you set it up with me in mind." They smiled as she went on. "I plan to relax here until Wednesday and then drive to the city for a few days with Sarah. Then I will return here and spend some time before I go back to school. You remember that I have a two week track clinic beginning the third week of August." She continued, saying, "Sarah doesn't get to do much except work. I would like to take her up to the Poconos for the weekend if that's all right with you. You remember that big lake we went to a few times when I was small?"

"That sounds nice," her mother said. "Just be careful driving."

Reeta's father asked if she needed money. "No thank you," Reeta smiled. "You keep adding to my checking account. I have over fifteen thousand in it and I already made the fall tuition payment." Then she said, "Well, thank you again for the nice trip." And with that she returned to her room.

Reeta took a long, hot bath which made her even more conscious of her exhausted state. Still, before going to sleep she stood at her window and looked out at the large yard of their beautiful home. She could see that the sprinkler heads had popped up throughout the lawn and were at work watering the lush green grass. She looked at the large in-ground pool with the diving board at one end. Next her eyes focused on the ten-foot high wooden fence that enclosed the entire backyard and suddenly she felt a twinge of guilt. The fence seemed to remind her of the protected and privileged life that she led. She thought of the fact that she had never had a job. Except for the days that she helped Sarah at the mission she had never worked at all. Well, school work, but that she didn't count. She had never had a real job with a schedule and responsibilities. And it was there at her window that hot summer night when Reeta Sorvino decided that next summer she would find a job. Feeling better about herself she went to bed and promptly fell asleep for over fourteen hours.

It was nearly noon when she awoke. She ate toast and a banana, drank a glass of orange juice and decided to walk through the familiar paths to her old school. She was disappointed as she looked into the darkened classroom of Coach Brink. She had hoped to see his familiar figure behind the large desk working among his books and papers. She started to leave when the voice of a maintenance man said, "He was here this morning. He's here almost every morning from eight until noon. Mr. Brink doesn't know about summer vacation."

"Thanks," Reeta said. "I'll come back tomorrow."

* * *

She set the alarm for seven thirty and promptly got out of bed. By nine o'clock she was walking down the hall of her school and she smiled as she saw the open door and the light coming from his room. They shook hands. She was hoping to give him a hug, but she knew Coach Brink was careful about such things. She had never known a teacher as admired as he. He was a man of integrity. Even the "bad kids" behaved in his class. Reeta had often thought that his picture could appear in the dictionary beside the word "respect."

They talked easily for over an hour. Mostly he asked her questions. She told him that it had been difficult being far from the best on the college track team but that it had made her work harder and that she saw improvement. She told of her decision to major in nursing and that she hoped to minor in environmental science. She told how much she enjoyed her course in world literature and that she hoped her schedule would allow for more literature courses. She talked about her friend Sarah and the work at the mission. She told him about her trip to Europe and the upcoming track clinic. She remembered to ask him about his family, his classes and the track team.

As she was about to leave he said, "I am pleased that you have a good plan for your future. Be sure to enjoy the journey. It is as important as the destination."

They shook hands again and she went to the door where, surprising herself, she turned and said to him, "You have been a big help to me. I don't know where I would be if you hadn't talked to me out on the track that day. I really didn't have a life until then. You gave me one."

From behind his desk Coach Brink smiled and said, "Live it well."

* * *

When Reeta announced that they were taking a long weekend in the Poconos, Sarah resisted. "It's too expensive—we can go to Central Park or maybe the Cloisters." But she soon could see that her protests were in vain. Reeta said that reservations had been made for three nights at a motel overlooking a large lake. They would leave after lunch on Friday to avoid the worst of the traffic and return on Monday morning. "You need a break," Reeta said. "All you do is work."

Everyone else must have had the same idea, for the traffic was terrible. The trip which, at most, should have taken three hours ended up taking nearly six. Fortunately Reeta's air conditioned Honda Civic coupled with good conversation made the traffic delays tolerable. By early evening they were standing on the second floor balcony outside their room looking southward down the lake. It was hot, even for the Poconos, but a breeze made it comfortable. They walked to a nearby Chinese restaurant and brought back sweet and sour chicken with rice and vegetables. There on the balcony they ate and then talked until midnight. Reeta told of the European vacation and showed pictures of the Bavarian Alps. Sarah talked of her work at the mission and the AIDS ward of the hospital. It was a pleasant time, although at one point Sarah sensed an uneasiness in Reeta and asked if she was all right. "Just feeling a bit guilty," Reeta answered. "My life is so easy—so materialistic. I sometimes wonder if I make a difference to anyone—I mean in a positive way."

And as she always did, Sarah answered in just the right way. "Do you know how many volunteers come to the mission once and never return? You came back and you keep coming back to help feed smelly homeless men. And at the hospital you are really gifted. The patients love you. They feel like lepers. Most people are afraid to touch them. You give them a sense of worth.

Don't you realize how special that is?" They sat silently for a few moments and Sarah continued. "It's good for me too. It's nice to have a best friend. You know that don't you—that you are my best friend in the whole world. I thank God every day for you. Don't ever feel guilty."

* * *

The following day, Saturday, was oppressively hot. They spent the day in the lake. There were two large rafts located approximately one hundred feet from the shore and separated from each other by nearly fifty yards. All morning they would swim from one raft to the other, climbing on to rest and visit until the heat would force them back into the water. In the afternoon they rented tubes and floated in the lake, again often falling off into the water to cool themselves. Sarah said that it was the most relaxing day she had spent in years. When Reeta asked where she would like to go for dinner Sarah said, "How about pizza and soda on the balcony?"

Sunday's weather was the same. At ten o'clock they boarded a large canopy-covered boat and, with twenty-some other guests cruised for nearly four hours around the entire lake. The guide said that the mile long lake was manmade and that several old buildings stood pretty much intact at the bottom. They learned that the lake served not only as a recreational facility but also as a major water supply for the area. Further the guide said that when area streams fell to a certain level, water from the lake could be released to ensure the protection of the streams' ecosystems. Reeta wondered to herself if this manipulation of nature was good or bad in the long run. Perhaps, she thought, she could learn more about it in the environmental courses she was about to begin in the fall semester.

The boat had a luncheon bar and while they cruised the lake Reeta and Sarah ate garden salads served with chips and iced tea. They arrived back at the marina at two o'clock and spent the remainder of the afternoon swimming. Their evening was spent in a nearby town clearly geared for tourism. They ended up at an amusement center where Reeta amazed Sarah with her prowess in the batting cage where she consistently connected with baseballs thrown at sixty miles per hour by the machine. Following a game of miniature golf and ice cream cones, they returned to the motel ready to sleep.

Monday morning they slept late, signed out of the motel at eleven and returned to the city. Traffic was light and the trip was completed in half the time it had taken to come. For the next three days Reeta spent mornings at the hospital talking and reading to the AIDS patients. The remainder of each day was spent at the mission first serving meals and cleaning the dishes for use the following day. On Friday Reeta returned home. It was hard for her to leave. Partly she knew that she would miss her friend but moreover she knew the extra work it would mean for Sarah. "I'm all right," Sarah assured her. "This is what I do—it's what I want to do, at least for now."

The trip back to Long Island was spent thinking of Sarah. Reeta wondered if she was ever sorry for the life she had chosen. Sarah was such a good person. She was an attractive woman. Reeta wondered if she ever thought about what it would be like to have a boyfriend—a husband—a family. Someday perhaps she would muster the courage to ask her.

* * *

It became Ben's habit to drive to George Rogers' place each day to check on the heifers. There was really no need to, for George checked on them constantly. Mostly Ben went because he had a special interest in them. He knew that Slim and Mary had decided on the project for his benefit, and he was determined to make it succeed. Ben often arrived around ten, after morning chores were completed and before second cutting was dry enough to bale. Other times he drove over in the evenings. Always George would come out to visit. He was certain, he told Ben, that the heifers had grown already. This night Ben parked out near the barn and counted to see that all ten heifers were together. He checked the watering trough and the salt block. He was nearly ready to leave when he noticed that George had not hobbled out to see him. George was sitting on the porch holding the newspaper in front of him. As Ben approached the steps of the porch George turned slightly away from him and said quietly, "Don't come near me, boy—I think I'm catching a summer cold."

"Sorry," Ben said. "Anything I can get you?"

"No, I'll be okay in a day or so. "I'm going to bed soon."

"I will stop by tomorrow," Ben said as he started to leave. "Hope you're feeling better by then."

George turned slightly towards him and it was then that Ben saw the cut on the corner of his mouth. Not knowing what to say, Ben said nothing and climbing into his truck he drove away. When he reached home, Slim and Mary were in the garden watering the tomato plants. Ben joined them and said that George had acted strangely and appeared to have a cut on his face.

"He tried to hide it from me," Ben said. "I think he may have fallen and was embarrassed to tell me."

Slim and Mary looked at each other and said almost simultaneously, "Junior's been around." Ben looked confused and they explained that Junior was George's son. They speculated that he had come home demanding money, and when George had refused, the boy hit him. Ben was stunned, Mary was concerned and Slim was angry.

"We should go over right now," Mary said. Slim left the garden and headed towards the garage to get the car. Mary looked at Ben and said, "Why don't you stay here, Ben. We will be back in a few minutes if he is all right."

* * *

"We were right," Mary said when they arrived back at the house an hour later. Junior had an overdue gambling debt and was facing serious threats from his creditors. George didn't want to bail him out again and that was when Junior exploded.

"What happened?" Ben inquired.

"George gave him a check for five thousand dollars," Slim answered. "What choice does he have when he won't go to the police? Junior will wipe him out if he doesn't kill him first."

"Was he angry that I squealed on him?" Ben asked.

"No," Mary answered smiling. "He said to tell you he was sorry for fibbing to you."

"Junior doesn't like our heifers there," Slim said. "He thinks George should be charging us rent. He told George that I am trying to get the place from him."

"What are you going to do?" Ben asked.

"Think about it for a couple of days," Slim replied. "Just think about it for a couple of days."

* * *

The three of them passed through the garden gate and headed toward the apiary located in the rear. They all wore netted hats. Mary and Ben wore gloves that came far past their elbows. Slim's hands were bare. As Slim had instructed him, Ben wore a light colored shirt and his jeans were tucked inside his socks. He carried the smoker that Slim had given him. It was a metal container with small bellows attached to the side. Smoke from the smouldering baler twine inside came out of the spout at the top. Mary carried two cameras, a thirty-five millimeter and one with a zoom lens attached. Slim carried only a small metal tool, flat on one end and curved on the other. He referred to it simply as a hive tool.

The day was sunny and Slim said that was good since thousands of the worker bees would be out of the hive collecting nectar. As Slim worked, he talked. Ben knew that the monologue was for his benefit and so he watched closely and remained mostly silent. "The boxes are called supers. Each one contains eight frames which is where the queen lays her eggs and also where the worker bees make and store the honey. All the smaller bees are workers. They do a variety of jobs. Some feed the drones and the queen because they can't feed themselves. Others flap their wings to regulate the hive temperature. Some guard the hive entrance to keep out intruders. The majority leave the hive in search of nectar which they bring back to use in the production of honey. The drones are much larger. They are the males whose only job is to fertilize the queen. The queen is larger also. You won't see the drones or the queen today because they are in the bottom two supers."

"Why don't they come up to the top?" Ben asked.

"Because I have an excluder between the bottom two supers and the top two. It is a wire mesh that is big enough for the worker bees to crawl through but too small for the drones and queen. I don't want the queen up in the top because I don't want any egg larvae mixed in with the honey that I want to extract. You better give them a few shots of that smoke. They are getting a bit frisky."

Mary took some pictures while Slim worked and Ben watched but mostly she observed the bond that had developed between Slim and Ben. The transition of Ben from hired hand to son had gone so smoothly. She knew that some in the community had openly said that they were making a mistake, but those people were wrong. Ben's presence with them seemed completely natural. There had been no serious adjustment problems. It was as if the events of the past year were meant to be, and Mary was convinced that they were.

Slim closed up the hives and as they left the apiary he said, "We will have a good crop of honey this year. We'll start extracting as soon as we finish the haying."

The day had been another scorcher. They were all soaked with perspiration as they took off the beekeeping gear. The clock said three thirty and Slim suggested that they sit on the porch with some iced tea until four thirty when they would begin evening chores. Clouds began to move in from the West. "Maybe the forecast for thunderstorms was right," Mary commented.

"It won't help us get a third cutting of hay," Slim said, "but it would still help the ears develop on the corn." Then looking toward Ben he said, "Take Anabel and get the cows down from the pasture. Maybe we should get started early in case we get a bad one."

Ben was still fastening stanchions when he heard the first clap of thunder. Within five minutes it was pouring. The center of the storm was close by as evidenced by the fact that the lightning and thunder were nearly simultaneous. The rain was accompanied by strong winds that sent the rain nearly sideways against the barn. After a particularly sharp strike of lightning, the lights went out and the milking machine shut down. "I think that one took out a transformer," Slim said. "We might as well switch over to the generator. I doubt if we get power back for a while."

Ben was fascinated by the generator. He had never seen it work—had not even known it existed. He watched as Slim pulled the breaker from the main power source and plugged in the generator cord. Then pushing the button on the gasoline powered generator, the machine started up and immediately the barn's lights and milking machine resumed functioning. "Have you always had one of those?" Ben asked as they began the milking.

"About twenty years," Slim answered. "Before that we had to milk them by hand if we lost power. We had to do it for three days once during a February blizzard. It was no fun. Just ask Mary. We have a generator for the house too. Mary probably won't turn it on until we go in. She has always been spooked by electricity."

The storm passed in approximately fifteen minutes. The sky brightened and Mary came into the barn. "You all right out here?" she asked. Seeing that they were, she continued. "The gauge registers three quarters of an inch. That should help your corn. Can you come in and start up the generator so I can make dinner? Maybe the lights will help get Anabel out from under the bed. She is still terrified from the thunder. By the way, I had the portable radio on and it said we may get more storms until about ten. Then it's supposed to clear and be cooler."

The radio was correct. Two more storms passed through, neither as strong as the first one had been. The gauge indicated that one and a quarter inches of rain fell altogether. "That should guarantee at least an average corn crop,"

Slim said as he stood on the porch. "It hasn't been a great year for corn or hay but we will have enough to get by. Feel that air. It's almost cold. We'll probably hay with long-sleeved shirts tomorrow."

Two trucks from the power company passed by with lights flashing. A few minutes later the power returned and except for some small limbs on the lawn, it appeared that the storm had done minimal damage.

Chapter 28

It had been a difficult trip for Reeta. Three times she had been forced to pull off the highway because of the poor visibility caused by heavy rain. Once on the New York State Thruway she had been able to find the safety of a rest area but later near Bennington the rain came so quickly that she had to pull onto the shoulder and with her emergency lights flashing hope that no one ran into her. The same thing happened again just North of Manchester and by the time she reached campus she was late, tired, hungry and frazzled. She took time to say hello to her track teammates before having a dinner of soda and peanut butter crackers, and with that she crawled beneath the blanket of her unmade bed and went to sleep. The car could be unpacked tomorrow.

* * *

College track had been an eye-opening experience for Reeta. The natural ability that had served her so well in high school was a common denominator among her college teammates. It seemed that they all had natural ability. Here the difference between success and failure had less to do with ability and more to do with dedication to training and excellence of technique. Coach Brink had warned her about it. "It's like going from the minor leagues to the majors," he said. "You have learned the basics here, but college track is another level. Many good high school athletes drop out at the college level because they are unwilling to accept the challenge."

He had been right. She had seen several people quit the team because they couldn't accept a diminished role from that to which they had become accustomed. Reeta herself had found the situation difficult, but her personality did not allow her to walk away in defeat. Rather she was determined to do whatever it took to rise to the level of collegiate track. This determination had inspired her to run regularly throughout the summer. She also had maintained her stamina with endless laps in the family pool. Even on the European holiday she had run three times a week. Now she was back at college for a two-week clinic before the fall semester. And she knew that throughout the fall and winter she would continue her training for the spring track season.

The first session of the clinic began promptly at nine o'clock. The morning was spent in the training room where a visiting coach spoke for an hour on the types of exercises and weight lifting that were most beneficial for track athletes. Following the talk they spent two hours trying the new techniques and setting up individual conditioning programs. Lunch was served from noon to one, after which Reeta spent two hours learning a new technique for passing the baton during relay races. At three o'clock they finished the day with a two mile run. Reeta was back in her room at four thirty, exhausted. That evening she finally unpacked the car and organized her room. The thought to call Benjamin was on her mind, but she chose to wait another day or two. She was asleep by nine o'clock.

For the next two days the routine was the same: guest speakers in the morning and field work in the afternoon. The weather was cool, actually cold in the mornings, but reports called for a return to summer weather on Friday. Reeta found herself enjoying the clinic. During the evenings she went to the training room with a few of her teammates to do stretching exercises and weight lifting.

Friday afternoon the track coach announced that there were no practices scheduled until Monday morning. He told them that week two would be very rigorous with more field work and fewer speakers. The meeting ended at four o'clock and as she walked back to her room Reeta looked forward to the next two days. She had plans, although as yet they were only in her mind.

* * *

When the second cutting of hay was complete, August was more than half gone. By then the swampy areas of Slim's farm were hard and dry. The waist-high hay was turning brown from maturity but the stems were still green with life. Most farmers no longer bothered with these areas. At best they mowed it down with a brush hog and let it lie. For bedding under their cattle they purchased sawdust by the truck load; it was the way things were done now. Slim saw things differently. He had approximately two acres of swamp land on his farm and nearly the same amount on the neighboring place. Early in the day, after morning chores were complete, Slim would mow a section of the swamp. If the day was sunny, the hay would cure by the following afternoon. He would rake the hay into windrows and using a large flat bed wagon load it loose by hand.

The loose hay was stored in an area near the milking barn where it could be easily transported for bedding under the cows. This year Slim did not have to do the difficult task alone. With the tractor and wagon parked between windrows he would load hay from one side while Ben loaded from the other. While they worked, they talked—mostly about random topics that came up naturally. Slim said that soon they would begin cutting and hauling firewood from the mountain across the stream. He explained to Ben the process for chopping corn and storing it in the silo for ensilage. Ben smiled as he recalled his first day on the farm, throwing the ensilage down from the cold, dark silo. They discussed the growing herd of young heifers on the Rogers place and how some would soon be mature enough to breed and sell. Ben asked questions about the honey bees and Slim took him to the edge of the field where they watched the bees hard at work on the goldenrod.

The process of harvesting the swamp hay took just over a week if the weather cooperated. It was hard work and by day's end Ben's arms and shoulders ached from the effort. Still, he loved those days. Busy but not hurried, he thought, with much good conversation besides.

One evening after just such a day, Ben sat at the desk in his room looking out the window at the fields beyond. He had written in his journal and was attempting to read a controversial chapter from a book by Howard Zinn on the treatment of Native Americans. He could hear Slim and Mary talking from the front porch where they relaxed on the warm August evening. Ben heard the phone ring and a few moments later Mary's voice from the bottom of the steps said, "Ben, it's for you." With his heart beating fast he went across the room to the phone beside his bed and said hello. From the other end of the line he heard her voice.

Chapter 29

She didn't know him well yet, but Reeta Sorvino was a bright and perceptive young woman. She knew that he would be nervous, wouldn't know what to say, and so she was prepared. For almost five minutes she talked nearly non-stop. She told him that she arrived back at college on the previous Sunday and that the trip was difficult because of recurring thunderstorms. She said that the track clinic was already worthwhile with excellent speakers and good workouts. She talked about her trip to Europe and how beautiful Germany was, especially Bavaria. She said that she had taken some pictures that turned out well and she would show him some of them sometime. She said that she was certain he was tired of storing her skis, and she was anxious to get them out of his way.

"I don't have any meetings or practices until Monday," she said. "I was thinking that maybe you could bring them over to campus this weekend. Like tomorrow night might work. We could get something to eat—my treat. Any time after five would be good for me. I could be in my room. Same dorm as last year. First floor, room A-14." And then she said, "Maybe that's not good for you—I know you are busy with your work."

Ben finally spoke. "Yes, that will be good. We usually finish chores around six, but I can leave early. I can probably be there by six or six thirty."

"Are you sure I am not messing things up?" she said. "I know it's short notice, but I thought it might be fun. There is a lake near here where we can sit outside if you like."

"That would be good," Ben answered. "I will see you tomorrow night."

* * *

He sat in his room for several minutes after he hung up the phone. He was both excited and nervous. Random thoughts raced through his mind. He tried

189

to picture her face but the memory was blurred. He wondered what she would wear, if he should park on campus or on the street. Should he take the skis to her room when he arrived or wait until later? He walked to the closet and looked through his clothes. Blue jeans would be best with the yellow shirt. But it was very warm. Maybe shorts would be better, with sandals. He was irritated that he could not focus on any issue and come to a decision. Why would she ever be interested in him? He was shy and insecure with no abilities socially. Feeling depressed he went downstairs where Mary and Slim were sitting in the kitchen.

"That was a girl I met at the college," Ben said. "I kept her skis for her over the summer. They wouldn't fit in her car when she went home last spring."

"Where is she from?" Slim asked.

"Long Island," Ben replied, adding, "Her name is Reeta. She spells it R-e-e-t-a. I am taking the skis over tomorrow night. She wants to take me out to eat."

Mary said, "I will help Slim with the chores so you can get there without rushing. And take the car. You don't have to drive the truck everywhere you go."

* * *

Fortunately he was very busy the next day. After morning chores he drove to the Rogers place and, using the weed whacker with plastic blades, trimmed the grass beneath the electric fence. It was typical Vermont weather for August—extremely hot during the day but cool, almost fall-like when the sun went down. By the time he finished trimming it was nearly noon and he was soaked with sweat. He stopped to talk with George for a few minutes before hurrying home where, after a quick lunch, he helped Slim complete the gathering of swamp hay. The last two loads were difficult because the storage area was nearly full and they literally had to force the loose hay into the rafters. They finished just before four o'clock and already the cows were working their way back from the pasture in anticipation of evening milking. By four thirty Ben had stanchioned the milkers and given them their grain. He was about to start feeding the calves when Mary came to the barn and shooed him out.

"I brought the car out of the garage," she told him. "You go have a good time. Be careful," she added. "Watch for deer when you drive back tonight."

* * *

Ben left for campus at five o'clock. He wore the blue jeans and yellow shirt. Knowing that the evening would be cool, he took a gray sweatshirt and put it in the back alongside the two pairs of skis. As he drove the forty-five minute trip to the college he felt very nervous. By the time he arrived he was in such a state that he had no idea what he would say. The sight of the college coupled with his lack of social skills nearly made him physically ill. His saliva stopped flowing and his mouth was completely dry. He stopped at the water fountain in the foyer of the dorm. The cool water refreshed him as he walked down the corridor until he stopped in front of room A-14.

He knocked softly on her door and heard her feet as she walked across the room. "Hi," she said as she opened the door. "Come in." She was wearing jeans with a red top. Her hair was longer than he recalled, but it still fell casually around her face. Her eyes, large and brown with dark lashes, smiled at him warmly, and he felt himself relax slightly. Reeta would always send messages with her eyes and tonight's message seemed to say she was glad to see him. "You look great," she said. "What a terrific tan you have, and you've grown. Have you been lifting weights?"

Ben smiled. "Lifting bales of hay," he said. "Several thousand of them."

"Well, it suits you," she said. "Have a seat. I have to run down the hall to the girls' room. I'll be ready in a minute."

Alone in her room, he looked around. It was neat and clean. One wall was completely covered in pictures and illustrations of stretching techniques. A chart with dates showed the record of her training regiment. On another wall were three posters of scenes from the European countryside. One was a scene from Ireland, the second a picture of the Italian Alps and the third said "Bavaria." Her desk contained several pictures. In one she was standing with two people whom Ben assumed to be her parents. The others were mainly of a young woman. Since in one picture the woman was wearing a habit, Ben guessed that she was the girl Reeta had referred to as her best friend, the nun, Sarah.

"Ready," she said as she returned to the room. They walked quietly to the car. Ben tried desperately to think of something to say but nothing came. Reeta broke the silence when she saw the car. "You didn't drive your truck today. I love trucks. My parents think I'm crazy."

"Sorry," Ben answered. "I'll bring it next time." Immediately he thought his statement was a mistake. How was he to know there was going to be a next time?

But before he had time to worry she said, "So tell me about your summer.

What's new with your life? Do you still like your new career? Read anymore Schumacher?"

Surprising himself Ben began to talk, and the talk came easily. "I love the farm," he said, "and the farm work. It is hard for me to believe sometimes that I fell into it almost by accident. We have worked hard—harvesting hay, growing corn for the silos, milking twice a day. Besides the regular work, we cleared some fields that an old man Slim knows can't take care of anymore and we keep heifers over there."

"What are heifers?" Reeta asked innocently.

"Young cows," Ben replied, "who are about ready to have calves and start producing milk."

By then they had reached the main street. "Left here," Reeta said. "Just stay on this road about five miles and we will come to the lake. Sorry I interrupted. Heifers—young cows. I have never seen a cow up close. Are they mean? They don't look mean. The baby ones are so cute, at least in pictures. Maybe you can show me yours sometime."

Her comment calmed Ben and he said, "I would like that—anytime you want."

"I interrupted again," she said, "sorry, so you love farming even though it's hard work. What about the people you work for? Are they still nice? You still get along good?"

"So much has happened this summer," Ben said. "I don't know where to start, plus I don't want to bore you too much." He glanced toward her and the message in her eyes told him not to talk of boring her again.

"Tell you what," she said, "we are almost there. You find a table down by the lake and I'll get the food. I always get the chicken tenders, and they have great coleslaw. Is that all right for you?"

"That sounds good," Ben replied as they pulled into the parking area. Finding a picnic table proved to be a challenge. It was a popular place and the tables were all taken. A family left just before Reeta arrived with the food.

"I forgot to ask about drinks," she said. "I hope you like iced tea."

The small lake, nearly a half a mile long and about half as wide, was beautiful. The public beach that accompanied the snack bar was still filled with mostly young children swimming while their parents watched from the shore. Reeta was right—the food was good, and Ben felt at ease enough to eat. And then she asked him to tell her about his summer. And he did. He told about his father arriving unannounced at his door. He told his father's sad story and how it had made him feel sorry rather than angry. He told of Slim and Mary's reaction: how they had taken him from the trailer into their beautiful home. He described his room and the first soft bed he had ever slept in. He said that Slim and Mary had asked him to call them Mom and Dad and how much at home he felt with them.

When he finally stopped he was shocked to see that they were alone in the picnic area—that the beach was empty and the sun was gone. Suddenly he felt cold and he noticed the goose bumps on Reeta's arms. "You're cold," he said. "It's getting dark. How long have I talked? What time is it? I'm sorry."

"It's all right," she said. "You needed to tell me that. I feel honored that you could talk so openly." As she said those things she reached across the table and gently laid her hand on his arm. It was the first time she had ever touched him, and he was stunned by the emotional impact of her simple act.

The ride back to campus was quiet. He had given her his sweatshirt which she had wrapped around herself. "Are you still cold?" he asked her as they approached campus, and she said that she was fine.

She carried one set of skis to her room and he took the other. At the door she found her keys and turned on the light. She placed the skis that she carried against the wall, and taking the pair he was carrying she did the same with them. Then knowing that he had no idea what to do next she said, "So, do I get to see you again?"

And with a weak voice he said, "I was hoping so."

A moment of silence passed and she said, "Tell you what—I'll call you on Wednesday and maybe we can arrange something for next weekend." And with that she told him to drive carefully and sent him on his way.

* * *

It had become Mary's habit to come to Ben's room each night to "tuck him in" as she said. On this night she carried with her a folder. Giving him a look of hesitancy she said, "Slim and I would like to arrange for a stone to be placed on your mother's grave. I brought some brochures from the funeral director in town for you to look at. We are hoping that you will choose one that you like along with the words you would like engraved on it. Please don't feel we are trying to invade your privacy by wanting to do this. If you think we are, please tell me so."

Ben answered, "I don't feel that way at all. I think it would be nice. I have wanted a stone placed on her grave for a long time but I knew it would be too expensive. I appreciate that you will do this for me—and her."

"Good," Mary replied. "You see what you like and show us how you want it to look. Do you know the name of the cemetery and the address of the funeral director?" Ben said that he had the information in a box in his closet. "You are such a good boy," Mary said and kissed his forehead. "You never disappoint me."

When she left his room Ben looked at the large variety of monuments presented in the catalogs. After a while he chose a gray granite stone. Its dimensions were two feet across and fourteen inches high. At its base it was nearly a foot thick after which it tapered on an angle so that its top narrowed to about two inches. Choosing the inscription proved to be more difficult. The brochure gave examples but Ben found most of them to be too superficial— almost silly. Poems that didn't sound at all like his mother. It was nearly midnight when he finally made his decision. The stone would read, "Ellen Marie Thomas." Below her name would be the dates "1960-1993." And below the date it would simply say, "Remembered."

He showed the stone, with its inscription, to Mary the following night. He could tell by her smile that she liked it. "Simple yet profound," she said softly, almost to herself, and Ben watched as a single tear formed in the corner of her eye and ran gently across her cheek.

A few weeks later Ben received a snapshot of the newly mounted stone, and he placed it in a box in his closet where he kept special things.

Chapter 30

There was no need for them to preserve fruits and vegetables. Slim was a successful farmer and Mary's careers in teaching and photography made them more than comfortable economically. Yet by late August the shelves in the cellar and the huge freezer that stood beside them were nearly filled with jams and jellies, carrots, corn, beans and pickles. There were also jars of stewed tomatoes and even beets. A large bin beside the shelves would, in less than two months, be filled with potatoes, squash and pumpkins. Partly they did it out of tradition. Partly it was from Mary's concern that food produced for large scale marketing was contaminated with pesticides. And partly it was simply that their own fruits and vegetables tasted better. The process of freezing and canning was always a joint effort, and either Slim or Mary could do any step of it as good as the other.

The idea of preserving one's own food was completely new to Ben. Even the concept of it had never crossed his mind. He had grown up in a world where food was purchased in a store and that was all there was to it. As he watched the process unfold that first summer in Vermont, he found it completely appealing. First there was the economics of it. Ben had always, by necessity, been conscious about money. The idea that by investing a few dollars in seeds one could provide for nearly every physical need was attractive to him. Even more appealing was the feeling of independence and self-reliance that it brought. It was, for him, the ultimate insurance policy because it literally insured survival for another year.

And so on a Wednesday evening in mid August Ben stood at the kitchen counter cutting sweet corn from the cobs, which Mary would parboil and place in plastic freezer bags. From the kitchen window they watched Slim standing at the end of the driveway and looking across his lower fields that bordered the stream. "My guess is that he is thinking of the crop of third cutting he won't get because of the dry spell," Ben remarked.

"My guess is that you're right," Mary replied, and she continued: "There is no part of farming more important to Slim than a good crop of hay. He wants high quality and plenty of it. The barns are already full and with the fields at George Rogers' place there is plenty for our herd with extra to sell. Still he wanted that third crop of alfalfa. It's like gold to him and this is the third dry year that he hasn't been able to gather one." Then pausing she added, "Maybe next year."

The two worked in silence for a few minutes. Slim returned to the front porch and sat in the large wicker chair that was his favorite. It was then that the phone rang. Mary quickly rinsed and dried her hands and reached the phone on the third ring. "Yes, he is here," Ben heard her say and then looking across the room she said, "Ben it's for you." As he came to the phone Mary went to the porch with Slim and closed the door behind her.

Reeta told him that her week was grueling but great. She said that two students had dropped out of the program because it was too rigorous but that she was excited about the possibility of improving. She asked how his week was going and what he was up to. When he said he was preserving corn for the winter she asked, "What does that mean?"

Ben laughed and said, "I will show you sometime perhaps."

And then she said, "I am free all day Saturday. Do you think you could come over in the morning? I was hoping that maybe you would take me to your farm. I want to see the cows up close. I was hoping maybe I could pet them—at least the little ones. Do they bite?"

Ben's mind was racing. He hadn't thought of bringing her to the farm. Perhaps he should first ask Slim and Mary's permission. But he heard himself say, "Sure, that would be fine. I would like to show you the place. What time should I pick you up?"

Ben went immediately to the porch where Slim and Mary were sitting. Hesitantly he told them about Saturday and was pleased when Mary asked if he would like her to fix a lunch. "Do you know what she likes to eat?" Mary inquired.

"Healthy things mostly," Ben answered.

"Good," Mary said. "We will have lots of fresh vegetables." That said, the three of them went to the kitchen and continued working on the corn.

* * *

He arrived on campus at ten o'clock. She was waiting on the steps of her dormitory when she saw the truck. Before Ben could turn off the engine she had run down the walk and climbed in beside him. She wore blue jeans and a shirt that said "varsity track." As he had suggested she was wearing sneakers and socks. "Hi," she said. "I'm glad you have the truck. I love trucks." And then she said, "These are the closest things I have to farm clothes. Will they be all right?"

"They'll be fine," Ben answered as they pulled out on to the street and began the ride back to the farm.

Reeta knew that he was nervous. She made conversation as they drove through the Vermont countryside—mostly about the natural beauty of the place and how she loved the mountains, but there were periods of silence during which random thoughts raced through her mind. She thought that he looked especially handsome this day with his deep tan. The summer sun had lightened his hair until it seemed almost blonde. She thought how different he seemed from most young men she knew. He was more serious, more reflective. She found herself worrying about his nervousness and so she decided to be honest. "I'm nervous about meeting your Slim and Mary," she said. "How about you?"

"Yes, I'm nervous too," Ben answered, "but it's nice knowing I'm not alone. I hope you like the farm. I hope that you don't mind the animal smells. I have grown to love the odor of the barn but some people can't stand it. I really want you to have a good day."

He glanced across the seat at Reeta as she said, "I will." As she spoke she reached across and gently patted his arm. Ben felt the strange sensation surge through his body as once again he realized the emotional power of touch.

He stopped the truck at the top of the hill in the exact spot Jim Braxton had first shown him the place ten months earlier. He pointed out the dimensions of the farm and he could tell by her eyes that Reeta was moved by the scene before her. When she commented that it looked like a calendar, he smiled and told her that he had made nearly that exact comment the first time he had seen it. "See," she said, "great minds think alike."

It was eleven o'clock when they arrived at the farm. For Reeta the scene was as alien as if she had landed on another planet. For the remainder of the day she was like a wide-eyed child in an enchanting new world. Everything intrigued and delighted her. Slim and Mary were in the garden and it was there that she was introduced to them. Later she told Ben she was surprised by their youthfulness—that she expected an older couple. ("They are so attractive," she would tell Ben on the way back to campus that evening. "And Mary reminds me so much of my friend Sarah—so caring and sincere.")

Reeta asked many questions in the garden. She had never seen tomatoes on the vine or cabbage growing in long straight rows. She had no idea that one potato could produce as many as a dozen in one hill and had never considered that cucumbers grew on vines the way they did. For nearly an hour she toured the garden asking dozens of questions. It was high noon when they entered the home through the back door. Reeta loved the old farm house with its huge circular fireplace. She commented on what a great kitchen it was and how attractive the black ironware looked hanging on the walls. She was drawn to Mary's photographs and listened with interest as Slim told her of Mary's successful career in photography. They ate lunch at the kitchen table. There were sliced carrots and cucumbers fresh from the garden served with a ranch style dip. Slices of roast turkey were served cold with rye bread and Swiss cheese on the side. There were grapes in a bowl and sliced peaches lightly sugared. A large pitcher of iced tea sat in the middle of the table. Slim was quiet for the most part, letting Mary lead the conversation. She asked Reeta about the upcoming school term and about her family in Long Island. Ben mentioned Reeta's love for track and field and for the remainder of lunch Reeta described the clinic that she was currently involved in.

When lunch was completed Mary looked at Ben and said, "You run along and show Reeta the farm. Slim will help me with the dishes."

As they walked toward the barn Reeta asked about the two tall silos. "That is where we store the ensilage," Ben said adding, "Ensilage is ground-up corn—stalks and all. The cows love it." They entered the empty barn and Ben explained that the cows were grazing on the mountain, but he took her to the far end where the calves were tethered. A half hour later they were still there petting the calves. Reeta's conversation was like that of a little girl. She was intrigued by their Holstein markings and looked for specific designs. She liked the ones predominately black best but this she told Ben in a whisper so as not to hurt the feelings of the white ones.

When they finally left the barn Ben asked if she would like to see the stream that bordered the lower fields. With Anabel running ahead of them they followed the well-worn path across the field until they reached the tree-lined creek. Reeta looked with interest at the five piles of rocks strategically placed across the stream. "Slim calls that the poor man's bridge," Ben explained. "It is how we get across and keep our feet dry." He watched as she quickly jumped from pile to pile and then leaped gracefully up the bank on the other side. Ben followed and together they walked the path up stream until they came to the swimming hole. Reeta said that she had never been swimming in a creek. She remarked how clear and fresh it looked and without asking she took off her shoes and socks and waded along the shore. It was mid afternoon when they returned to the house. Mary came to the door as they approached and said to Reeta, "We hope you will stay for dinner. We are going to barbeque chicken on the garden patio."

While Ben and Slim did the afternoon milking Reeta talked with Mary. Mostly they were in the garden where Reeta picked and husked her first ear of corn, picked her first tomato from the vine and watched with amazement while Mary dug fourteen brown potatoes from a single hill. Their visit was casual, with topics ranging from the garden to teaching and photography. Together they walked to the barn and as Ben and Slim milked, Mary showed Reeta the entire milking process. "I can't believe how big they are," Ben heard her say as she looked down the two long rows of stanchioned milkers. And before she left the barn Reeta came to where Ben was working and said, "You are right. It's smelly, but I think I'm getting used to it."

By the time Ben and Slim had showered, the meal was ready. Together the four ate on the garden patio beneath the large umbrella. Reeta asked Slim about the hives at the far end of the garden and for several minutes listened as Slim explained the basics of bee keeping. Ben watched her eyes as they revealed her interest in a topic that, like so many others that day, had never before crossed her mind. At one point she expressed her amazement at "how little I know about all this."

It was after seven when she said goodbye and walked with Ben to the truck for the ride back to campus. The dusk was setting in but enough daylight remained for Reeta to point at the mountain and say, "So that is the mountain you love so much."

Ben pointed to the spot where the pasture ended and the woodlands began and said, "See where the trail begins? It runs up the mountain for about a quarter mile to a huge rock. From there I can see down to the farm and look off for miles into the Green Mountains. I go there to read and think." She stood there for several minutes looking up at the mountain and then said quietly—almost to herself—"Sometime soon, I hope."

He could feel the tension rising in his body as they rode back to campus. His problem embarrassed him to even think of: he had never kissed a girl— wasn't even sure what to do. She sensed his nervousness and smiled to herself because she already knew the problem. He was so smart, so nice, so good looking but in many ways a frightened little boy. She almost brought the subject up. She almost told him that she had barely kissed a boy since her crazy middle school days. That she had found most boys her age boring and sophomoric. But she said nothing. It was to prove one of the few times she was indecisive.

They walked silently up the sidewalk to the front of her dorm. There, alone, she turned and looked up at him. It was then that his panic struck. "I have to go," he said, and turning quickly he nearly ran down the sidewalk to his truck. She wanted to call to him, but she said nothing as she watched the truck pull away. She went quietly to her room. She needed to think.

The ride back to the farm was a blur. He was too embarrassed to cry. He could feel his face burning. His clothes were soaked with sweat. Mostly he felt despair. The thoughts raced through his mind. She was so beautiful. It had been such a wonderful day. And now it was over. She had seen him for what he was—shy to the point of abnormal. He trembled at the thought that he would never see her again. His whole body ached as he thought of her finding someone else—that he had lost the dream of a lifetime. And it was then that he felt the tears running down his face.

Fortunately when he arrived home Slim and Mary had retired for the night. He went quickly to his room and fell onto the bed. That night he did not sleep at all. He decided that for a few days he would do nothing—say nothing. Hopefully Slim and Mary would ask no questions until he had more time to think. At five o'clock he dressed quietly and walked through the darkness to the barn. As daylight approached he looked out at the fields he had so quickly learned to love but somehow this day they did not look the same.

Reeta's night was also restless but in a different way. At first she worried about his drive home in his terrible state of mind. She thought of calling but dismissed the idea. She knew what he was going through and the thought of his emotional turmoil saddened her. She almost called Sarah for advice but in the end she knew what needed to be done, and she knew that the job was hers alone. With her decision made she said a prayer that God would keep him safe until tomorrow.

* * *

Ben ate his breakfast quickly. Slim noticed that he was quiet but assumed he was tired from the previous day. Mary knew that something was wrong but kept her thoughts silent. "I'm going up to the mountain," Ben said as he placed his breakfast dishes in the washer. "I will see you after church." Slim watched as Ben and Anabel disappeared up the mountain trail. Already dressed for church he sat on the porch with the morning paper. It would be an hour before they needed to leave for town and Mary was at the kitchen table still in her robe, sipping her second cup of coffee. Later when he heard Mary go to the bedroom he followed to get his wallet and keys. It was then that he heard the car enter the driveway. "Who can that be at this hour?" Slim said as Mary went to the window.

"It is a small red car," she said, and after a moment added, "Why, it's Reeta. Slim, go to the door and let her in. I'll be out in a minute."

"I am sorry to bother you so early," she said to them as they sat at the kitchen table. "But I need to see Benjamin."

Mary looked at her directly and said, "He seemed upset this morning. Is he all right?"

Reeta smiled a nervous smile and said quietly, "He is so shy," and pausing she added, "but he will be all right when I see him."

"He has gone up the mountain," Slim told her. "I can take you up there or go and get him."

Reeta answered, "Thank you, but I can find him. He pointed out the trail to me yesterday."

"Well, I will take you to where the pasture ends," Slim said. "The milkers are up there and they might get curious when they see someone unfamiliar."

"Thank you," Reeta said, "that would be good."

They said very little as they walked through the pasture. The morning was still cool although as the sun rose higher it would be a warm August day. When they reached the place where the fence ended and the mountain trail began, Slim held the barbed wire while Reeta slipped through. "Don't be surprised if Anabel bounds out at you," he told her. "She is up here somewhere." Reeta smiled and thanked him again as he turned back toward the house and she started up the trail.

Ben lay on the huge flat rock and stared up at the sky. He heard Anabel's bark from down the trail but thought nothing of it. Convinced that he would never see Reeta again he tried to plan how he would explain the situation to Mary and Slim but he was so distraught that his mind was unable to focus. Instead he kept replaying the feeble scene from the previous night in front of Reeta's dorm. Nearly oblivious even to where he was, Ben felt Anabel's nose against his hand which hung off the side of the rock. He reached to pet her head and it was then that he saw Reeta standing only ten feet away. Stunned, he sat up instantly and stood beside the rock. As she walked toward him he began to stammer. "About last night... I'm sorry... It's just that..."

Standing before him she placed her finger across his lips and said, "Shh." He stopped trying to talk and heard her say, "You owe me a kiss and I have come to collect." Again he tried to speak and again she stopped him. She slipped her arms around his neck and looked up at him. At first their lips barely touched and as she leaned back and looked into his eyes he felt his body began to relax. Again their lips met—this time longer, and instinctively his arms slipped around her waist. She leaned back again and this time when he spoke she let him continue.

"It has been horrible. I have never had such a terrible night. I thought that I would never see you again and the idea was terrifying."

She spoke. "It was a tough night for me too. I was so worried about you. But it is over now. I'm here—you are here. Everything is good now. Smile—please smile—I want you to be happy." And he did smile and then he held her close and they kissed again, and it was as natural to him as breathing.

After a long time Reeta looked up at him and said, "I looked straight ahead when I came up here. I felt as though I was going to a sacred spot and I wanted my first glimpse of the view to be with you." Slowly he turned her around and she looked in silence first at the farm below and then off into the distance. Finally she said, "It is beautiful—your spot here. Do you think maybe someday it could be our spot?"

Slipping his arms around her waist he said, "It already is." And there atop the mountain—his favorite place on earth and with Reeta in his arms—Ben still wasn't sure there was a heaven. But if there was, surely he was having a taste of it right now.

Chapter 31

Slim Smith was never known as a talker. He was an exhaustive reader, although even his closest acquaintances couldn't have told you so. Mostly he was a quiet observer of the world around him—both people and nature. His ability to see and understand that which went unnoticed by others was a quality deeply admired by Mary. Often it was little things. Once, on a sunny January morning, standing in front of his barn door, Slim pointed to a tall white pine standing atop the mountain to the east and said, "The sun always rises directly behind that tree on January sixth." Mary often recalled to herself how a chill had moved through her body when Slim had made that remark. For her, it represented so well the essence of what he was—a man so in touch with the creation around him that he seemed in complete harmony with it. His life, she often thought, had a marvelous balance to it. And as Mary observed these qualities in her husband, she found that her love and respect for him increased.

Slim used these powers of observation on the days following that meaningful Sunday in mid August. With quiet interest he observed the two most important people in his life. In Ben he saw a change that was subtle yet distinct. Always serious about his work, Ben now appeared even more so. Learning the art of farming now had an added importance. He approached each task with a heightened sense of purpose—a more urgent reason to succeed. Slim further observed in Ben a growing confidence. The insecurities so apparent in the young man's eyes were being replaced with other qualities. Slim saw eyes filled with hope, perhaps even joy. It was as though the young man was, for the first time, seeing life as a glass half full rather than half empty.

It was with equal interest that Slim watched Mary. She never ceased to amaze him. He had been concerned that the entry of Reeta into Ben's life would upset her. She had waited, after all, for over thirty years for a child of her own. Now after having Ben in her life for only a short time it appeared that she would have to share him with Reeta. But Mary appeared to have no such reaction. Rather she was clearly pleased that good things were happening to Ben. And from the start there was plainly a bond between her and Reeta. The reason for that bond, Slim pondered.

* * *

Reeta had been on the phone with Sarah for nearly two hours. "I never meant for this to happen," she said over and over. "Most guys are such jerks. I always found them so boring. But he is different. I can't really figure him out. In some ways he is like a little boy, innocent and afraid. Still in other ways he is deep and thoughtful. I can tell that he is smart. I know that he reads endlessly. He knows more than the guys here on campus who think they're so smart. What do you think my parents will say when I tell them I'm seeing a farm boy?"

Sarah let her talk. Sometimes several minutes would pass by without a word from Sarah's end of the phone. Reeta's monologue turned to Slim and Mary. "They seem so young," she said, "but they must be in their fifties. I didn't know people like them existed. It's like I'm on another planet. They are not hicks—quite the opposite. Mary is a teacher and a great photographer. You should see her work—really great nature things. Do you know that they grow most of their own food? They have it in the freezer and in big glass jars in the basement. It doesn't spoil somehow. I never knew you could do that—actually I never thought about it."

When she finally looked at the clock she apologized to Sarah. "I had no idea that I talked so long," she said.

"It's all right," Sarah replied. "You needed this talk and anyway I am interested. By the way, I don't think your life will be the same again. You have had a watershed moment, and I am happy for you."

When Reeta hung up the phone she found herself not only thinking of Ben but also of Sarah and what an important friend she was.

* * *

The first week in September Slim began making calls. Several of the large heifers at George Rogers' place had already been bred and Slim informed more than a dozen farmers in the area of their availability. Further, he checked with the local auction to determine the fair price for a registered Holstein milking cow. Sale was certain. It was simply a matter of finding the best price. As the process unfolded, Slim kept Mary and Ben informed. One evening at the dinner table he reminded Ben that in the near future he would begin to receive payment for his efforts in the project. Ben commented that he hoped to use the money toward some type of health insurance. He quickly noticed the glance between Slim and Mary and then he heard Mary's voice. "Ben," she said, "that is something we want to discuss with you. After a thoughtful pause she continued. "Slim and I would like to make things official. We are hoping that you will let us legally adopt you."

The words echoed in Ben's mind. He heard the sound of Mary's voice again and again. "We are hoping that you will let us legally adopt you." He sat very still for what seemed a long time and finally he said simply, "Wow." More silence and then he said, "Wow, I can't believe this is really happening. How could it be done?"

Slim answered, "It should be quite simple. First of all you're nineteen and besides there is really no one to contest it. I suspect that it's just a matter of signing some papers." Again there was silence, but it was a peaceful silence because it was clear to both Slim and Mary from the glow on Ben's face that he would soon officially be their son.

Ben spoke quietly, "For some reason my mom never gave me a middle name. Benjamin Thomas—that is my name. Now I will have a middle name—it will be Thomas." And after a long pause he said simply, "Benjamin Thomas Smith."

Mary reached over and took his hand. "It has a wonderful sound to it," and she repeated the words, "Benjamin Thomas Smith. We will call the lawyer tomorrow and get the paperwork started. Oh and by the way now you will be covered by my health insurance at school—at least for a couple of years. So I guess you will need to spend that heifer money somewhere else."

Again there was silence. When Ben finally spoke he said, "I am going to tell Reeta." And with that he bounded up the stairs to his room.

Chapter 32

Slim used his largest John Deere tractor, the one with the canopy to protect him from the sun. He had once told Ben that the canopy was a gift from Mary, that at the time he had considered it a waste of money. But, he then added, as usual Mary was right. It protected him from the blazing sun during haying season and it kept him dry if he needed to work in the rain. "I would never get a tractor without a canopy again," he said. Behind the tractor he pulled the chopper. It was a machine that cut the stalks of corn approximately six inches from the ground, chopped it up, ears and all, and blew the ensilage into the huge wagon with high sides that he pulled behind the chopper.

Slim wasted no space in his fields. Limbs from the trees that bordered the fields were cut to a height that enabled his machines to pass beneath unencumbered. The corn itself was planted to the very edge of the fields. Most farmers left a space of fifteen or twenty feet around each field but losing that much tillable land was, in Slim's way of farming, unthinkable. It did, however, create extra work. Before he could use the chopper it was necessary to cut fifteen to twenty rows of corn by hand and feed it into the chopper manually. He used a tool that resembled a miniature scythe to do the cutting. It was a rigorous task, but one that Ben soon discovered he loved. Together they would cut the corn, mostly in silence, and stack it in piles. Frequently they would rest and visit. When the strip around the field was completed, Slim drove the tractor from pile to pile and they would feed the corn manually into the chopper.

Slim owned two of the large ensilage wagons. They were designed in similar fashion to the manure spreader. A track ran along the bed of the wagon. Small fins were connected to the tracks and when the power takeoff lever was engaged, the tracks pulled the ensilage toward the rear of the wagon.

Slim showed Ben how to position the wagon over the auger-driven conveyor. As the ensilage fell slowly from the rear of the wagon the auger drew it to the base of the tall blue silo where a powerful blower sent it up the pipe that was attached to the side. For nearly two weeks in late September they harvested the corn. Slim would circle the corn fields chopping and blowing the corn into the wagon while with a second tractor Ben would haul the other wagon to the silo and deposit its contents. By the time he returned to the field with the empty wagon, Slim would have another load waiting for him. When the harvest was completed, both silos were filled to capacity and nearly three loads that would not fit were piled near the barn to be used first.

* * *

September found Reeta under an extremely heavy work load. In addition to the hours spent training and conditioning for track, she now had a full schedule of classes. The nursing program was both academically rigorous and time-consuming. Besides the classroom instruction that was the staple of all college courses, there were long and exhaustive laboratory sessions. It was typical for her to eat dinner in her room between eight and nine o'clock because her lab work would extend through the cafeteria hours. Reeta quickly learned that while her first year of college had been difficult because of the new adjustment to being away from home, the second year was even more difficult because of the enormous amount of work assigned. Her recreation consisted mainly of two things: each night at ten o'clock she talked with Ben on the phone; and on Saturdays he came to campus and they spent the day together. Rarely did they remain on campus. Occasionally they went to a nearby city or to a large shopping mall near it. More often they returned to the farm where after playing with the calves they took long walks—sometimes up the mountain behind the barn, sometimes across the field and along the stream, and sometimes along the county road well past the neighboring farm that Slim maintained.

Reeta watched with interest as Ben grew in confidence. She discovered in him a playful quality that for his entire life had been hidden beneath layers of fear and insecurity. He began to talk openly about the change remarking one day that in many ways the events of the past year, especially the last few months were much like being released from a prison. "It's like," he told her, "my body was free to move about but my spirit and soul were imprisoned." He added, "It is probably a good thing that I did not fully realize how unhappy I was. I guess I always figured that was just the way things were."

But there were, for Ben, also moments of fear that bordered on panic. Reeta could sense them immediately and without asking she knew that he was wondering when the dream would end and he would again descend to the loneliness of his earlier life. Once when he lapsed into one of those moments he felt her take his hand and heard her say, "You don't need to worry. It won't happen."

Ben looked toward her and said, "I didn't know you could read minds."

To which she replied, "Just yours," and stood on tip-toes to kiss his cheek.

* * *

By the first week of October the nightly calls and Saturday dates had become routine. It was during that week that Reeta surprised Ben with the fact that it was her birthday. He felt badly that he had never inquired before as to when it was, but before he could say so she knew what he was thinking and said, "Stop worrying. You have had a lot on your mind."

Ben said, "I know but still—well, would you like to do something special on Saturday?"

Without a pause Reeta said, "I thought maybe we could go to a fancy restaurant for dinner."

"Do you know of any?" Ben asked.

To which Reeta replied, "Hey pal, that's your job."

Almost immediately Ben began thinking of an appropriate gift. His thoughts went to the shelf in her room where he had seen her collection of Audrey Hepburn films. He recalled her comment that Audrey Hepburn was not only her favorite actress but also one of her favorite people. "She did great things for children all over the world," Reeta had told him. With these thoughts in his mind, Ben drove to the mall the following evening and purchased a very expensive book filled with pictures and stories on the life of Audrey Hepburn. Mary wrapped the gift for him and he took it on the following Saturday. When Reeta opened the gift he could tell that she was pleased. It was a thoughtful gift. And it made no difference that the exact same book sat on her shelf back in Long Island. She would give that one to Sarah.

Ben was more dressed up than usual. He wore off-white pants with a dark blue shirt and casual black loafers. He watched television while Reeta changed from her usual jeans and sweatshirt. When she emerged from the bathroom Ben felt ceratin that he was looking upon the most beautiful girl in the world. She was wearing a tan khaki skirt that came slightly above the knees. Her top was a bright yellow jersey with sleeves that stopped just above the elbows. Around her neck she wore a necklace that consisted of a very thin gold chain with a single white pearl. Matching gold earrings were barely visible beneath her dark brown hair. Her appearance left him nearly speechless, but he managed to say something to the effect that yellow was her color.

They entered the restaurant at seven o'clock. Neither had been there before but Mary had told Ben that it was nice. The room was very large, but three foot dividers with plants on top created the feeling of several rooms. In the front there was a slightly elevated platform upon which sat a baby grand piano. The man at the piano played quietly and without effort. He did not speak and skillfully shifted from one piece to the next without interruption. The meal was pleasant and Ben felt at ease. He ordered salad followed by broiled flounder with seafood dressing. When the waiter looked her way, Reeta said, "That sounds good—I will have the same." At one point during the meal Reeta commented that most of the music was from her favorite old movies. Ben asked about her love for the old films and who her favorite actors were. "Well you know about Audrey Hepburn," she replied, "but let's see, among my other favorites would have to be Grace Kelly, Cary Grant—and oh yes Humphrey Bogart and Ingrid Bergman. And then I would have to include Tracy and Hepburn, as in Katherine. And let's see, oh I love Sidney Poitier. There are others too," she continued, "but I guess those are the top of my list. How about you?" she inquired.

"To be honest," Ben answered, "I don't know much at all about the movies. Most of my life we didn't even have a television. And you probably won't believe this, but I have never been in a theater. Well, except last year when I came to your campus with Dave Burnham."

A well-dressed man came to the microphone. "Tonight," he announced, "I am proud to welcome vocalist Johnny Ray for your listening and dancing pleasure." The pianist played and the vocalist began. After several numbers the dance floor was filled. "I've never danced," Ben said, "but if you are willing I will try."

It turned out to be easy. The crowded floor meant that mostly each couple stayed in one place moving only slightly. For several numbers they danced, saying nothing. "Would you like to sit for a while?" Ben asked finally, but looking up at him, Reeta shook her head no.

"Please let's keep dancing," she said.

The vocalist began a new number. "Moon river, wider than a mile," he sang.

"This is from *Breakfast at Tiffany's*," Reeta told Ben. He looked confused and she said, "Movie—Audrey Hepburn—one of my favorites." Reeta let go of his hand and slipped both arms around his neck.

Her head was nestled between his head and shoulder and he felt her draw even closer as the man sang, "Two drifters off to see the world, there's such a lot of world to see, we're after the same rainbow's end, waiting round the bend..."

She looked up at him and asked, "Do you think that could be us? Two drifters looking for the rainbow's end?" But before he could answer she reached up and kissed him. And there in that crowded room it seemed there were only the two of them.

It had been a rather simple evening by most standards—dinner followed by dancing to the music of old love songs. Certainly it failed to meet the tempo usually associated with college-age people. Still as the night concluded, both knew that it was a memorable time for them and one of immense significance. Back in Reeta's room they sat together in the La-Z-Boy recliner. Following a period of silence Reeta said quietly, "I was wondering—would you be my steady guy?"

Ben smiled and replied, "I have been your steady guy since that first night on the bridge when you asked me about Schumacher."

"And I'm your steady girl," Reeta responded. "Yours—just yours."

Chapter 33

This October morning Slim had business to attend to in town. He left the farm as soon as the morning chores were completed and he had eaten breakfast. Ben's instructions for the morning were to go to the upper pasture where he was to cut cedar posts. He had learned the system well—cut the tree down, remove all the limbs and stack them in a neat pile—measure and cut the trees into eight-foot lengths. Later he and Slim would split and sharpen the posts and carry them to the pasture fence where the bulldozer would haul them to the barn below. Some of the posts would be used to upgrade the pasture fence but most would be sold to local farmers. "I would like to get at least twice as many as last year," Slim had told him. "The upper pasture needs thinning plus it's a good money maker." Slim's only other instruction was, "You be careful with that chainsaw. I'll see you at lunch time."

An hour of rigorous work left Ben thirsty. He walked to a nearby place where the spring water bubbled up out of the ground, and bracing his arms on a large stone, he lay nearly prone and took a long drink. As he stood up he looked off at the bright red, yellow and orange leaves that presently adorned the Green Mountains. The scene reminded him of a picture he had so often contemplated as a young boy living in the South. The caption beneath that picture had said simply, "October in Vermont." The words of his mother echoed down through the years. "Someday Benjamin," she would say, "someday we will see Vermont in October." For her it had never happened and that fact saddened Ben. Still she would be happy to see him there. He was certain that his current situation would bring her much peace and satisfaction. That belief comforted him.

He had now seen Vermont in all twelve months. He had experienced the distinct changing of the seasons, a series of events much more vivid than in the South. He tried to pick a favorite, but it was impossible. The thought of

211

winter thrilled him—frigid air rushing into his lungs, snow blanketing the fields, hauling wood from the mountain across the stream, the odor of ensilage in a barn warmed by the bodies of huge Holsteins. He looked forward to it all. But what about spring? There was the gathering of maple syrup, plowing and planting, mending fences and turning the cattle out to pasture. Perhaps that was his favorite. Then again, what could be better than summer?—watching the empty barns fill up with hay, fresh vegetables, working with the honey bees, swimming in the creek. No, he could not choose. He loved them all.

The quiet of the morning prompted other thoughts, thoughts concerning this particular plot of land. How, Ben wondered, could he feel so much a part of it in such a short period of time? The answer, at least in part, came from his admiration of Slim. Ben was certain of that. Slim's approach to this farm bordered on reverence. And it was clear to Ben that it had little to do with ownership. Slim knew that he held the deed, but in his mind he also felt that the trees and animals owned the land as much as he did. The feeling of guardianship clearly surpassed that of ownership. The title signified responsibility to, rather than power over these woods, this stream, these fields and all the inhabitants they contained.

Slim had never expressed any of these sentiments to Ben verbally for words were scarce with him. Mary had once said to Ben, "Slim doesn't preach sermons with his mouth but rather with the way he lives." And she added, "And if you watch him carefully those sermons can be both powerful and profound."

* * *

Ben looked at the pile of posts and thought that he should have accomplished more. It was nearly twelve thirty, and he knew that Slim would be home by now. This afternoon they would give the milk house a thorough cleaning even though it appeared spotless already. Slim wanted no bacteria. The state inspectors who often came around would shut down an operation for several weeks if they didn't like what they found. Slim knew that it happened often to farmers less conscientious about hygiene.

When the farm came into view Ben saw the old gray pickup in the driveway and knew immediately that it belonged to George Rogers. Entering the kitchen he saw George and Slim sitting at the kitchen table. One glance at Slim revealed to Ben that something was very wrong. A few seconds of awkward silence ended when Slim said, "George lost his son last night." He paused for a moment and added, "killed—police found him in a motel—foul play, they suspect." Ben knew that he should say something but silence overcame him.

The quiet was broken by George who looked up at Ben and said, "He was always in trouble—had lots of enemies—I hoped he would straighten himself out as he got older but he just got worse. I'm glad his mother doesn't know."

Ben managed to mutter the words "I'm sorry," but no more would come.

Slim looked at him and said, "We have to go claim the body. I have already called Mary. It will be late when I get back. I want you to take care of cleaning the milk house. You know what to do. Then drive over to George's and check on the heifers. By then it will be time to do the milking. Mary will help if you get behind."

They left within minutes. Ben ate a quick lunch and went to the barn. He had much to do and much on his mind.

* * *

Ben ran the farm for the next three days. Mary helped with the evening chores. Slim spent all his time helping George make the arrangements for his son's burial. After claiming the body, Slim arranged for it to be transported to the local funeral home. George requested no services but a plot had to be purchased, a vault and a coffin selected, money transferred from savings to checking to cover the expenses. "My mind's not clear," George said to Slim. "You take care of things. Just tell me where to sign." There were also the authorities to deal with. The police had many questions and mostly George sat silent while Slim answered as best he could. When the police ended their investigation they said that very little evidence was available. The murder appeared to have been done professionally and quite probably the case would never be solved. When they informed George of this probability he said simply, "Just as well—best just to let it go—I can't take much more of this anyway."

The burial was on Saturday morning. Only George, Slim, Mary and Pastor Braxton attended the brief service. Complying with George's wishes, Pastor Braxton only read the twenty-third Psalm and said a prayer. He was glad for the request because he didn't know what else to say anyway. The long sad life of George Rogers Junior was over and in truth most people were relieved.

Chapter 34

The days of late October grew shorter while the nights grew longer. Ben loved the evenings. They became times of great security for him. By six forty-five the evening chores would be complete, showers taken and the meal prepared. Conversation at meal time came easily with Mary telling interesting stories from school and always remembering to ask both Slim and Ben about their day. Clean up was a community effort, and by seven thirty the three of them were ready for a leisurely time by the living room fireplace. Ben learned quickly that Slim was a voracious reader. Each night he would settle into his overstuffed chair, place his feet on the hassock and, after a few minutes with the daily paper, pick up his book. His reading interests were remarkably diverse. One would have surmised that non-fiction would dominate his attention but such was not the case, for his book shelf contained at least an equal amount of fiction. This night Ben could see that he had begun a new book entitled *Whirlwind* by an author named Clavell. Slim's love of reading was another point of admiration for Ben, whose current choice was a controversial look at United States history by the author Howard Zinn. Written from the point of view of people exploited by the system, this night Ben read a scathing indictment of Andrew Jackson and his systematic destruction of Native Americans and their culture. Zinn criticized the terms used to describe Jackson by most historians—terms that usually included "frontiersman," "democrat," and "man of the people." Zinn's view was that the words "slave holder," "land speculator," and "exterminator" would be more appropriate.

It was on this topic that Ben was reading and thinking when the clock reached ten and he heard the phone ring. Picking up the kitchen phone, he heard the voice he had been waiting for. Reeta was exhausted and a bit down. Her work load was impossible to keep up with. She studied until midnight every night and still seemed to fall behind. Twice this week studies had forced her to cancel her workout and that too depressed her. "If I can make it till Friday," she told Ben, "I will be all right. Before then I have two exams, another long lab and a paper due."

"Anything I can do to help?" Ben asked.

"No thanks," she replied. "Just come as early as possible on Saturday. I need to escape from this place."

They talked of the upcoming weekend. "If I get a good night's sleep on Friday night," she said, "maybe we can take a long walk on Saturday. I have to go," she said at last. "I will talk to you tomorrow night." She said that she was lonely.

When Ben told Mary about the rough week Reeta was having she said, "If she wants to get away for the weekend she is welcome to stay here. We have the extra bedroom just sitting there."

"I'll ask her about it tomorrow night," Ben said and when he did he found that he only had to ask her once.

* * *

Reeta was exhausted but relieved on Friday afternoon. Somehow she had managed to complete the work and she felt confident with the results. A long workout in the training room removed the tension from her body. Back in her room by eight o'clock, she warmed some leftover pizza in her microwave, drank a large glass of apple juice, and by nine o'clock was sound asleep. One hour later her alarm rang. She made a quick call to Ben, told him that she would be ready by ten the next morning and almost immediately fell back to sleep where she remained until seven the next morning.

He pulled up in front of the dorm at five minutes before ten. He saw her immediately walking down the sidewalk, carrying her weekend bag. She climbed into the truck beside him, leaned across and kissed him gently. Despite the good night's sleep she still looked tired. "I can't believe this week," she said wearily. "Please get me out of here."

* * *

Together they walked, hand in hand, across the field and toward the stream. Ahead of them ran Anabel, looking back often to see that they were coming. The late October day was unusually warm. They wore only jeans and

215

short-sleeved shirts. At the stream's edge Reeta pointed north and asked if they might walk that way. "I have never seen the farm from that direction," she said. Initially the path was rough and low hanging evergreen branches required them to force their way through. The difficult stretch ended after a few hundred feet and they entered into an area of hardwoods dominated by maples. Foliage season was in its final stages and the leaves remaining on the trees were mostly dull browns and oranges. It reminded Ben of the scene riding north in an eighteen wheel truck nearly a year ago. Deep in thought, Ben failed to realize that he had ceased walking. He heard Reeta's voice, "You okay?" she asked. "You have been a million miles away."

"Sorry," Ben replied. "I was thinking about my mother; Florida; the trip here; Jim Braxton; the trailer where I first lived; farming; Slim and Mary; Dave Burnham; your college; you…" He paused. "It's the trees; the falling leaves; the colors—they look like they did when I arrived." Again he was silent. She let him think. Finally he said, "What if I hadn't come? What if I had stayed there? I wouldn't know any of this. I wouldn't even know that you existed."

She could see the fear in his eyes, and she came to him. Placing her arms around his waist, she looked up and said, "You did come. You are here. This is real. Don't be afraid. I want you to be happy."

They continued along the stream, mostly in silence. Ben pointed to a metal stake in the ground. "That marks the northern end of our farm."

"Are we allowed to go further?" Reeta asked.

"Yes," Ben told her. "We harvest all the hay on this place. And this is where we tap trees for maple syrup. The house up by the road is vacant. I have never seen the owners. Mary says they haven't been up for a couple of years. Slim pays the taxes on the place in exchange for the use of the land."

Ben placed the leash on Anabel's collar. They walked across the field toward the county road. When they reached the house Reeta asked if they could look through the windows. The rooms were completely empty. The two rooms visible to them appeared to be a living room and a dining room. Walking around to the back of the house, they could see into the kitchen. It was quite small. There appeared to be at least two rooms on the second floor, but from their vantage point they could not be certain. Together they walked down the road toward Slim and Mary's. Ben, in his innocence, had seen the house for what it was—vacant and interesting. But Reeta was already dreaming of other things.

* * *

It was four thirty on Saturday afternoon. Slim and Ben were already well into the afternoon milking. The process was still in a summer mode. Although it was too late in the season for the cows to be pastured, a temporary electric fence had been placed around the field closest to the barn and the cattle spent their days grazing on the late alfalfa. Soon all of that would change and the herd would be restricted to the barn and barn yard. Large scale feeding of hay and ensilage would commence. But for now the milking process remained in its simplified summer state, and by hurrying, the two men could do the entire procedure in less than two hours. Slim said little about it, but he saw a huge difference in his work load since Ben's arrival. Life was much easier. Best of all he had more free time to spend with Mary. They were already planning a long weekend on the Maine coast for the Columbus Day weekend. Mary had booked their room at a hotel in Old Orchard Beach.

While the men worked Reeta slept soundly on the living room couch, still recovering her strength from the difficult week just ended. She awoke to the sounds of Mary coming in from the garden where she had picked fresh lettuce for the evening meal. Mary was glad when Reeta joined her in the kitchen, because she wanted to talk. After some initial conversation about the soon-to-end fresh vegetables Mary said, "Ben is very bright. I'm sure you have concluded that by now."

Reeta responded, "He is so well read. I can't believe how many books he goes through each month. He puts me to shame in that regard."

Mary smiled and said, "He is so much like Slim in that way that sometimes it seems they really are related." She continued, "Most people don't know what a voracious reader Slim is. He never talks about it—but that's Slim. Anyway, about Ben. Slim and I would like him to try a college course. He has never taken SAT's so it would need to be some kind of non credit situation. We were hoping that you would check with the registrar and see what your school offers. We may be looking for something that doesn't exist." Mary had already observed, as Ben had, that Reeta talked with her eyes. It was clear that at the words, "Slim and I would like him to try a college course," Reeta's eyes had clearly approved of the idea. Her words confirmed it.

"I think that is such a terrific idea," she said. "I will look into it on Monday. Should I call you? Is it a surprise?"

"Yes," Mary answered, "We would like to make it a birthday present—if we can talk him into it. He still lacks confidence as I am sure you have noticed."

"Yes," Reeta replied, "but it's growing all the time. You and Slim have done so much to help him." Her mind drifted momentarily and then she added, "It's amazing, just amazing."

* * *

It was a fun evening. The four of them played Chinese checkers. It was the one game Slim would play. "Quick and painless," he would say. It also fit his ability to see lines and angles. He won the first two games and Mary won the third. At ten o'clock Slim and Mary went to bed. Ben and Reeta turned on the television and curled up on the sofa. Neither could have told what the program was about.

"Benjamin," Reeta said. "I want to ask you something. Actually I was hoping that maybe you would do something for me—with me." He listened intently but did not answer and so she continued. "I was thinking that maybe you would take me to Slim and Mary's church tomorrow."

Reeta saw the immediate look of concern cross Ben's face. "I have never been to a church service," he said. "It sounds a bit scary to me. I wouldn't know what to do. Would I have to say anything?"

Reeta smiled. "You have to sit beside me, stand up and sit down when I do, and no, you don't have to say anything." She looked up at him and said, "Please." And from the look on his face she knew that he would go.

* * *

They sat with Slim and Mary, four rows from the back. Mary's father and stepmother sat with them also. It was the same pew used by Mary and her father since she was a little girl. When the service began Ben discovered that Reeta had been right. He simply did what others did and carefully followed the program handed to him at the door. Things moved quickly—welcome, announcements, a hymn, something read in unison called the Apostles' Creed, an anthem by the choir, the morning prayer and the offering. Ben felt his body relax in the friendly and unthreatening atmosphere. A song which Ben remembered from somewhere was sung after the offering. The program referred to it as the Doxology.

The people were asked to be seated and Pastor Braxton asked the children to come forward. He came from the pulpit area and sat on the floor as more than a dozen children gathered around him. His own son, now a toddler, climbed up onto his lap. The message was simple. The pastor thanked the children for the card they had collectively made for his recent birthday. He had the large card with him and several of the children pointed out the pictures and words they had contributed to it. He told them how nice it made him feel to be remembered and then he reminded them that it was important to do nice things for people every day. When he dismissed the children they were taken to another part of the church for activities. The program next called for a scripture reading and Ben was surprised when Mrs. Braxton, very pregnant with their second child, approached the pulpit. She had a beautiful speaking voice and with great sincerity she began to read:

"Once when some mothers were bringing their children to Jesus to bless them, the disciples shooed them away, telling them not to bother him. But when Jesus saw what was happening he was very much displeased and said to them, 'Let the children come to me, for the kingdom of God belongs to such as they. Don't send them away! I tell you as seriously as I know how that anyone who refuses to come to God as a little child will never be allowed into his kingdom.'"

She returned to her seat. Pastor Braxton approached the pulpit. Ben looked down at the program and saw the words: "Sermon: 'The disciples shooed them away.'"

"Today three children will die as a result of child abuse in the home. Probably they will be less than six years old. Child abuse is the leading cause of death for infants and young children. An incidence of child abuse is reported every ten seconds and experts feel that the actual cases of neglect and abuse are at least three times greater than those reported. The obvious immediate pain and suffering are just the tip of the iceberg. Results of abuse tend to be long term—in many cases permanent. Children who suffer abuse often become abusive themselves. Their chances of turning to a life of crime, drugs or alcohol multiply. Indeed, men and women serving time in our nation's prisons report a higher incidence of abuse as children than does the general population.

"We look at these facts and statistics with a combination of horror and disgust. We grieve for the young children—the victims of this plague. But I feel that I need to say today that our concern is not enough. We need to look ourselves squarely in the eyes and ask. As the church of Christ—as modern day disciples—are we like the disciples of old—guilty of shooing the children away? Sometimes it is good for us to remember that there are two kinds of sins—sins of commission and sins of omission. In terms of today's topic, a sin of commission would be the act of abusing a child. Now we members of this particular church may be able to say that we are not guilty of that. But what about sins of omission—that is, failing to take action against the evils of abuse—the causes of abuse? And from a personal standpoint I also feel that I stand guilty."

The minister continued. He talked of the enormity of the task. He talked of the complexity of the issue.

"Sometimes we want to do something but we feel confused and overwhelmed as to where even to start. We feel inadequate to the task. It is easy to wonder what a small congregation in rural Vermont could possibly do to impact an issue national, even global, in scope. Well I wish to submit to you this day that we need to take action. We need to throw a pebble into this sea of despair. We may not create a giant wave of reform but perhaps the small ripple will help the children of our area. Yes we need to create a place where at risk children can find security. A place where they know they are wanted. A place to play, a place where basic health issues are dealt with, a place to be supervised while parents work. It needs to be affordable—free if necessary. We need to stop shooing the children away. It is time for us, like Jesus, to say, Let the children come to me."

The pastor paused for a moment and then he said, "We need a place—a children's place—and I think we need it now. Therefore I have arranged with Dr. Taylor for a potluck supper at his community center for next Saturday evening. If you share our concerns about children I invite you to attend. Please bring a covered dish to share, but more than that, bring ideas as to the direction we might go."

The service ended with a prayer and a final hymn. Ben felt nervous as he left the building. Several people shook his hand and said that it was good to see him. With Mary's help they made their way to Nellie Zenger, to whom he introduced Reeta. At the door he also introduced Reeta to Pastor Braxton. Ben had feared that the minister would make an issue about his first appearance at church, but nothing on that subject was raised. "Hey Ben, how are you doing?" was all Jim Braxton said as he shook his hand.

Ben was quiet on the ride back to the farm. The service had left him confused. To be honest, Jim Braxton had always puzzled him. He was the antithesis of everything Ben had forever associated with religion. He was positive rather than negative, uplifting rather than depressing. Even today's talk—it was presented more as a challenge than a criticism. True, the pastor had looked the issue straight in the eye, but somehow Ben did not sense that the motive was to make the congregation feel guilty. More it was a call to action. Ben wondered to himself if Jim Braxton was an exception to the rule when it came to religion or if perhaps there were others like him.

Reeta had a million questions. They started in the car and continued through lunch time. She wanted to know about Mary's father—what his clinic was like, where it was located, when he had established it, and if she could visit it sometime. She asked about his role in this new idea presented by Jim Braxton. Mary told her that it had been a long term goal for her father. "He has long dreamed for a comprehensive children's program complete with a building and playground. There is space available by the clinic, but he has never been able to get funding to build and staff it. I know that he is excited that someone else is joining his crusade. And if anyone can pull it together, it is Jim Braxton. He is an expert organizer."

* * *

That Sunday afternoon the sky clouded over and a cold wind began to blow. "I think we have seen the last of summer," Slim commented. "It lasted longer than usual this year."

The afternoon was quiet. Ben and Reeta spent two hours looking at books filled with Mary's photographs. Mary did school work at the kitchen table. Slim went to the shed where the wood splitter was stored and serviced its engine. At four Slim and Ben started the evening milking. Mary ordered pizza for dinner and Reeta slept soundly on the living room sofa. By seven thirty Reeta's weekend bag was packed and Ben was ready to drive her back to campus. "It has been so good having you with us," Mary told her. "You know that you are welcome anytime."

"I love it here," Reeta said. "And I feel rested for the first time in days. Thank you for a great time." She paused and then said hesitantly, "Would next weekend be all right? I would like to listen in on that meeting at your Dad's clinic."

Reeta was unusually quiet on the ride back to campus. Finally she spoke. "Am I too pushy?"

Ben smiled and said, "Of course not."

"Really," Reeta continued, "I wonder if people think I'm pushy. After all, I did practically invite myself back next weekend."

"But I want you to come—don't you see, I want you to come every weekend." Reeta smiled as Ben continued. "You are invited every weekend. I will come to get you. See, now I'm the pushy one."

Chapter 35

The following day, Monday, began what proved to be one of the busiest weeks of farming that Ben could remember. The two men worked quickly through the morning chores, ate breakfast on the run, and headed for George Rogers' place. The next three hours were spent removing the electric fence from around the field and rolling it on large spools for winter storage. Next they pulled the posts from the ground, loaded them into the truck and hauled them to the shed where they were stacked neatly on two pressure treated four-by-fours. George watched them work. Ben noticed a look of tranquility in George's eyes. Oddly, the tragedy of his son's death seemed to have lifted a great burden form him. Fear and tension no longer etched his face. It was also obvious to Ben that George wholeheartedly approved of the Slim Smith method of farming. Many farmers, for example, never bothered to remove their temporary fences in the fall, resulting in rusty wire and rotting posts which needed constant replacement. Slim's fencing materials, on the other hand, remained "high and dry" during the off season and seemed to last indefinitely.

The heifers were confined to the barnyard where they would spend the fall and winter feeding on baled hay from the two large steel feeders. Later in the day Ben would return and direct the animals into the barn for the night. The larger heifers would be stanchioned while the smaller ones were confined to a penned area. Once a week Ben cleaned out the barn and applied new bedding. It was hard work, but work nonetheless, that Ben enjoyed.

They returned home at one thirty, ate a quick lunch, and began the process of fence removal in Slim's field. At three o'clock Slim sent Ben back to George's place where he housed and fed the heifers. By four thirty he was back at the barn to begin the evening milking. He climbed the silo for the first time this season. After one hundred and ten forkfuls he heard Slim's voice: "That's enough, Ben." He climbed down the chute thinking how farming for one year had increased his physical strength. Last year he had needed nearly thirty more forkfuls to equal the same amount of ensilage.

While he dumped ensilage in front of each cow, Ben saw that Mary had entered the barn and was feeding the calves, which enabled him to join Slim in the milking process. By six thirty they were exhausted but finished for the day. At dinner Slim told Ben that tomorrow they would complete the fence removal and then head up to the mountain to cut trees.

Tuesday, Wednesday and Thursday they cut trees on the mountain. The dead ones would be split and sold for firewood and the others sold for lumber. Slim told Ben that they would continue cutting for at least another week before they began the hauling process. As the week had progressed the weather had moderated, but the warm days of summer were gone for another year.

* * *

Mary hurried home from school on Thursday afternoon. She had no school on Friday and she and Slim were leaving for a two-day trip to the Maine coast. By four o'clock they were gone. Slim's instructions to Ben were simple. "Just take care of the cows here and at George's," he said. "Don't try to do anything extra."

Mary gave him a hug and said, "Our number is on a pad by the phone in the kitchen. Call if you need us. We will be back on Saturday in time for the meeting at the clinic. You be careful."

Ben began the afternoon chores as soon as they left. It was a long process working alone, but he was not nervous. First he threw down the ensilage and distributed it in the feeding area in front of the stanchions. Next he brought the four milking machines from the milk house to the main barn. Then he fed the calves. Only when those jobs were completed did he bring the milkers into the barn. Running four milking machines was almost more than he could handle. He literally ran from cow to cow to keep up. Despite the fast pace, it was seven o'clock when he finished milking. He then fed the cows their grain and went to the milk house to wash and sanitize the machines. By seven forty-five he was back in the main barn giving the cows their overnight feeding of hay. It was after eight thirty when he placed the plate of food that Mary had left in the refrigerator in front of him. By nine o'clock he was sound asleep on the sofa where he remained until Reeta called at ten. He told her how much he loved a day of farming.

* * *

Ben was in the barn at five thirty. The cows heard his arrival and mooed their approval. The hungry calves in the rear of the barn were less patient, so he fed them first. The morning chores went smoothly. As Ben cleaned up the equipment he heard the tanker pull into the driveway and begin the process of transferring the milk from the large stainless steel tank into the truck. The driver asked if Slim was sick and seemed surprised to hear that he was on vacation. "I didn't know that Slim knew about vacations," he said.

Ben finished his breakfast and went back to the barn. He filled the barnyard feeders with hay before releasing the milkers from their stanchions. When the barn was empty he cleaned it and replaced the bedding. He then attached the loaded manure spreader to the tractor and drove it to the field across the county road.

George was watching from his kitchen window when Ben arrived at eleven o'clock. He hobbled to the barn and looked over the fence while Ben took care of the heifers. "Let's get some lunch at Jensen's," George said when Ben completed his work. They sat at George's usual table and ate hot roast beef sandwiches and cherry pie. George knew nearly everyone and several people stopped to visit.

"Slim's finally getting a couple of days off," he told them. And with a look of pride he added, "The boy here is running the place and doing a good job of it too."

The two days passed quickly and smoothly. That he could manage things so well gave Ben a boost of confidence. That because of him Slim and Mary could get away gave him a deep feeling of satisfaction. At precisely noon on Saturday Reeta's red Honda Civic pulled into the driveway where an excited Anabel ran to greet her. "How are things going?" Reeta asked when Ben met her at the door. And when Ben said things were fine, Reeta responded, "You should feel so good about yourself. A year ago you knew nothing about this profession and now you are running the place."

"I have two really good teachers," Ben replied, and he meant it.

* * *

Jim Braxton was rarely nervous. Secure in his faith and his calling, he tended to remain calm whatever the situation. But tonight he was anxious. Last Sunday's sermon had been a leap of faith for him. True, he believed deeply in the need to help children, but was this specific concept of a children's center the direction to go? Would anyone attend the meeting? Would it be a meeting where people gave lip service to the concept but then went home only to see the status quo continue? Purposely he had made no calls that week to remind people of the meeting. He was convinced that if they came it had to be from a genuine concern for children.

Nellie Zenger was the first to arrive. She had walked the short distance from her home while there was still some daylight. In a small basket she carried two cherry pies. Soon Dr. and Mrs. Taylor arrived. For a few minutes it appeared that no one else would attend but then Mary, accompanied by Ben and Reeta, appeared. Slim, who never was much for meetings, told Mary that she could fill him in later. Three other members of the local clergy arrived along with members of their congregation. Pastor Braxton seemed pleased when several more members of his congregation appeared. There was a gentleman in attendance whom no one knew. He simply identified himself as Joseph Clauson, and he said that he had heard of the meeting and was interested in the issue.

There was plenty of food. Most people brought casseroles of one sort or another. The meal lasted about half an hour, after which Jim Braxton called the meeting to order. He asked the priest from the local Catholic church to open with a prayer and then, after reviewing the purpose of the meeting, he called on Dr. Taylor to speak. For nearly ten minutes the doctor talked of the urgent need for a children's center. His talk was very calm and very clear. Ben saw the looks of respect on the faces of the people listening. It was clear to him why Jim Braxton had asked the doctor to speak first.

When Dr. Taylor completed his talk on the need for a children's center he walked to a large flip chart that had been placed on an easel, and lifting the top page, revealed a blueprint of the facility they were currently in. He reviewed with them the parking area, the community room and the medical wing. Next he pointed to the open area behind the blueprints and said, "This is the lot adjacent to our facility. It is approximately one third of an acre in size, more than sufficient for a large daycare center and adjoining playground. Now most of you are not aware, actually my own daughter is not aware, that I recently purchased this parcel. If somehow we as a community can figure a way to construct and staff such a facility, I am prepared to donate the land for that purpose." There were looks of surprise on the faces of the audience— even a few gasps. Ben could see Mary's face from where he was sitting. He saw that she neither gasped nor looked surprised. She only smiled knowingly.

Next Jim Braxton called on a local contractor who was also a member of the Methodist congregation. The man discussed various kinds of building materials normally used in these types of facilities, the advantages and disadvantages of each, and which were most and least expensive.

The pastor then opened up the floor for discussion and after several questions noticed unexpectedly the raised hand of the stranger, Joseph Clauson. "You don't know me," he began, "but I live in the area and my occupation is that of writing grants for educational institutions." He explained that there were huge sums of money, both private and public, available for worthy causes such as this one. The problem, he explained, is that most people don't know such money exists or worse yet, they lack the skills for writing a successful application. Then he said, "That is where people like me come in. I spend my life locating grants for institutions and then preparing the applications. I have heard about your project, and I agree that the need is great. That is why I would be willing to assist you in securing funding for this center and I am further willing to provide those services *pro bono*."

Jim Braxton thanked the gentleman for his generous offer and suggested that, along with Dr. Taylor, they meet to discuss specifics. The pastor further suggested that the group meet again in two weeks to be updated on any new developments. He thanked all who had attended and adjourned the meeting. He immediately went to Mr. Clauson to arrange for a meeting. After a few minutes of conversation the minister said, "I am curious. How did you hear about us?"

Mr. Clauson replied, "A young woman contacted me this week and asked if I would be willing to attend the meeting. She is over by the door," he said, and pointed toward Reeta.

As they rode back to the farm, Reeta told them that she knew Joseph Clauson from school; that he had been instrumental in securing funds for their new track; that he worked for many colleges and non-profit organizations; and that he was active in the Presbyterian church located in the same town as the college. Mary thanked Reeta for her involvement and Reeta responded with the comment, "I hope that I didn't overstep my bounds."

Ben gently nudged Reeta and with a mischievous smile said, "Pushy Reeta."

Chapter 36

Slim, Mary and Ben entered the judge's office at eleven o'clock on a Saturday morning in mid November. The day was cool but not cold. At times the sun shone brightly, while occasional dark clouds passed over, bringing with them sprinkles and even some light rain. The judge was cordial but businesslike and the process took only a few minutes. "The paper work is all here," he said. "We only need to sign in the appropriate places to make this official. My secretary will act as witness."

Because Ben was nineteen years old and because there was no one to contest the action, the adoption process had happened quickly and without problem. In minutes they had signed the papers, and the judge looked at the three of them and said, "Congratulations. Benjamin, these are your parents. Mr. and Mrs. Smith, Benjamin is legally your son." Mary came to Ben and gave him a warm hug. She then turned to Slim and as she kissed his cheek Ben saw the single tear fall across her face. They looked toward Ben and knowingly he came to them.

Ben felt Slim's long arms surround both him and Mary, and in that moment they were truly a family. Ben wanted to say something meaningful for the occasion but fancy words failed him. And so he said simply, "Mom, Dad, let's go home."

They arrived home at noon time. Several cars sat in their driveway. It was not a surprise, for Mary had told Ben that they would be celebrating both the adoption and his nineteenth birthday, which had occurred a week earlier. Nellie Zenger was there, as were the Braxtons and Dave Burnham. George Rogers sat in a chair by the fireplace. Mary's parents were there, and of course, so was Reeta. Before they ate Mary looked toward Jim Braxton and he said, "Let's say a prayer." Ben felt embarrassed but he could not help but smile when the pastor said, "Lord, we thank you that Ben's car broke down somewhere in New Jersey; that he found a truck driver traveling to Vermont; that for some reason he chose to stop in our town. I thank you that I decided to work late in my office that cold November night; that Ben saw my light. Thank you that Slim and Mary needed someone to work."

He paused and before he could continue they all laughed when Nellie said, "And thank you that I lost my purse."

After a pause Ben heard the voice of Reeta say, "Thank you that I followed Ben to the bridge that night." No one except Ben knew exactly what that meant, but they knew it was important.

After a moment of silence the pastor simply said, "Amen," and the celebration began.

* * *

NOVEMBER 16
11 pm.

The house is still. Slim & Mary are in their room. Reeta is in the guest bedroom. Everyone is exhausted from the day. Yet sleep will not come to me, and so I write... Today I was legally adopted by Slim and Mary Smith. So much has happened to me in one year that sometimes it seems like a dream. When I arrived in Vermont I had few clothes and approximately one hundred and sixty dollars. I had no home, no job, and no plan. Any sane person would have told me that leaving Florida & coming here at the start of winter was sheer lunacy. In spite of all that, my life has fallen into place in a way more wonderful than I could possibly have dreamed. How often I think back to words that Nellie Zenger said to me shortly after I arrived here — she told me that none of this was an accident. At the time, I considered them to be the words of a sentimental old lady. No longer am I so sure... My bank statement came this week, & I saw that there is more than $6000 in my account. But the money is a minor thing. I now have two people who I can call Mom and Dad. I live in a beautiful home on a beautiful farm and with each passing day the profession of farming fills my being. Today Mom asked me if I would consider taking a college class. The idea is both exciting and frightening to me. I told her that I will need time to think about it. And then there is Reeta... I met her at the college at a moment of great embarrassment & humiliation to me. She appeared to me, out of the shadows, almost like an angel sent to lift me from my despair. Whenever I relive that night,

the words of Nellie Zenger return to me. ~~~~ Anyway,
about Reeta – I think that she is the most beautiful
girl in the world. She has been so good to me. We spend
every weekend together, but even when we are apart she
is never far from my thoughts. There is something that
I want to tell her, but I am frightened to say the words.
I wish that I had the courage. Maybe

Ben thought about what to say next and eventually fell asleep without finishing the sentence. He awoke the next morning with the journal still lying on his chest. Before going to the barn he placed it in the bottom drawer of his desk.

* * *

Sunday was a duplicate of the day before in terms of weather. Periods of bright sunshine were interrupted periodically by large dark clouds that brought sprinkles and light rain. Reeta was unusually quiet during lunch, as though deep in thought. When the meal ended, Mary and Slim took Anabel and walked across the field toward the stream. Alone in the house together, Ben heard Reeta's voice. "Take me up to the mountain."

"We might get wet," Ben replied.

"I don't care," Reeta responded. "Take me up to the rock."

They walked quietly across the pasture holding hands. At the fence Ben lifted the wire for Reeta to climb through, and she did the same for him. Again they walked in silence, this time in single file up the narrow path. When they reached the rock Reeta came to him. For a long time he held her close. Finally she looked up at him, and he saw that she was crying. Through her tears he heard her voice, quiet yet firm. "Tell me," she said. "Say the words that I have to hear. Say the words that I know are in your heart. Please say the words now. I can't wait any longer. I need to hear them now."

Suddenly a calm came over Ben. He was no longer frightened. Instead he smiled and looked directly into her eyes, and with more confidence than he had ever before felt he said, "I love you."

Reeta buried her head between his neck and shoulder in a way that Ben had come to love and he heard her say, "I love you too, Benjamin Thomas Smith, I love you too."

The sun was warm upon them as they stood on the mountain and they were surprised when off in the distance they saw the huge dark cloud with rain falling from it. And as they watched they saw it happen. The rainbow, bright and distinct, arched across the sky and disappeared into the Green Mountains. Instinctively Ben drew Reeta to him and through her tears appeared a smile. Then he heard her voice, and she said the words that would forever be their words, "We're after the same rainbow's end."

Printed in the United States
51294LVS00004B/241-258

9 781424 101955